The MONKEY PUZZLE TREE

The MONKEY PUZZLE TREE

A NOVEL

SONIA TILSON

A JOHN METCALF BOOK

BIBLIOASIS
WINDSOR, ONTARIO

FIRST EDITION

Library and Archives Canada Cataloguing in Publication

Tilson, Sonia
    The monkey puzzle tree / Sonia Tilson.

Issued also in an electronic format.
ISBN 978-1-927428-12-2
    I. Title.

PS8639.I557M66 2013   C813'.6   C2012-907644-9

Edited by John Metcalf
Copy-edited by Tara Murphy
Typeset by Chris Andrechek
Cover Designed by Kate Hargreaves

Canada Council for the Arts   Conseil des Arts du Canada

ONTARIO ARTS COUNCIL
CONSEIL DES ARTS DE L'ONTARIO

Canadian Heritage   Patrimoine canadien

Biblioasis acknowledges the ongoing financial support of the Government of Canada through the Canada Council for the Arts, Canadian Heritage, the Canada Book Fund; and the Government of Ontario through the Ontario Arts Council.

PRINTED AND BOUND IN CANADA

Gillian's mother, propped against the pillows, rapped the inhaler on the tray in front of her. "Why are you just standing there with the bottle open in your hand?"

Gillian jumped. Clumsy with jet lag, she fumbled at the little blue vial of *Je Reviens,* spilling some on her fingers.

Her mother raised her eyebrows. "I would like a spot. That is, if there's any left."

Gillian wiped her fingers, dipped the stopper back into its bottle, and touched the bulbous end behind each of her mother's earlobes.

"Now put a little rouge on my face, there's a good girl, and do my hair for me, would you?"

Quirking her mouth at the idea of being a girl at fifty-five, good or otherwise, Gillian smoothed the peachy powder onto her mother's cheeks, and fluffed up the sparse white curls. At a nod she applied a touch of lipstick. Her mother rubbed her lips together and studied her reflection in the hand mirror Gillian held for her.

"Isn't she wonderful, at her age, to take such care of her appearance!" Sunita, the nursing assistant, had said when Gillian arrived earlier that morning at Saint Anne's Nursing Home; despite a couple of private reservations, including that seventy-seven did not seem nearly as old to her as it obviously did to Sunita, Gillian had, of course, agreed.

A rattling cough shook her mother's rib cage. Smoking, taken up she said in the stress of the Blitz, had left a legacy of chronic bronchitis. According to her, a stay at the nursing home would enable her to go back to living on her own, but looking at her, pale and gasping after the coughing fit, Gillian had her doubts. She might recover. Apparently she had bounced back often enough before, albeit a little lower each time. Then again, she might not.

Her mother spat into a tissue and took a deep breath. "That's better! Now pass me my silk bed jacket and a hankie. The doctor should be here any minute." She examined her nails. "Perhaps you'll sit in the hall while I talk to him."

Gillian eased on the delicate garment, controlling the urge to give it a yank, and left the room. She might as well humour her, she thought as she settled into the brown vinyl armchair by the hall window. She could talk to the doctor later. She winced, remembering her mother's earlier greeting. "My goodness, you've aged!" the old woman had said, receiving Gillian's kiss on her tissue-paper cheek. "I couldn't believe it when your brother told me you were coming. You must have thought I was dying, and I wouldn't have thought you'd have come even then. Anyway, it'll take more than a cold to see me off, you'll be sorry to hear."

Gillian had left Wales for Canada at twenty-two, feeling that she might as well put an ocean between herself and her mother. Now, sitting out in the hall, she was already regretting the panicky rush from Ottawa that had followed Tom's phone call the day before.

He had met the early morning arrival at Heathrow, greyer and stouter than when she had last seen him in Ottawa, fifteen years before, but beaming with delight as he enveloped her in a bear hug before seizing her luggage. At his insistence, they had set off immediately for Swansea.

"It's lovely to see you, Gill! You're looking well." He kept his eyes fixed on the M4 as they flashed past fields of blinding yellow canola. "How's Bryn?" He overtook a mover's truck at terrifying speed.

"He's okay, and so are Carol and Alice." The thought of her son and daughter-in-law and her five-year-old granddaughter calmed her somewhat until Tom entered on what seemed to be a drag race with a motorcycle.

"How's that Simon?" he shouted as the motorcyclist finally blew past, turning his head to grin.

"He's fine. He's lovely. But slow down, Tom, please!"

He chuckled. "We don't poke along the way you do in Canada you know. But look here, Gill, I've got something to tell you."

He slowed minimally, and looked across at her. "Vanna wants to see you."

"Vanna does? After all these years?"

"She wants you to have dinner with her tonight at her place, just the two of you. Something quick and simple, she said, because you'd be tired." He looked across at her. "You will go, Gill, won't you? I'll take you there and pick you up."

She glanced at his still-handsome profile. "You haven't given up then?"

He picked up speed. "Never!"

"Okay, I'll go. I'd love to see her again actually." She sat back and closed her eyes, opening them with a start as he gunned the engine to zip around a Volkswagen. "Hey! Take it easy!"

"Sorry! Look here, Gill, you're tired. Bag of nerves! We'll go to Langland first, to Mum's bungalow. You can see her later, after you've had a rest."

ONLY HER BODY RESTING, she lay on the over-soft bed in the curtained gloom of her mother's bedroom amidst faint smells of mothballs and aging cosmetics. She had been sure for most of her adult life that she and her mother had nothing more to say to each other, but evidently she had been mistaken, about herself at least. Why else had she left her family, and Simon, to rush back here after over thirty years' absence? Nearly knocking a frilly, pink-shaded lamp off the nightstand as she pushed away a pillow, she turned on her side, hoping a change of position might entice sleep. She lay prone again, trying to concentrate, first on breathing deeply and evenly, and when that failed, on the swish of the high tide washing against the cliff. Finally she had to accept that there was still something left for her to do, and that, moreover, she knew what it was. She owed it to her mother, as well as to herself, to try to turn that deeply buried stone. If she succeeded, it could help explain the reserve and even hostility she had always shown towards her mother, which she knew must have made her hard to love. Possibly she could hear her mother's side of the story too: why she had kept her only daughter at arm's length throughout her whole life.

She had showered and changed, and told Tom, dozing in the chintz armchair by the beige-tiled fireplace, that she was ready to go.

TRYING TO DISTANCE HERSELF from her mother's rancour, she looked down from the nursing-home window onto slate rooftops sloping towards the glinting sea, a view almost the same as that from her childhood bedroom in the house where she had been born, just up the hill from Saint Anne's: the five-mile sweep of Swansea Bay stretching in a perfect arc from what used to be the docks on her left, now a marina, to the Mumbles lighthouse on the right. Around the coast from the lighthouse lay Langland Bay, where her mother's bungalow perched on another hillside.

Closing her eyes, she leaned back, wearily rubbing a hand over her face. The intense, flowery perfume on her fingers, the essence of her mother, overwhelmed her, sweeping her back nearly fifty years to the night of September the third, nineteen thirty-nine; her last night at home before being evacuated, and the last time she had spoken to her mother with an open heart.

A GLIMMER DANCED ON GILLIAN'S bedroom wall. She could hear the silky whisper of her mother's dress and smell her perfume curling like an invisible mist around the half-open bedroom door, a fragrance which she knew came from a little blue bottle lying amongst the wonders of her mother's dressing table. She had held it like a round flat pebble on her palm just the day before, studying the label and puzzling over the letters.

"J-e R-e-v-i-e-n-s," she had spelled out. "What does that mean, Mummy?"

"It's French. It means 'I will come back.'" Her mother had put on her lipstick and rubbed her lips together making a kissing noise before saying, "Stop fiddling with my things, there's a good girl. You might break something."

As the flickers of light became brighter, and the scent grew stronger, Gillian raised her head and whispered, "Mummy, I can't sleep!"

Darkness fled into corners as her mother entered the bedroom. The folds of her blue dress gleamed as she set the stubby brass candlestick down on the night table. "What's the matter Gilly? You ought to be fast asleep by now."

Gillian sat up, took a deep breath, and looked straight at her mother. "Why do we have to go away, Mummy? Why do we have to go to the Macphersons'? Why can't we stay here with you and Daddy?"

Her mother sighed and sat on the bed. "You know why, darling. I told you. It's because of the bombs. All the children have to be evacuated. It's the law."

Gillian grabbed her mother's skirt. "But couldn't you come with us then? Like Auntie Vera's going to Canada with Josephine and Tony?"

Her mother stood up, removing Gillian's hand. "No. I have to stay and look after Daddy and help with the practice. And, before you ask; no, you can't stay with Grandma and Grandpa either. Grandma's still not well enough after her operation. You have to go to the Macphersons', and quickly too, and that's that." She moved towards the window.

Gillian's chin began to wobble. "But Mummy, what about you and Daddy? Will you be bombed?"

"No, no. Don't worry about us. We'll be all right."

"Then we'd be all right too, if we stayed with you, wouldn't we?" Gillian grabbed her frizzy mop of hair, pulling it hard, trying not to cry. "Please, Mummy, don't send us away!"

Her mother turned around. "For shame, Gillian! A clever girl like you! You're six years old, not a baby. I expected more of you. You know there's a war on, and we all have to do our duty, even you children. And your duty, Gillian, is to be brave and not whine, and to look after your little brother. Now leave your hair alone." She loosened Gillian's fingers. "You know I'll come to see you. It won't be long before this silly old war is over, and then we'll all be back together again." She turned to the window and yanked the thick black curtains to make doubly sure no chinks of light could escape. "Now lie down and go to sleep, there's a good girl." She kissed her cheek quickly and left the room.

"Don't go, Mummy! Stay with me!" Gillian whispered, but her mother did not come back.

SINCE THEIR FATHER WAS BUSY with the practice, their mother drove the children to the little village of Croesffordd, 'Crossroads', by herself. Everyone, or at least Olwen, the maid, and Mrs. Jones, the daily cleaning woman, had told Gillian that she and Tommy were very lucky. Their parents had connections, so they didn't have to go on the special bus like the other evacuees. Their mother would drive them all the way from Swansea, even though that would use up a whole week's petrol ration. They did not have to stay down in the village either, with families living in the cottages around the crossroads. Olwen, who knew someone there, said those people were *common*, a word Gillian thought about a lot, and that she should be glad they were going to live with Dr. and Mrs. Macpherson up at Maenordy, "the manor house," the big house up on the hill.

Mrs. Jones's daughter, Gladys, however, who was nearly seven and knew more about everything than Gillian, had not been so nice about it. "Ooh, there's *posh*!" she said, her black eyes flashing as she slammed a ball against the garden wall while waiting for her mother. "You'll be able to see the flames lovely from up by there."

Gillian dropped the ball. "What flames, Gladys?"

"The flames of Swansea burnin', silly." She ran off laughing, taking the ball with her.

ARRIVING AT CROESFFORDD, they made a turn between a sweetie shop and a grey chapel with the word *Ebenezer* carved over the door, and drove up a steep hill. A winding drive, edged by mauve rhododendrons, led to the house where they were to live until it was safe to go home.

It was indeed grand, Gillian saw. It was tall and white, with a dark slate roof and small windows, their blinds part down like half-shut eyes. On one side was a rose bed and a lawn, and beyond that, a view of a far-off river winding its way through fields towards distant hills. Just over those hills, Gillian thought, Swansea might lie. She tried not to think of flames. On the far side of the house stood a wooden barn shaded by a clump of leafy trees.

They pulled up near the front door, under a very different sort of tree. Gillian stared at it, her stomach still queasy from the long drive. It didn't seem like a proper tree at all. It looked dark, almost black, its branches like giant bottle brushes sticking out at crazy angles. All wrong somehow.

"Look!" said their mother, taking out the suitcases, "A monkey puzzle tree! How unusual! Isn't that nice! Aren't you lucky children to be coming to a lovely place like this?"

Mrs. Macpherson, tall and pale, with black hair in a bun and sharp little dark eyes, stood at the door of Maenordy. Even though it was hot for September, she was wearing a tweed costume. On her lapel was a brooch made from an animal's paw, like a little furry hand with a wide silver cuff around the wrist. In the shadowy hall behind her loomed black furniture on a shiny, dark wood floor. Gillian could smell polish and carbolic soap. Tommy clutched her hand.

"Now, my darlings," their mother stood behind them, putting her hands around their shoulders, "This is Mrs. Macpherson, who's going to look after you while the bombings are going on. You must be very, very good and not give Dr. and Mrs. Macpherson any trouble." She hugged the two of them and kissed them. "Take care of each other, sweethearts, and be sure never to do *anything* to make me ashamed of you. Do you promise me now?"

"No Mummy, we won't. We promise." Gillian was echoed by Tommy as they struggled to control their tears.

"That's my brave darlings! I'll come back to see you as soon as I can." She kissed them both again. Hurrying to get back to Swansea before the blackout, she jumped into the little grey car and was gone.

Mrs. Macpherson looked down at them, sighing hard through her nose. "Come along then." She picked up their suitcases. "Follow me." She led them across the hall, down a cold, mouldy-smelling stone passage, up a steep wooden staircase on which she bumped the suitcases at every step, making cross puffing sounds, and along another gloomy passage to what was to be their bedroom. After showing them the way to the bathroom and telling them to stay in their room until she came back, she left them.

The room was dark, and very high and bare, the only furnishings being the huge four-poster bed, covered with a slippery-looking, pale purple eiderdown, a black, mothball-smelling wardrobe, big enough for the two of them to live in, and a matching chest of drawers, also empty.

Tommy was sniffling worryingly, so Gillian helped him up onto the bed, where they tried some half-hearted bouncing before he gave up and started to cry in earnest. Afraid that Mrs. Macpherson would come back, she ran to pull up a window blind, hoping to distract him with a sunny field or maybe even some animals. The blind stuck at first, but then rose slowly onto a maze of dense, prickly branches.

Peering through gathering tears into the dark heart of the monkey puzzle tree, she wondered what would actually happen to a monkey caught in those branches. Would it be able to get out? Was that the puzzle?

LIFE WAS STRANGE AT MAENORDY. They had to stay out of the house all day except for meals. In the house they had to be quiet and never do anything to annoy Mrs. Macpherson. If by some accident they did, she would spank them, pulling down their underpants and hitting them hard on their bottoms, making Tommy wet himself, which made her even angrier. They only saw Dr. Macpherson at meals. He had rusty grey hair and a dark, mottled nose, and never said anything.

Angus, their son, who was eighteen, was away at boarding school.

Gillian had hopes of the village school, but everything was in Welsh, and she hardly knew any. Even worse, Gladys had been evacuated to the village too, to one of the stone cottages in the whitewashed row down by the crossroads, where loud-voiced, cheery women in flowered pinnies hung out their washing in gardens full of cabbages and chickens. Still jealous of Gillian being at the big house, she would whisper to the other girls in Welsh, making them stare and giggle.

"You's only there 'cos you dad's a doctor, like 'im up by there," she said to Gillian one day in the schoolyard. "They *'ad* to take somebody, and they asked for you two special. They din't want us *common* kids. That's what my mam said." After that the other girls turned their backs on Gillian and wouldn't let her join in their hopscotch and skipping games.

Things were better after school and at weekends since Gillian and Tommy could go wherever they liked outside, and could play in the barn if it rained. At first it was warm and sunny most of the time, and it was exciting to be free to wander in the woods and fields. In one field there was a white calf which would let Gillian climb on her back. In another there was an old cart-horse who did not seem to mind sharing his space with them. On the hill behind Maenordy they found an abandoned cottage which at first they joyfully imagined making into their own house, but the dried-up dead crows and stained, ripped mattress in the bedroom gave them such a bad feeling that they never went back.

Another time they heard screaming, thin and high, and searched the field until they found the rabbit, its leg caught in a trap. They managed to lever the trap open with sticks and watched the poor little thing limp trembling away, after which they dropped stones on all the traps they could find to spring them until the farmer complained to Mrs. Macpherson, who said he would shoot them if he caught them at it again.

There was a fox's den, too, in the woods, with a stink that made Gillian want to blow out hard through her nose. Once they saw the fox himself, so fine and delicate, with his gleaming eyes and pointed snout, twenty times better than Red Riding Hood's wolf. They watched and waited for him for weeks, but they never saw him again until the day they found him hanged. A trap had been laid for him too, and he swung from a tree by the neck, stiff and snarling.

"Why was the fox hanged?" Gillian and Tommy stood hand-in-hand in front of Mrs. Macpherson.

She squinched her eyes at them. "For a warning," she said.

They stared back at her. Tommy turned to Gillian, his mouth wobbling. "What'd we do?"

"Nothing." She held his hand tight. "It wasn't us. It was a warning to the fox."

He gaped at her before running off with his chin in the air and his arms flung out behind, being not a goose but a Spitfire, the low sun shining red through his sticking-out ears.

THE GOOD WEATHER CAME TO an end in October, and there were many days of wind and rain when they played after school in the almost empty barn. In a dark corner of that shadowy, sweet-smelling place where the odd ray of sunlight lit up the dancing dust, they built, out of leftover bales of straw and metal milk crates, a little golden room. Straw-covered boards made a roof, two bales served as seats, and an upside-down crate became a table on which Gillian put a jam jar full of Michaelmas daisies. An old calendar with a picture of baby rabbits on it made it even more home-like.

Sitting on the prickly bales along with Tommy, Glory Anna, her doll, and Tommy's teddy bear, Rupie, she would teach Tommy his alphabet with a slate and chalk, rewarding him with miniature Dolly Mixture sweets doled out one by one while Dinah, the Macphersons' brown and white spaniel, who was going to have puppies, drooled in expectation of her share. Gillian would make up stories there about The Little People who lived right beneath them in The Kingdom Under the Earth, or she would read to Tommy from her big red book, *The Children's Golden Treasury.* Sometimes they would sing: *London Bridge is Falling Down, A Bicycle Made for Two,* or, still one of Tommy's favorites, *Incy, Wincy Spider.* They would study Dinah, too, wondering about the puppies.

They decided to call this secret den Cartref, 'Home', like their grandparents' house, and for months, from autumn until the Christmas holidays, they were safe and free and happy enough there.

THERE WAS EXCITEMENT AT MAENORDY. Angus was coming home from boarding school for the Christmas holidays. Mrs. Macpherson bustled around, getting ready for his arrival, polishing and baking, and, astonishingly, bursting into a carol once in a while. She even put up a Christmas tree, rather dingily decorated in Gillian's opinion, and gathered holly and ivy to stick around the newel post and drape along the mantelpiece.

The children first met the great, grown-up boy in the lamplit, wood-panelled dining room that smelled of the rabbit pie Mrs. Macpherson was cooking for dinner.

"Well, hello! What have we here?" He was smiling a funny sideways smile and rubbing his big hands together like Jack-in-the-Beanstalk's giant as the children stood, hand in hand, on the patterned carpet looking up at him. Gillian saw that he was tall and thin, with thick, red-brown hair and a long nose.

"Are they good?" he said to his mother. "They *look* good. Matter of fact, they look good enough to eat." He laughed and fished in his pocket to give them each a black toffee.

TO THEIR SURPRISE, ANGUS SPENT a lot of time with them. He would take them for walks through the bare, silent woods and fields, talking and even sometimes listening to them. One afternoon he scared Gillian by taking a gun with him and pointing it all over the place, but to her relief all the birds and animals hid from him. It was hard to keep up as he strode along in his tall, shining boots, especially for Tommy, but when Angus suggested one day that only Gillian should go for a walk with him, Tommy set up such a racket that the subject was quickly dropped. Bicycle rides, though, were for Gillian only, since Tommy was obviously too little for that.

"Just you and me, eh?" Angus would say, as they hurtled down the hill to the sweet shop on the corner, Gillian perched on the crossbar. "You like that, don't you?" She did too, especially when they bought a bar of Cadbury's Fruit and Nut, or a triangular packet of sherbet with a liquorice straw.

Angus was kind to them all right, and they enjoyed the sweets he bought, but they were never by themselves anymore, and could not get to their den for nearly a week. Finally, however, the day came when he had to go to Brecon with his mother to do some Christmas shopping, and they were free at last to go to Cartref.

In the gloom of the barn, Gillian saw that their den had stopped shining. She looked at the dusty, straw-scattered boards and the dried-up Michaelmas daisies. The place definitely needed cheering up. "I know what, Tommy!" She clapped her hands. "Let's decorate Cartref for Christmas!"

He gawped at her. "But what'll we do for decorations?"

"Just you see!"

Using an old pair of clippers they found in the barn, they gathered armfuls of holly and ivy from the woods, Gillian even managing to wrench a bunch of mistletoe off the low, twisty apple tree which Angus had shown her how to climb. They stuck the stems into crates and between bales and planks until Cartref glowed with shiny, dark green leaves, red and white berries, and golden straw. When they finished, they stared at it in awe. It was as beautiful as Aladdin's cave in the pantomime.

Tommy wiped squashed mistletoe berries off his hands onto the front of his new coat. His nose was running, but his cheeks were bright red and his blue eyes were blazing. "Gilly!" he whispered, "Let's show it to Angus!"

"But it's our secret, stupid."

"Oh, please, Gilly! He's our friend. He won't tell. And we can have a party! Pop n' sweets n' things! It'd be fun!"

Gillian looked around at their gleaming creation. She wanted to keep it safe and secret forever, but in a way she wanted to share it too. She wanted it to be admired. And it was true, Angus was their friend. "If you like," she said. "It'll probably be all right."

"I SAY! JUST THE THING, EH?" Angus was impressed. He crouched in Cartref and looked around with his twisted smile. "You mean to say, you clever little monkeys, you've had this smashing place all to yourselves all along, and you never told anyone?"

They declared proudly that no one had any idea of their secret, and they all settled down comfortably, bulgy Dinah included, to share a bottle of fizzy *Tizer* and the striped humbugs Angus had brought, and to examine the disc of ice, clear as glass, which had come off Dinah's drinking bowl.

As they sucked the sweets, Angus did a strange thing. He slid his hand under Gillian's jersey and stroked her back, moving his hand around, over and over, as if learning the shape of her bones off by heart. She squirmed away from him, but he kept on stroking.

"Tell us about the puppies," Tommy said, dribbling. "How'd they get in there?"

Angus stopped his stroking. He looked at Dinah, and then at Gillian.

"Tell you what, old chap," he grinned at Tommy. "Be a sport and go look in my bike basket for some more sweeties."

Tommy scrambled off, and Angus turned back to Gillian, getting his hand under her skirt that time. "Come on, Gilly! Why won't you let me do that? I won't hurt you. Now this doesn't hurt at all, does it?"

She shot to her feet. "Angus, that's rude! Don't be so ... so *common!"* She was shocked. He should have stopped all that sort of thing when he was little, as she had. "Grown-ups don't do things like that."

"Is that so?" He seemed to think that was funny, but then grabbed her arm, his face suddenly serious. "Listen. Come here tonight, after he's asleep."

What was he talking about? "No, I can't. Let go! You're hurting me, Angus!"

He looked down at her, frowning. "You must. If you don't, I'll have to tell my mother about this place. You'll get a royal beating for being so sly, and you'll never be allowed to come here again. I bet she'd tell on you to your mother too."

Gillian thought about it. The beating she could stand perhaps. She had already survived some of those. But to make her mother disappointed in her? That would be awful. And what about Cartref? Mrs. Macpherson was so mean, she'd surely put an end to it. But how could they live without their den? Where would they go? What would they do?

"Come on. What's it going to be? Make up your mind." He let go of her arm and stroked it gently, smiling at her, nice again. He lifted her chin with his finger. "I won't hurt you, you know. I'm your friend. I won't even touch you, I promise. Cross my heart and hope to die."

That was a real promise. No one would say that if they didn't mean it.

"All right," she said, as Tommy stumbled in, proudly waving a Fry's peppermint sandwich bar. "I'll come."

THEY WERE IN BED BY SIX O'CLOCK, as usual, and it was not quite dark. It was cold in their bedroom, and Tommy had trouble getting to sleep. "Don't go," he whispered. "Stay here with me."

"I must go. I said I would. If I don't, he'll tell on us. I'll only stay for a bit, though. I won't be gone long."

As soon as they had warmed up under the heavy blankets and lumpy eiderdown, and Tommy had finally fallen asleep, Gillian slithered from the high bed onto the icy floorboards and put on her sheepskin slippers and the red wool dressing gown her grandmother had made her. She tucked Glory Anna under her arm and crossed the shadowy room to the door. From there she looked back at Tommy, deep in his hot sleep, with Rupie beside him. He looked like a baby, not like a big boy of four at all, his cheeks red and his dark hair stuck to his forehead.

She managed the stairs, avoiding the creaky bits, tiptoed past the sitting room where she could hear people on the wireless, laughing, and crept along the dark hallway to the back door. Slowly and carefully she lifted the latch and slipped out into the cold night.

By the upward-leaping shadows from a hurricane lamp on the floor, she saw that Angus was in Cartref already. He was sitting on one of the bales, white and strange-looking, as though he too were scared. The hands he held out to her trembled as he pulled her to him between his knees, and she could feel his heart thudding. A smell of mothballs came from the rough blanket he had brought. He reached up under her nightdress and put his hands right around her waist and shook her.

"Why did you come?" His voice was shaky, and his breath smelt funny, like his father's.

"What?"

"Why did you come?" He stared hard into her eyes. "It was because you wanted to, wasn't it?" He shook her again. "Wasn't it?" The fierce expression and the upside-down lighting made him look like the Demon King in the pantomime she saw last Christmas.

Gillian nodded dumbly.

"That's right. You came because you wanted to."

Dinah whined and struggled out of her *cwch.*

Angus pulled Gillian hard against him. This felt all wrong, and she was frightened. She struggled to escape, trying to think what to do. If she screamed loud enough, Mrs. Macpherson might hear her and come, but she would be furious with her for being in the barn at that time, and would probably tell her mother, who would also be very angry. She knew, too, that Mrs. Macpherson would never take her side against Angus. Grown-ups always stuck together.

"Stop it Angus, please! You're scaring me!"

Kicking Dinah out of the way, Angus pushed Gillian down on the blanket and undid the snake clasp on his belt.

Was he going to beat her?

As she tried to scramble out of Cartref, he reached after her, grabbed her ankle and pulled her back in. "You can fight if you like," he said, holding her down with his knee and grabbing both her flailing fists with one hand. "But you can't win."

"THAT WASN'T SO BAD, NOW, WAS IT?" he said later, doing up his belt. "You see, I didn't hurt you, did I?" He brushed the straw and dust off her and dabbed with his handkerchief at the sticky mess, like squashed mistletoe berries, on her thighs and stomach.

"Don't look at me like that, Gilly. It's your fault really, you know, the way you look, so little and skinny, with that soft, frizzy hair and those big green eyes, making me feel this way. Anyway, we're special friends now, right?" He fixed his hot, red-brown gaze on her. "But this is to be our secret. D'you understand? You breathe a word of this, and I'll tell them it was all *your* idea; that you suggested it. What would your mother think of that, eh?" He grabbed her wrist. "Now come here, I want to play some more."

A high scream came from the house, and another, and another. Angus dropped her wrist and ran to the back door of the barn. Looking back, he bared his teeth at her. "Remember what I said!"

Trembling, Gillian crept with Dinah to the other door. Lights came on in the house. The side door opened, and she saw the Macphersons come out with torches, calling her name. The screaming kept on: "Gilly! Gilly! Gilly! Where are you?"

She ran towards the screams. When a beam from a torch picked her out, Tommy shot past the Macphersons into her arms.

"It was the fox!" he shouted between hiccupping sobs, as she grabbed him under the monkey puzzle tree. "The fox was alive, and he was blowing the house down. And then he ran away with you on his back! And then I woke up, and you were gone, and I thought the fox had really got you!"

She held him tight and looked around at the grown-ups, Angus somehow included, who were staring at them indignantly.

Mrs. Macpherson was coldly angry. "What's the meaning of this shameful behaviour, you sly, disobedient girl? Would you mind informing us where you were, and what, exactly, you were doing?"

Gillian looked helplessly at Angus who seemed lost in staring up at the twists and turns of the tree. There was a frozen silence while her brain raced from one barrier to another. Then she heard herself say, bold as brass, "I just wanted to see if Dinah'd had her puppies."

BACK IN BED, STILL SHIVERING and stinging from the slaps, she slowly calmed down. With Tommy finally asleep again beside her, she began to think about herself. Mrs. Macpherson had said she was sly and disobedient, and she'd obviously become an awful liar. And what about what Angus had done? Was she *common* now? It must have something to do with that secret, too shameful to be talked about, that only grown-ups knew. What was more, her mother, besides asking her to be brave and not whine, had most particularly asked her never to do anything to make her ashamed of her. Gillian knew, as well as she had ever known anything, that if her mother ever heard what had happened that evening, she would be horribly ashamed. "I can't love you if you are not good," she had said more than once. So Gillian would not tell her, ever.

Before she finally warmed up and calmed down enough to go to sleep, she remembered that she had left Glory Anna in the barn, but decided she did not care.

THE DAY ARRIVED FOR THEIR mother's Christmas Eve visit, her first since she had left them at Maenordy. She had telephoned once, causing Tommy to be so upset that Mrs. Macpherson had asked her not to do it again. Their father had written a letter, almost indecipherable despite being printed, which Gillian would take out and work on from time to time, planning to write a reply. He had been supposed to come for the Christmas visit too, but had phoned that morning to say he had an emergency at the hospital.

Tommy had pestered Gillian for weeks about how many days were left until they came, and she had been as excited as he was, but now that the time was nearly here, the tight feeling that took hold in her chest at the thought of seeing her mother again closed in until she could hardly breathe.

FIRST THEY HEARD, AND THEN saw the car crunch up the drive to park under the monkey puzzle tree. Then there was their mother, beaming with love and joy, holding out her arms. Tommy hurtled into them to be hugged, kissed, and exclaimed over. But when her mother opened her arms to her, Gillian could not move. When she took Gillian's chin in her hand, Gillian had to force herself to look into her puzzled eyes.

"What's the matter?" Her mother smoothed Gillian's hair. "Are you forgetting all about your poor mummy?"

"No, Mummy. I'd never do that."

Her mother hugged her. "That's my good girl. I'm so proud of you. Daddy says he's sorry he couldn't come—you know he had to go to the hospital—but he sends his love to you both. He said to say he's proud of you, too."

As the day went on, with Angus nowhere to be seen, and Mrs. Macpherson being weirdly nice and kind, not saying a word about shameful behaviour, and even telling their mother how good the children always were, Gillian began to be able to breathe more easily, to talk to her mother again, and even to smile once or twice.

Before she left, her mother brought in from the car the gaily-wrapped Christmas presents, not to be opened until Christmas Day. The huge one for Gillian would turn out to be a life-sized Shirley Temple doll, all dimply smile and curls, doomed to be stuck at the back of the wardrobe to simper alone.

As she was getting ready to leave, and they were all, Angus now included, standing by the car, Gillian's mother put her arm around her. “Gill, you’re very quiet. Is everything all right? You *are* happy here, aren’t you?”

This was it. She had to be strong and brave. She stood up straight.

“Yes, I’m very happy here, thank you, Mummy.”

But she had bargained without Tommy.

“Mummy!” He stood in front of their mother, hands on hips. “Angus makes Gilly go to the barn with him in the night!”

The two mothers drew in their breath sharply. Gillian hung her head and closed her eyes. She wanted to disappear forever.

“Gilly is this true?” Her mother opened her eyes wide at her. Gillian stood there, frozen, unable to move.

“Is this true, Angus?” said Mrs. Macpherson.

“No! No! I never!” Angus’s face was white.

“Yes he did!” Tommy shouted. “She had to go last night, an’ the night before!”

“Angus?” Mrs. Macpherson’s voice had a dangerous lift to it.

“It’s her fault.” Angus looked as if he was going to cry. “She suggested it, not me. I won’t do it again, I promise.”

“Get in the house!”

Gillian knew she must stop the truth coming out! “We didn’t do anything, Mummy,” she said. “We just talked.”

Mrs. Macpherson and Angus stopped on the steps and looked at her.

“Angus.” Her mother’s voice was sharp. “Tell me the truth now. Why did you take Gillian into the barn with you at night?”

Angus clasped his hands together in front of his chest and smiled his twisted smile.

“Well as a matter of actual fact, Mrs. Davies, to tell you the honest truth, we did go there a couple of times just to have a look at Dinah, who’s going to have puppies any day now, you know. Gillian wanted to see if the puppies were here yet.” He blinked at her. "And it wasn't, really speaking, all that late. Not even seven o'clock."

Gillian saw her mother draw herself up to her full height, an expression on her face that meant trouble. "And you think that's a suitable subject for a child her age?"

Angus did a sort of squirm. "No, of course I don't. I see that now. It was a mistake on my part. I'm terribly sorry, Mrs. Davies. Honestly, I'll never do anything like that again. I promise you. Cross my heart and hope to die."

Gillian felt herself being led around to the far side of the car. "Is that really what happened, Gillian? Was it just to go and see Dinah? Tell me the truth now. It's very important." Her mother knelt down to hold her chin so that she could not look away.

"Yes." Gillian was sure of only one thing in all this confusion. "That's why we were there."

Somehow she managed to look straight at her mother, her back stiff.

"Mrs. Davies, I'm going to send the dog over to the farm," Mrs. Macpherson said, adding to Gillian's misery, "That way there'll be no more temptation."

Her mother looked up at the sky, biting her lip and thinking. After a pause she stood up. "Well, I suppose that's all right then." She stared, frowning, at Angus who gazed back, his eyes wide open.

Turning again to Gillian she said, "But there must be absolutely no more going out at night. All right, Gilly? None whatsoever! Do I have your promise?"

Gillian nodded, numb with misery.

"Goodbye, my darlings." Their mother gathered them both to her. "Oh, I do so wish I could take you home with me, but it's much too dangerous."

Tommy began to cry. "Take us home, Mummy! Please! Don't leave us! We don't want to be evaporated!"

She covered a smile, exchanging a glance with Mrs. Macpherson. "Now, don't be a tiny-whiny, Tommy. You know there's a war on, and you have to be safe, the two of you. I'll come back as soon as I can." She kissed them both, thanked Mrs. Macpherson again, and in a swirl of silk and *Je Reviens,* got into the car.

"Goodbye, sweethearts. Merry Christmas! Be good children now."

Still keeping her chin up as Tommy sobbed beside her, Gillian watched, dry-eyed, as the little grey car disappeared down the drive.

"You must be Mrs. Davies's daughter from Canada." The doctor walked briskly down the hallway towards Gillian, smiling, pristine in his white coat, a stethoscope around his neck. "I'm Dr. Gabriel."

Getting up to greet him, Gillian saw glossy hair greying at the temples and deep lines in his cheeks, becoming parentheses when he smiled. He must have been a lovely little boy, she thought: black curly hair, dimples, quick to laughter; like Tommy in that photo of him at four years old just before their evacuation, with his dark curls, big ears, and wide grin.

"Let's take a look at the patient." Dr. Gabriel stepped back for her to enter the room. He raised his voice as he followed her in. "You must be so pleased that your daughter's come all this way to see you, Mrs. Davies."

Her mother snapped to attention at the sound of the doctor's voice, her hollow eyes suddenly bright, and her smile at full wattage.

"Doctor! You've come to see me at last!" Ignoring Gillian, she held out a still elegant hand. "I've been waiting for you all morning."

"Well, you see, Mrs. Davies," he winked a dark eye at Gillian, who had slipped around to the other side of the bed, "I keep the best for last." He put the stethoscope to the old woman's chest and listened, his eyes on the ceiling, his smile slowly fading. He moved the instrument around, repeating the procedure several times.

"How do you feel, Mrs. Davies?" He trained a pencil flashlight into her eyes.

"All the better for seeing you, Doctor!"

Oh for Heaven's sake! Does it never end? Gillian turned away to busy herself with the flowers, a type of small lily, she had brought. A refrain from her childhood, "Your mother could charm the birds from the trees," entered her head as she pulled the red, trumpet-shaped blooms to the front and pushed the paler ones to the back.

"Can you turn on your side, Mrs. Davies?"

She seemed to lack the strength to move her own weight, little as it was. The doctor pushed her half over and asked Gillian to hold her there, a bundle of bones, while he listened to her back. He straightened up and helped Gillian ease her on to the pillows before turning to leave.

"You're going, Doctor? So soon?" The old woman held out her hand again.

"I'll be back to see you again before long, Mrs. Davies." He smiled at her, then looked at Gillian and glanced at the door.

"I'm worried about your mother." He had pulled the door shut after them as they left the room. "Her lungs are still very congested, her heart is weak, and her temperature is up. It's not a good combination, but we're going to try a different antibiotic to see if that might do the trick." He walked off down the hallway, coat flapping, through the smells of eau de cologne, Johnson's baby powder, and Depends, to descend the wide, curving stairway.

Her audience gone, her mother dropped the façade. "I don't feel well at all," she said breathlessly. She lifted her sunken eyes to Gillian's, their faded pupils rimmed with a raised whitish circle. "I'll be better soon, though, won't I?"

You have an infection, your lungs are shot, and your heart is giving out. What do you think?

"You'll be all right, Mum," Gillian said. "The antibiotics will fix you up. They always have, haven't they?"

Her mother relaxed into the pillows, until she was seized again by another paroxysm of coughing. When she had caught her breath, she said, wheezing, "Grandma was here, you know. She was here for two months before she died." She shot a look at Gillian. "But as I told you, *I* have no intention of *dying*. I'm going home to my little bungalow, and to my Tweetie-Pie and Sylvester, who are pining for me."

Neither the cat nor the canary had shown any signs that Gillian could see of decline. "They're just fine, Mum."

Her mother pursed her lips and shook her head. "They really feel the separation, you know, animals do. Grandma's old cat, Twm, died while she was here. I remember her talking about it. It was very sad."

This could be the opening she had been waiting for. Gillian sat down beside the bed. "Mum," she took her mother's hand and stroked the raised blue veins and brown age-spots on its back, "did you and Grandma talk much while she was here?" She could tell her mother that children felt the separation too; that she and Tommy certainly had. After which she could bring up the years when they had been evacuated at her grandparents' home; and that, perhaps, could lead back to the previous year at Croesffordd, at which point she would be able, at last, tell her mother what had happened there.

Her mother removed her hand. "Yes we did. We talked about old times, and about Grandpa, and about your father of course, and my family, and people in Tregwyr. She talked about you and Tommy too; those years you spent with them, and how happy you were there." A theatrical sigh brought on a fit of coughing. "As a matter of fact," she resumed after she had caught her breath, "I always felt that you two loved being there so much, you didn't want to come back home to live with your father and me." She shook her head, flicking a sideways glance at Gillian. "It was very hard on me, you know, Gillian, being separated from you children for so long."

What was that? Gillian stared at her. *We didn't want to come home?*

She stood up. *It was hard on* you?

"I've got to go." She grabbed her coat and purse off the foot of the bed, and before her mother could raise any argument, was at the door. "I hope you'll feel better tomorrow."

Her mother seemed to shrink, suddenly looking even older and frailer. Raising her eyebrows she looked out of the window. "Don't you worry about me! You go off and enjoy yourself. I'll be all right."

"I'll be back in the morning."

"If you have the time." Her mother studied the ceiling.

Hearing the rattling cough as she reached the stairs, Gillian stood still, her hand on the polished banister and her head turned, until she saw Sunita slip into her mother's room and heard the coughing die down.

She hurried down the stairs and out onto the quiet street, the words *You didn't want to come home* playing over and over in her head. It had been all they had ever wanted, both at their grandparents' house, kind as they had been, and of course before that, at Maenordy where she and Tommy had kept a calendar, crossing off the months, weeks, and days of their exile until the great day finally arrived when they left Croesffordd for good.

GILLIAN SAT IN THE SHADE on the steps of Maenordy, clutching her cardigan around her and staring at a daisy that had struggled through the gravel at her feet while Tommy, panting and red-faced in the August sunshine, galloped back and forth between the steps and the bend in the drive. He was watching for their parents' car to come into sight and chanting, "We are going *ho*-ome! We are going *ho*-ome!" at the top of his funny, gruff voice.

Gillian narrowed her eyes at him. "Shut up, you idiot!"

He skidded to a wide-legged stop on the gravel and stared at her, his wet, red mouth open.

"What? Whassa matter? Don't you want to go home?"

"Course I do, stupid! I hate it here. It's just…" Why did she wish that the car buzzing unstoppably along the road towards them would turn around and go back? It didn't make any sense.

"You look like a dumdum running around like that," she said, as Tommy went on staring, his mouth drooping, "You're all red, your socks have fallen down, and your shirt's hanging out at the back. Mummy and Daddy will think you're a mess when they come." She shrugged. "*If* they come. I heard the clock strike one ages ago. They're late. They've probably changed their minds, and they're not coming."

"They *are* coming!" Tears filled his eyes. "I know they are! You're *horrid!*" He picked up a handful of gravel and threw it at her just as a toot came from down the drive.

Brushing off the gravel, Gillian picked the daisy and scrutinized the slender, fuzzy stem and pink-tipped petals while Tommy slobbered over their mother in the front seat.

A crunch of footsteps announced her father's approach.

"Hello, Gill." Balding sandy head on one side, he was stuffing tobacco into his pipe. "What's the matter? Aren't you glad to see us?"

"Yes Daddy." She glanced up at the grey flannels, and down again at the pattern of little holes in his polished brown brogues. The fragrance of his tobacco, mixed with that of Imperial Leather soap, brought back the sensation of being held giggling in his arms as he rubbed his scratchy chin against her cheek. In the old days.

"I expected a bit more of a welcome." He lit his pipe, smiling and frowning at the same time, as she squinted up at him. "But perhaps you're overwhelmed. Is that it?"

"What does *overwhelmed* mean?" There was comfort in being able to talk the way they used to.

"It means 'overcome'—feeling it's all a bit too much for you. Is that the problem?"

"Yes." She was grateful for the word and stashed it away for future reference. "I'm overwhelmed."

After the suitcases and bags had been loaded into the boot, Mrs. Macpherson shook hands with their parents and made to kiss the children goodbye. Tommy hid behind their mother, and Gillian, stiff as a post, turned her head away at just at the right moment as Mrs. Macpherson's long nose and sharp chin approached. Her mother raised her eyebrows, but said nothing.

As her father started the engine, Angus came running out of the barn. "Here," he thrust Glory Anna at Gillian, panting, "You forgot this."

Gillian looked at the dirty, straw-covered doll she had not played with since before Christmas, and pushed it back at him. "I don't want it. Keep it yourself." She wound up the window and flung herself back in her seat. As they drove away, she saw him watching from under the monkey puzzle tree, the doll dangling from his hand, and thanked her lucky stars she had escaped from him and from what he had said he was going to do the next time.

"That was very rude!" Her mother looked around at her. "I thought it was really nice of Angus to fetch your doll for you. What's the matter with you?"

"Yes," her father said, "What was that all about?"

"I'm sick of the stupid doll. It's babyish." She wrinkled her nose at Tommy and they drove on in silence.

As they passed through the village, she saw Gladys, weighed down by a full basket, come out of the greengrocer's shop. Leaning out of the car window, Gillian thumbed her nose and stuck out her tongue. Gladys dropped the basket and ran into the middle of the road to make what Gillian knew was a very *common* gesture after the car.

The silence in the car persisted for a while until Tommy began bouncing around in the back seat, starting up again with his *We are going home!* song. Their mother turned around in the front seat. "You're not going home, darlings," she said. "It's not safe yet for you to come back to Swansea. Grandma's better now, so you're going to live with Grandma and Grandpa in Tregwyr! Won't that be fun? We can come and see you at weekends, and you might even be able to come home for the day sometimes!" She beamed at them, seemingly thrilled with the arrangement.

Tommy shrank like a punctured balloon. Gillian bit her bottom lip and picked the scab off her knee until it bled. Only the day before, Mrs. Macpherson had told them their parents were taking them away. And now they really were leaving Croesffordd, but not to go home.

"Is *underwhelmed* a word?" she asked, lifting her head, but received no reply.

BY THE TIME THEY REACHED TREGWYR, their grandparents' village, which lay about six miles from Swansea, she was getting her mind around to the idea. Even though they would not actually be at home, they would be closer to it and away from Maenordy anyway, and she would be safe at last from Angus and his terrifying plans.

She remembered helping her grandmother with the baking, putting wings on butterfly cakes and placing glacé cherries just right on queen cakes. Perhaps Grandma would teach her how to knit. Also, school would be taught in English, and, even better, there would be no Gladys. Tommy was cheering up too, asking if Grandpa would take him to the market to see the animals. By the time they got to the brick house on the corner they were ready to run into the arms of their grandparents.

Her grandmother took one look at Gillian. "Oh *cariad*!" She put her arms around her. "My darling! What have they done to my little girl?"

It was all Gillian could do not to burst into tears, but she stiffened her back. She must not allow her grandmother to get too close. She could see too much.

"Look at this child, Iris!" Her grandmother turned her around to face her mother. "She's as white as a sheet and there's nothing to her. We'll have to see what we can do about that, never mind that old rationing. Tommy doesn't look quite so bad, although he's not the plump little fellow he was, either."

Their mother glanced at them. "It's just their age, Mam. They're bound to be thinner."

THAT EVENING, AFTER THEIR PARENTS had left and Tommy had calmed down, they sat in the living room, Tommy sprawled, hic-cupping, on their grandfather's lap in the big leather armchair, and Gillian perched next to her grandmother on the brown velvet loveseat. Their grandmother wanted to hear all about Maenordy, and Tommy cheered up enough to tell her about the horrible pigeon pies which always made him sick, the burnt porridge, and lumpy custard. He started prattling on about the barn but caught Gillian's eye and veered off the subject, and, when they were asked about Angus, did not contradict her statement that Angus was always away at school and they had hardly ever seen him.

In the morning, while their grandfather took Tommy to the station to see the train come in, Gillian helped her grandmother prepare the dinner. She was shown how to choose the best string beans from those growing up the garden fence; not too little and thin, and not too big and tough. They pulled up potatoes, which she scrubbed clean by herself, and then made Welsh cakes together, Gillian sieving the flour, and watching how to rub in the margarine. When the cakes were done, she was given one to take out into the garden.

Wary of bees droning and bumbling in the hearts of the roses, she inhaled and rated the various fragrances. She rubbed thyme, sage, and rosemary between her fingers and nibbled a sprig of parsley as she watched a white butterfly lazily open and close its wings on a lacy, dark-green cabbage leaf. At the bottom of the garden, she found she had grown enough to sit on a low bend in the trunk of the elderberry tree, now laden with umbrella-like clusters of little black berries. Swinging her legs in the dappled shade, she savoured a handful of the bitter-sweet fruit along with her still-warm Welsh cake.

That evening they listened to music. Their grandfather wound up the gramophone before carefully lowering the needle onto the old, familiar *His Master's Voice* records: Madame Adelina Patti, performing something with lots of trills and amazing high notes, and Dame Clara Butt, sounding just like a man at times, splendidly belting out *The Lost Chord.* Finally he put on a record Gillian had not heard before: someone called John McCormick singing, *I'll Take You Home Again, Kathleen.*

As the clear notes died away, Gillian saw tears in her grandfather's eyes. She knew all about homesickness, that piercing, paralyzing ache for the feel of home, and went over to him, putting her hand on his knee. "When were you away from home, Grandpa?"

"I spent a week in London once, with the choir." He wiped his eyes with a spotted handkerchief. "Nearly killed me."

"Is that why you're crying?"

"No." He put his arm around her. "It's that voice brings tears to my eyes, Gillian *fach*. The voice of an angel!"

On other evenings, their grandmother would recite poetry by heart. She favoured really sad poems like the one about the death of the miner's only son, beginning, *The cottage was a thatched one,/ The outside poor and mean.* Gillian, who hated to be seen crying, would be out the door before her grandmother, her voice quavering with pathos, could get to *I feel no pain, dear mother, now/ But oh, I am so dry!*

Gillian preferred the funny poems and stories, and the everlasting quotations. *Heat me those irons hot!* her grandmother would exclaim, taking the poker out of the fire and waving it. Or, raising an eyebrow over her flashing glasses, she would hiss, *But Brutus is an* honourable *man*!

There were books too, mostly boring, apart from the heavy, leather-bound Bible, with its fancy metal clasps and bright, tissue-covered pictures; and *Pilgrim's Progress,* with its embossed cover and scary black and white illustrations. Like most children in the village, they could never have comics in the house or play on Sundays, so they spent much of the day poring over those two volumes, puzzling together over pictures like *The Sacrifice of Isaac*, or *Christian Struggles in the Slough of Despond***,** Gillian doing her best to follow the text. Sundays were not much fun, it was true, but it was a million times better than living at Maenordy.

Pushing the matter of Angus into the darkest corner in the cellar of her mind, Gillian began to relax. Tommy took his cue from her, and the whole thing seemed to be successfully forgotten, apart from the nightmare that sometimes tore her nights open.

In her dream, Angus was making her skate, although she did not know how, over thin ice with reeds growing through it, and cracks running across it, and bubbles moving under it. She could smell the ice and hear it cracking, but still she had to wobble on, in skates much too big for her, towards the bottomless middle of the pond, into which she knew she would fall. When she woke screaming as the ice broke, and her grandmother was comforting her and asking what her nightmare was about, she always made up a different dream.

One afternoon, after such a night, she heard her grandmother say thoughtfully to her mother, "Deep as the well that girl is!" and had held her breath. Her mother had looked up in surprise but then changed the subject, and the scary moment passed.

SHE LIKED THE SCHOOL AND MISS THOMAS, her teacher, who knew all about King Arthur, and the earth going round the sun, and all sorts of things. Nobody there behaved like Gladys. The other girls seemed to accept her, and Mary Bevan and Sian Lloyd had both asked her back to their houses to play and for tea.

Tommy liked the Infants' School too. Gillian's alphabet and numbers drills seemed to have paid off, and he was not behind. She had seen him kicking the ball and playing conkers with the other boys and knew he was not being picked on or shut out, so it was annoying that he still clung to her, following her about and telling on her when she sent him away.

THE YEAR AFTER THEY CAME to live with their grandparents, there was great excitement in Tregwyr. An Apostolic convention was to be held in Swansea, a huge event, not to be missed, their grandparents said. Since the convention would take up a whole Saturday and Sunday, it was arranged that the children would spend those two days with their parents, going back on the bus to Tregwyr each night in case of bombs.

They could hardly believe it. Two whole days at home! Tommy could not control his excitement, and clattered down the stairs, jumping the last three steps, running down the passage, shouting and singing at the top of his voice. He was making up for his year of imposed silence, their grandfather said, but their grandmother declared her nerves could hardly stand it. Gillian kept it all in, quietly savouring the prospect.

Once home, they did the rounds. They inspected their indoor den, the mousy-smelling secret cupboard with its spiral ceiling under the attic stairs, the torn eiderdown on the floor still spilling feathers. They checked the attic and found their dapple-grey rocking horse still there, with his flaring red nostrils and real horsehair mane and tail, as was the German helmet from the first war, and, best of all, the skull. Putty-coloured and shiny with a wired, moveable lower jaw, and eye sockets and nose-hole you could poke your fingers through, it made a wonderfully gruesome puppet. At first, Gillian had imagined that some poor person must have died unnoticed in their attic, until she was told the skull was just something left over from her father's medical studies. All the same, she thought, it was what was left of somebody's head and still pretty thrilling.

In the afternoon, left to themselves and fascinated by what they had been told about bomb sites, they set off to explore the changes in the neighbourhood. They had heard that big safe houses much like their own, houses they had been in, some of them, had been blown to smithereens. This they had to see. They did not have to look far, either; there was one such site just a few doors down.

Defying parental warnings and threats and stern notices from the town council, they squeezed around the plywood fence to find their way onto the property. Inside they stared around at the exposed wallpaper, once so private, the twisted bedstead, the broken kitchen sink. Their brown Oxfords crunched on sparkling glass shards. They had a good laugh at the lavatory which had landed upright in the flattened rose bushes, but fell silent at the sight of a china doll lying amongst the stones, its glass eyes, the same bright blue as Tommy's, staring up at the clear sky from its cracked face. A bony black cat watched their every move from under a one-legged chair.

Giddy with the strangeness, the unlawfulness, the richness of it all, they poked around in the debris. Gillian found a high-heeled, peep-toed shoe and tried it on, giggling, while Tommy pretended to drink beer from a battered pewter mug, smacking his lips, and staggering about like Great-Uncle Tom.

Sensibly resisting the lure of the stairs, they began to search for treasure, an emerald necklace maybe, or a bag of sovereigns, and found it when Tommy discovered a sixpenny piece, and Gillian picked up a shiny, black music box which played *We'll Meet Again* every time she opened the lid, and which she stashed away in the satchel she had brought along in hopes of finding something amazing.

They were getting ready to go back on the bus with their grandparents when their mother picked up the satchel and discovered the music box. Having got out of Gillian where they had found it, she clutched it to her breast.

"You took your brother onto that bomb site?" She stared at Gillian, the whites of her eyes showing all around. "After everything we told you? For shame, Gillian! You could've been blown up by an unexploded bomb, both of you, or crushed under a collapsing wall! And I'll have you know, miss," she wagged a pointing finger, "this music box belonged to old Mrs. Beynon, who was *killed* in the blitz, right there, where you were walking around. And you want to keep it and play with it? I don't think so!" At seven years old, she said, Gillian should have known better. She had been irresponsible and disobedient and should be thoroughly ashamed of herself. She confiscated the box, telling them they would be forbidden to leave the house by themselves the following day. She was not sure they should be allowed to come home at all, she said, if they could not be trusted.

The bus back to Tregwyr was packed with chattering, beaming people, so excited by the convention that Gillian, still smarting from the music-box scrape, was afraid they were going to hold another stupid prayer meeting right there on the bus. As soon as the bus reached the outskirts of Swansea, however, they began to sing: first Dai Jones, the baritone, "famous throughout the valleys"; then Ceinwen Rhys, the chapel soloist; then more and more, until they were all singing, their heads thrown back,

Mae popeth yn dda!
Mae popeth yn dda!
Mae Iesu f'ynghâru!
Mae popeth yn dda!

"Everything's fine! Everything's fine! Jesus loves me! Everything's fine!" They rocked in their seats, Grandpa's bass voice booming out behind her, Grandma's sweet shaky treble rising up in descant beside her. She heard Tommy join in at the top of his voice, getting thumbs up all round; and when the bus driver threw his trumpet-like tenor into the mix, she could hold out no longer. *Mae popeth yn dda!* she sang, along with the rest of them, and felt for a moment that, despite everything, it was true.

THAT NIGHT SHE HAD THE DREAM AGAIN, but this time her mother was there, dancing on the far side of the pond, long hair floating behind her as she sang to the tune of the music box cradled in her arms. She did not seem to see Gillian trying to skate over the crazed ice towards her, or to hear her calling, but circled around, crooning to the box. Gillian could see the edges of the black hole widen as dark cracks in the ice zigzagged towards her.

"There, there, *cariad*." Her grandmother was holding her. "Shush, shush. *Mae popeth yn dda nawr.* Everything's all right now. You're safe as houses here with me and Grandpa. What was that old dream then? Tell Grandma."

Snuggled in her grandmother's arms, drinking hot milk with honey, Gillian told her a story about a wolf with red eyes and big teeth that was following her.

STILL BROODING ON *You didn't want to come home*, Gillian hurried away from Saint Anne's, her footsteps clicking on the pavement. She ran her hands through her hair before thrusting them deep into the pockets of her raincoat, tightly belted against the wind from the sea. Turning the corner, she came to the garden wall of her old home, now used, Tom had told her, for law offices. She stopped to put her hands on the rough stones, sheltered from the wind and warmed by the afternoon sun. The cushions of bright green moss between the stones still sprang back when pressed. The same clumps of tiny flowers, blue with yellow throats, like miniature snapdragons, trailed from the crevices. Breathing more slowly, she placed an awkward, adult finger and thumb around the throat of a single bloom, squeezed gently, and, *bow-wow*, the flower opened and closed its mouth.

The wall was far older than the house, her father had told her. Like the huge pear tree that used to grow against it, it had been part of a farm that had been there for centuries before the town swallowed it up.

VANNA FARRELL, HER CHILDHOOD FRIEND, lived further up the hill in a tall, gabled row house looking down over Cwmdonkin Park. Passing the house where Swansea's poet, Dylan Thomas, was born and lived, Gillian entered the park where she and Tommy often used to play. The bandstand was still there, but the oval, bronze "Keep off the Grass" notices were gone, and the drinking fountain had lost the chained iron cup from which they all, germs be damned, had drunk as children, Dylan Thomas no doubt included.

Vanna had not played there as a child. Gillian had met her in primary school in Tregwyr. According to Tom, she had become a successful stage actress, had starred in a couple of films set in Wales, and was currently playing a feisty older-woman role in a BBC Wales television series. Gillian had not seen her since leaving Swansea, apart from the few photos or newspaper clips Tom had sent from time to time, in which her height and shock of red curls seemed undiminished, her bony, freckled beauty still arresting. Remembering the early intensity of their childhood friendship, Gillian wondered if they would fall back into their old ways together. You don't really change as you get older, she thought; you are what you have always been, only more so.

The walk had done her good. By the time she reached Vanna's house, out of breath from the steep climb, she had recovered her composure. Even if she had not succeeded in breaking any ground with her mother that day, she could try again the next. There had to be a heart-to-heart; that unfinished business had to be seen to; she had to find closure, and so on. Could she come up with any more clichés? But they were clichés for good reason: family secrets are common. She smiled at the once-dreaded word.

Vanna greeted her, elegant in slim black pants and silvery silk shirt, her smoothed hair a modified red-gold, and her face, despite three decades of emoting, still beautiful. "Gillian! How marvellous to see you again! I'm so glad you came! You look wonderful!" She held Gillian by the shoulders; "Still positively willowy" (a kiss on one cheek), "and delicately complexioned" (a kiss on the other), "and cloudy-haired, of course." She put an arm around her. "Canada suits you. Come. Tell me *all* your news."

They climbed the stairs to the sunlit living room, located on the second floor in order to afford a glimpse of the sea. The sea seemed to be everywhere in Swansea, Gillian thought. Rome might have been built on seven hills, but Swansea could have been built on seventy-seven, all jostling each other as if vying for the ocean view. You never walked on flat ground in Swansea, and never felt far from the ocean.

In Vanna's living room they drank Lapsang Suchong tea out of fine Belleek cups, from the same set perhaps as the cup Gillian had seen all those years before in Tregwyr in the work-worn hands of Vanna's mother, sitting in her tattered chair amidst piles of books, surrounded by her five children. Sipping the hot, smoky tea, they talked of Gillian's life in Canada, and of Mrs. Farrell, and Vanna's brothers and sisters, all of whom, like Vanna, had done well, despite their unpromising start in life.

Vanna walked over to the window. Looking back with a brittle smile, she said, "And how is dear Tom? Did he get his divorce from that Swedish air-hostess?"

"I think it's been made final." The question puzzled Gillian. Vanna had known since Tregwyr days how Tom felt about her, but while never lacking for male company, had always averred contempt for men in general, and had kept him, in particular, at arm's length.

"That's two now. Her and Gladys," Vanna said.

"Let's not go into that."

"Third time lucky, maybe."

To change the subject, Gillian began reminiscing about their schooldays in Tregwyr, and Miss Thomas, their teacher. Skirting the touchy subject of the Eleven-Plus exam, they settled on the slightly less painful one of Gillian's grandmother's unfortunate prejudice against not only Catholics, but also the poor, and, worst of all, the Irish.

Her grey eyes sparkling, Vanna came over to sit by Gillian. "D'you remember when we lost Jesus?"

Gillian looked out of the window, smiling.

"D'YOU WANT TO COME to my house?" The new girl chewed on the end of a dark red plait and slid a sideways look at Gillian.

Gillian's grandmother had forbidden her to play with "the little Papist girl" who had come with her family that September to live in Tregwyr; but Gillian liked her; and she liked the look of her tall, thin mother with her bony, beautiful face and proud way of holding her head. Gillian had seen her in the grocer's shop with a little girl and a toddler beside her, and a baby in the pram, and had known by her hair that she must be Vanna's mother.

"Just for a minute then. My grandma said I had to go straight home after school."

They stopped in the middle of a row of narrow brick houses staggering up the hill by the railway cutting, houses facing right on the street, only the lowest of thresholds between them and the skimpy pavement.

"Mama, we've got a visitor!" Vanna threw open the battered front door. "Gillian's come to play with me!"

THERE WAS BARELY ROOM FOR the two of them to stand together in the gloomy hallway. Looking down, Gillian could make out bare floorboards through holes in the linoleum. Beside her, jagged white streaks marked where the brown anaglypta covering on the lower half of the wall had been bashed in. A strip of wallpaper had let go its hold halfway up the staircase and was flopping onto the stairs. Underneath the odours of nappies and cabbage lurked a strange smell: dark and sour, a bit tarry.

Mrs. Farrell came along the narrow passage from the back room into the hallway, pushing a fiery wisp of hair off her face with her wrist, a small, dark green book in her fingers. She moved as if underwater, slowly and gracefully.

"Hello, Gillian. I'm very pleased to meet you." Her voice was slow and lovely too, like the rest of her. Her eyes were long and grey, and her smile lit up the hall. A knight would gladly slay a dragon for her, Gillian thought.

"Mama! They were picking on me after school again today!" With a bang of the back door, a dark-haired boy, about six years old, rushed sobbing through the house. "They said to go back where I came from."

His mother knelt down and put her arms around him. "Oh, Francis, darling, don't cry. It'll get better."

"You said that yesterday. It's getting worse, not better! I hate it here in Wales, Mama! I *want* to go back where I came from. I want to go home to Dublin!" He looked tearfully around his mother at Gillian. "Hey, that's Tommy's sister! He's in my class at school. He's nice."

Mrs. Farrell stood up. "There you are, you see, darling boy. Not all of them are mean. You'll have a better day tomorrow." Something was tugging her skirt back against the length of her legs. She put a hand behind her. "Come and say hello to Gillian, Bridie. She's Vanna's friend." The little dark-haired girl Gillian had seen at the grocer's edged, scowling, into sight, still holding onto the brown serge skirt with one hand, and clutching the ragged blue jersey of the even smaller child with the other.

"This is Patrick." His mother smoothed his straight, red-gold hair. "He's two and a half, aren't you, darling?" Patrick beamed up at Gillian as a wail came from the back of the house, and Mrs. Farrell floated away, followed by the three younger children, Francis whining, "I'm so hungry, Mama!" as they disappeared into the back room. Gillian could not understand that. Despite the rationing, she and Tommy never went really hungry. There was just not enough food here to go round, she supposed.

"There's an awful lot of you, isn't there?" she said.

Vanna fiddled with the elastic band on the end of a plait. "How many are you?"

"Just me and Tommy. We want to go to go home too, like your brother. We're only living with our grandma and grandpa until the war ends, or even before, maybe. We go home on weekends sometimes." Annoyed, Gillian remembered how the last time they had been there, she had found Gladys in the kitchen with Mrs. Jones, smirking because she had been allowed back home for good, and they had not. "And then we're going back to Swansea to live with Mummy and Daddy again all the time. Where's your home?"

"Not here anyway! We're only here until Dada makes enough money at the steel works, and then we're going back home to Dublin."

"Vanna, my lovely girl, will you watch Kathleen for me? I have to change Patrick's trousers." Mrs. Farrell passed them, carrying the little boy who waved bye-bye to Gillian over his mother's shoulder, looking pleased with himself. Tommy would never have got away with wetting his pants at that age, she thought.

The baby's blue eyes, fringed with long black lashes, stared up at Gillian from the fastness of her cradle in the back room until her mouth pulled down, and she began to cry again.

"I've got to mind her for a minute. Will you stay, Gillian?"

Gillian hesitated. She should not have been in what her grandmother would have called 'a den of iniquity' anyway, and, interesting as Vanna's home was, with those piles of books standing around on the floor, it did not look as if there would be much playing.

"Sorry, I've got to go."

She ran all the way back to her grandparents' house with its flowery curtains, soft chairs, and shining furniture. A mouth-watering smell came from the kitchen of *cawl*, the soup her grandmother was making from neck of mutton and vegetables from the garden.

"You took your time coming home from school." Her grandmother looked at her over her glasses as she seasoned the soup. "I hope you weren't playing with that little Irish girl."

"No, I didn't play with her." Gillian chose not to go into details. "Grandma, why won't you let me be friends with Vanna? I really like her."

"No, Gillian. I don't want you to have anything to do with her, and neither does your grandfather. Those people worship idols." Her grandmother tasted the soup with a wooden spoon before briskly removing her floral apron.

"But they worship Jesus, Grandma, like us." Gillian had seen a carving of Jesus on the cross in the Farrells' back room, as well as a picture of him wearing a crown of giant thorns and pointing to his bleeding heart. There was a lovely little statue of the Virgin Mary, too, up on a shelf with candles.

"They don't worship Him in the right way, Gillian, and I'm telling you again, I don't want you to have anything more to do with her. D'you hear me now?" She pointed the spoon at Gillian, quite fiercely for her.

"But Grandma, everyone's mean to them. I'm the only girl who'll talk to Vanna, and the big boys are nasty to Francis."

"Yes they are!" Tommy charged in, grabbing a Welshcake. "They pull down his trousers."

"He's only six, Grandma, like Tommy." Gillian put her head on one side and looked up at her grandmother. "Didn't Jesus say to suffer the little children, and to love our neighbours? And they're *five* little children, and they are sort of our neighbours, aren't they? Would Jesus say I mustn't be friends with her? Would he, Grandma?"

"That's enough arguing, Gillian. You're not to play with her, and that's that. Go and get me some more rosemary from the bush and help me lay the table now, there's a good girl. We have to be quick tonight because Grandpa and I are going to a meeting at the Apostolic Hall."

Gillian put out the soup bowls and spoons, brooding. She and Tommy had been to one of those meetings in the shack that was the Apostolic Hall. She remembered how the rain drummed on the corrugated iron roof as if trying to drown out the cries of the congregation: "*O Dew annwyl!* Dear Lord! Forgive me, Jesus!" they shouted, with scatterings of "Amen!" and "Alle*lewl*ia!" which she knew was not how you were supposed to say it. Tommy, overcome by the warmth, fell asleep, leaning against Grandpa, but Gillian kept her eyes open to watch.

After an endless sermon pleading with people to repent and be saved, some people went up to the front and announced that they had taken Jesus into their hearts. Others stood up and begged Him, in tears, to take them into His, there and then. One woman fell down, thrashing about and moaning, and a whiskery old man with pink, watery eyes and breath like bad meat turned around and whispered to Gillian, "Have *you* found Jesus, little girl?" to which she had thought it best to whisper back, "Yes, thank you." She had been very glad when her father later ruled that they were not to go there again.

Worrying about her friendship with Vanna as she put out the bread plates, she wondered if she should, after all, try asking Jesus what to do, as her grandmother was always telling her she should. In the end she decided there was not much point. She had rather gone off Jesus anyway. God was another matter perhaps, more for grown-ups, but wasn't Jesus supposed to be the little children's friend and protector? *There's a friend for little children,/Above the bright blue sky,* and all that, but he had not protected her from Angus, even though she had prayed to him with all her might to make her invisible. Nor had he got her and Tommy home again, away from the Macphersons', or if he had, he had taken his time about it. And what was he doing about the Farrell children?

This was not the first time she had had her doubts about him, either. At Eastertime, while the congregation moaned,

We do not know, we cannot tell,
What pains he had to bear,
We only know it was for us
He hung and suffered there.

she had wondered why, since she, personally, would never, ever, have asked Jesus to do such a thing, she was supposed to feel guilty. Why would he want her to?

She banged a plate of bread down on the table. She would go on seeing Vanna. Her grandmother just did not need to know.

AT SCHOOL THE NEXT DAY, the two girls studied the hole left by a stone falling out of the wall in a corner of the girls' yard. About ten inches each way, it made a perfect little room, just waiting to be set up. Watched from across the yard by a couple of sniggering girls from the next class up, they spent the morning break laying down a carpet of moss, picked off the wall.

After the dinner break, Gillian came back with a fire-place: a pillbox filled with chunky jet beads from her grandmother's button collection, interspersed with scarlet cellophane flames cut from a sweet-wrapper. Vanna had brought an outsized matchbox, filled with cotton wool. Covered with a square of gold damask from Gillian's grandmother's scrap bag, it made a perfect bed. Her other contribution had been a tiny naked china baby, which she said had come out of a Christmas cracker.

They swaddled the baby in cotton wool, tucked it into a cradle made from half a chestnut shell, and placed it by the fire. Vanna clapped her hands together, a wide smile on her thin, freckled face. "This is somebody's *home*! Let's get some more stuff and make it really beautiful!"

AT VANNA'S HOUSE, AFTER SCHOOL, they found Mrs. Farrell reading in an armchair. Patrick was playing with blocks, while Bridie drew letters on her slate and the baby slept in her cradle. Gillian suppressed a memory of her grandmother's friend, Mrs. Thomas-the-Post-Office, saying "That woman just sits around reading like a lady, when she should be scrubbing her filthy house."

Beside Mrs. Farrell, on a rough wooden box covered with a lace cloth, was a cup and saucer with a pattern of clover leaves scattered on a cream background, so delicate you could almost see through the cup. It was even finer than Gillian's grandmother's best tea-set, the one with yellow butterflies for handles.

"Mama, we found a hole in the wall and we're making it into a home!" Vanna opened her eyes wide and spread out her hands in a '*ta-da!*' gesture.

Mrs. Farrell put down her book and looked at them with her slow smile. "Isn't that a fine thing then," she said, "to make a home out of a hole in the wall! Tell me about it."

The girls described the carpet, and the bed, and the fire. "And we've got a cradle!" Gillian told her. "With a beautiful little china baby in it that Vanna got from a Christmas cracker."

The shout of the old rag and bone man rose up out on the street. "*Rah-BO*!"

"We never have crackers." Mrs. Farrell said. She raised her eyebrows and looked at Vanna who was twisting the toe of her sandal into a hole in the carpet. "Evangeline, did you take the baby Jesus from the box with the crèche?"

Vanna turned crimson. "I was going to put him back, Mama. I just wanted to see what it looked like to have a baby in the cradle."

"Well then, you run straight back to school and fetch it. Quickly now!"

As Vanna dashed off, Mrs. Farrell held out her hand to Gillian. "Stay here with me, will you, Gillian. We can have a chat."

Gillian sat on a three-legged wooden stool beside Mrs. Farrell, and glanced around at the shabby bits of furniture and the piles of books. What looked like art books were stacked on the floor beside Mrs. Farrell's chair. Columns of matching dark blue volumes stood each side of the door to the hallway. Smaller books were jammed onto rough shelves under the window, and a set of little leather-bound ones, maroon with gold lettering, stood between bronze horse-head bookends on the mantelpiece. Beside them a photograph in a tarnished silver frame showed Mrs. Farrell, in a long white dress, beautiful as a film star, smiling up into the face of a tall, dark-haired man.

"Is that Mr. Farrell?" Gillian could have kicked herself for asking such a stupid question. "He's ever so handsome!"

"Yes, that's Michael." Mrs. Farrell turned her head away to look out of the window. "Indeed he is handsome." She looked back at Gillian with a sudden smile. "But I see you're noticing my books, Gillian. Vanna tells me you like to read."

"Yes I do. More than anything!" Gillian looked at the small green book on the makeshift table beside Mrs. Farrell. "What's that you're reading, Mrs. Farrell?"

The thin, work-roughened hand held out the book, the words *Pride and Prejudice* written in gold on the spine.

"What does 'prejudice' mean?"

"It means judging people by someone else's ideas of them, not your own."

Gillian thought about that for a moment, before returning her attention to the book. On the first page she read, "To Deirdre with love from Papa". She sounded it out in her head. *Deirdre.* It was the saddest name she had ever heard. Underneath that she read, *Everyman's Library*, followed by the words, *EVERYMAN, I will go with thee, and be thy guide, In thy most need to go by thy side.* She looked up at Mrs. Farrell. "What does that mean?"

"It's in all the Everyman books. It means that a good book is a friend and teacher for life."

Gillian read the words again: *In thy most need to go by thy side.* It sounded better than Jesus. "Is it true?"

"As true as I'm sitting here, Gillian. Everything you need to know is in books." Mrs. Farrell took the book in her hand. "And there's another thing. When I'm reading this book, for example," she held it up, "as I've done many times, I may seem to be sitting in this room, in the middle of all this," she waved the book at the shabby room, "but in my mind, I'm in another place and another time, in the world of this book."

"I know! And you don't want to come back! I was like that with *The Wind in the Willows* when I finished it."

Mrs. Farrell smiled at her as if she had known her all her life. Looking like someone called *The Blessed Damozel* in a book at home in Swansea, she glanced down at the sleeping baby. "But now, Gillian," she said, "Vanna says that you're living here in Tregwyr with your grandparents because of the war. Tell me, do they not mind that she is Roman Catholic? I know the feeling is against us in the village."

"Um, well . . ."

The back door burst open, and Vanna rushed, white-faced, into the room. "Everything's gone!" she cried, "The baby, and the bed, and the fire, and everything! And it's all my fault! I've lost the baby Jesus!" She began to sob, yanking fiercely on her plaits.

Her mother stood up. "Calm down, Vanna. Don't be so dramatic. You shouldn't have taken it, but it's not the end of the world. Did you look all around?"

Vanna shook her head, gulping.

"Well off you go to have another look."

"I'll never find him! Never! Now our whole crèche is spoiled! It's no good without Jesus! I've ruined all our Christmases *for ever!*" She wrung her hands, sobbing and gasping.

"I'd go look, Mama, but I don't know where." Tears spilled down Francis's cheeks.

"We've lost the baby Jesus!" wailed Bridie, followed by howls of "Jethuth! Jethuth!" from Patrick, and screams from the startled baby.

Mrs. Farrell picked up the baby and fetched a small packet of Smith's Crisps which she began to dole out, one at a time. When they had all stopped crying, Gillian slipped out of the back door and ran to her grandparents' house.

She found her grandmother and Tommy weeding the front garden.

"Grandma!" She stood as tall as she could. "I'm going to Vanna's house right now. And I'm taking Tommy with me. Come on, Tommy." She grabbed his hand and glared at her grandmother. "We're going to help Vanna and Francis find Jesus."

Her grandmother, open-mouthed, but speechless for once, stared at Gillian over her glasses.

Hand in hand, Gillian and Tommy ran down the garden path and up the road. When Gillian looked back from the corner, she saw that her grandmother had come out onto the pavement and was standing, trowel in hand, still staring.

Vanna got up to light another cigarette. "We did have some happy times together there in Tregwyr, didn't we? For years really, until all that Eleven Plus business." Her face became somber. "I know I did well enough for myself in the end, but I totally believed then, of course, that passing that exam was going to be my only ticket out of poverty."

Gillian put down her teacup. "I know. That's what everyone said. You had to pass if you were ever going to make anything of yourself." She sat back. "You know, I never did understand what happened to you then, Vanna. It was all very strange."

In their last year at elementary school, Gillian and Vanna had thrown themselves into being Miss Thomas's star pupils. They read and swapped every novel they could find, the latest being *Ivanhoe* from Mrs. Farrell's collection, and *Anne of Green Gables* from Gillian's. They wrote sensational stories and deeply affecting poems, which they read to each other, and to anyone else who would listen. They drilled each other before spelling and vocabulary quizzes and tested each other relentlessly in mental arithmetic, firing quick questions out of nowhere such as "Seven times thirteen?" or "fifteen plus eight, plus seven, divided by six?" which had to be answered almost as quickly.

Gillian's father would sometimes play this game with her at weekends, unlike Vanna's father who always told them to "piss off." Her mother, however, until the new baby came, would find time to read their compositions, giving equal attention to Gillian's efforts. She encouraged them both to take the exam very seriously. Their whole lives might depend on it, she said, a theme that was echoed by their teacher.

IN SEPTEMBER 1944, AT THE BEGINNING of their last year at that school, Miss Thomas spoke seriously to the top class. "In May of this year," she looked slowly around the room, "you will all be sitting the new examination. You'll be tested to see if you should go on to the grammar school, and then possibly to university, or if you'd be better suited to a secondary modern or technical school."

The children shifted in their seats and looked around at each other.

"You must start working hard *now*," Miss Thomas went on. "You may think eight months is a long time, and that you needn't worry yet about preparing for the exam. But I promise you, my dears, the time *will* pass, and one day, if you're spared, each of you will be sitting here, in this very room, with the test paper on your desk." Gillian and Vanna smiled smugly at each other. They were not worried. They had everything under control.

AS THE MONTHS WENT BY, Gillian missed her talks with Mrs. Farrell now that there was another baby taking up all her time.

When she told her grandparents that Mrs. Farrell had given herself a black eye bumping into the newel post, they had puzzled her by exchanging a meaningful glance and rolling their eyes. To Gillian's relief, however, her grandmother had softened towards Vanna, even allowing her in the house at times. Gratified by her reaction to the story of Little Jim, and disarmed by her sobs on hearing *I'll Take You Home Again, Kathleen,* she had said, "That poor little girl! You can bring her here more often, Gillian. Perhaps she can learn something from spending time in our house."

Gillian chose not to think about what her grandmother was up to, happy that she and Vanna could spend time together in the parlour in the evenings and on weekends. Whenever Vanna's mother could spare her, they would settle down there together, among the antimacassars and china dogs, to do homework, read, and talk.

In time, however, Gillian became increasingly annoyed by Tommy who would barge in to sit, cross-legged and open-mouthed, staring at Vanna, apparently mesmerized by her hair, her freckles and her accent. Vanna did not seem to mind; she was used to worse things, Gillian knew, but it drove Gillian crazy. It seemed as though she was never free of him. He followed them everywhere, listening to them talking, telling tales if she went out of bounds or was mean to him. It did not help, either, that he had palled up with Francis. Next thing, she supposed, Francis too would be in the parlour with them of an evening. Her grandmother was already talking about his beautiful eyelashes.

AS THE CLASS SAT AT THEIR DESKS, back straight, feet crossed, pens and blotting paper at the ready, waiting for the first part of the Eleven Plus exam, the Composition question, to be given out, Gillian remembered with a start Miss Thomas's words, way back in September, about time passing. She had understood, of course, in theory, about the passage of time, but had applied the principle in a day-to-day way only, not to large chunks of time. To have everything happen exactly as it had been foreseen months before came as a shock. Miss Thomas had spoken true: the time had passed, all eight months of it, and here they were, sitting at their desks, just as she had said, waiting for the test papers to be handed out. Gillian nodded her head, registering the momentous fact, and lifted her eyes to their teacher standing at the front of the room, her white blouse stiff with starch, the line of her parting straight as a ruler, the test papers in her hand.

In the next desk Vanna, freckles standing out on her sharp white face, sat with her hands tucked under her arms. She was not wearing any socks, and there was a purple bruise on her arm. She would be all right, though, Gillian thought; she nearly always had full marks for composition.

Gillian checked that there was plenty of ink in her inkwell and put a new nib in her wooden pen as Miss Thomas moved around the room, placing the papers face-down on the desks. Three-quarters of an hour later, after checking her composition for spelling or punctuation mistakes, and reading it through one more time, she put down her pen with a satisfied sigh. She had written about "My Favourite Place," the Ilston Valley, with its successive waves of snowdrops, primroses and violets, and bluebells.

Feeling as if she had just woken up, she looked over to see how Vanna was getting on, and saw, to her dismay, that she had written only a few smudged lines. She was looking dopily into the distance, the shadows under her eyes matching the ink stains on her paper.

"I couldn't think," she said as they fetched their milk in the playground. "My bloody pen nib had a bloody hair in it, and I couldn't get it out, and I didn't have another bloody nib." She downed her milk in one go and slammed the bottle back in the crate. "Ouch!"

"Why didn't you tell Miss Thomas?"

"She said no disturbances, remember, stupid?"

Worried, Gillian slurped the last of her milk with a straw. "Maybe you'll ace the other tests."

"I'm not doing them. There's no point." Vanna stumbled out of the playground in an awkward, knock-kneed run, the laces of her canvas shoes trailing.

After the tests were over, Gillian went to Vanna's house. She knocked their special knock on the back door, but no one answered until Bridie opened the door a crack. "Vanna doesn't want to see you," she hissed. "She says to go away." She banged the door shut.

Gillian stood there, biting her lip. Why was Vanna angry with her? It was not her fault that Vanna's nib had a hair in it. Why hadn't she brought a spare nib anyway, or asked Miss Thomas for one before the test started? She knocked on the door again, jumping back as Vanna pulled it open and stood blazing before her.

"Why don't you leave me alone?" White-faced, her red-rimmed eyes glaring, and her unloosed hair springing out around her head, she looked like that Medusa in their book of myths who could kill at a glance. "I expect you've come to gloat because you know you passed." She stamped her foot. "I'm sick of you! And I'm sick of your grandma telling me about Jesus being her personal saviour and giving me cabbages to take home as if we were a charity case. And I'm sick of Tommy always mooning around after me. I hate the lot of you!"

"I thought we were friends." Gillian swallowed miserably.

"How can we be friends? You've got so much more than me, and now I've got no chance to catch up. *Ever!* It's just not fair! It's not fair! Fuck off!" She burst into tears and slammed the door in Gillian's face.

Shocked, Gillian walked slowly back to her grandparents' house. She had never heard anyone she knew say that word out loud, not even Mr. Farrell. It was true, though. It was not fair. Why should she herself have a nice, comfortable place to call home, enough to eat, a good chance of getting into the grammar school, and everyone in the village being nice to her, when all Vanna had was the whole village looking down their noses at her and her family, which was from the wrong place and had the wrong religion. She had to live in that dark, cramped house too; full of little ones she had to mind, with not nearly enough food to go round, and a mean father to boot. She did have a lovely mother, though, Gillian told herself, but at the thought of Mrs. Farrell, her beautiful hair going grey and a yellow-green bruise around her eye, surrounded by hungry, crying children and the books Mr. Farrell said he was going to burn to save money on coal, she began to cry herself.

"Don't tell me you spoilt your chances at that old exam?" Her grandmother put her arm around her and gave her a rock cake. "Never you mind, *cariad*! Your daddy will see you right, whatever."

Gillian told her it was not that, and told her about the hair in the nib, and Vanna running away from the playground, and, omitting the 'fuck-off' bit of course, about her saying she hated Gillian, and slamming the door on her.

"Those Irish!" Her grandmother slapped invisible specks of dust off the Welsh dresser with a dishcloth. "Feckless, that's what they are. There's no helping some people. Why couldn't they have sent the poor child to school properly prepared like you? I don't suppose she even had a good breakfast."

"But, Grandma, they're so poor! And there are so many of them!"

"Well that's their own fault, isn't it?"

Gillian looked at her in surprise. "What, being poor? Or having so many children?"

"Both. They should work harder and look after their money better. And they should control themselves. We managed. Why can't they?"

Asking herself how Mrs. Farrell could manage better, and what good controlling herself would be, and finding no answers, Gillian took her rock cake out to the garden, planning to sit in the elderberry tree, now in full flower, and try to calm down. About to perch on the usual branch, she saw that the bark where she wanted to sit had come loose, and tugged at it with her free hand. She leapt back with a yelp, dropping the rock-cake. Woodlice, each about a third of an inch long, swarmed over the exposed limb, crawling away into crevices on their multiple hair-like legs, or curling into serrated grey balls and dropping off the tree into the dirt. Shuddering, she ran back into the house. She would retreat to her bedroom and read something, anything, as long as it was not about insects or exams, or people being mean to each other. Shutting the bedroom door, she took *Five Run Away Together* off her bookshelf in the vain hope of putting Vanna's strange behaviour out of her mind. "Why did she fail?" she kept asking herself, "Why didn't she even try?"

"You never told me what went wrong with that exam." Gillian waved away the plate of chocolate digestive biscuits Vanna was offering. "I remember I could see there was something the matter, because you hadn't any socks on, and your arm was all bruised. I know we sort of made it up some years later, Vanna, but we never went into what happened, and there was always that tension between us. And of course, I've been away for most of our lives. But I wish I could finally understand what went on."

Vanna stood up to light a cigarette, nearly dropping the heavy silver table-lighter onto the coffee table before stalking over to the window. "The night before the exam," she said, "My da came home even drunker than usual. He'd lost his job and couldn't face what that meant, I suppose. He saw all the things my mother'd bought for me—pencils, pen, box of nibs, ruler and so on—and my best blouse and skirt and white socks airing over the back of a chair by the fire she'd lit specially.

"And what's all this fancy bloody gear for?" he says. "Who paid for this, then?" And when my mother, God rest her soul, tells him it's for my big day tomorrow, and that she knows he'll be wanting me to do well, he says, "You know bugger all!" and throws the whole lot into the fire.

"That's how I burned my fingers, trying to get stuff out, and why I couldn't hardly hold my pen the next day." She took a quick drag on her cigarette and blew out a cloud of smoke. "Anyway, the little ones were all screaming, while himself was waving the poker and shouting about throwing away good money, as if he'd never in his whole bloody life done any such thing at all. Then he said I'd turn out to be a useless, head-in-the-air, bluestocking like my mother, and he wasn't having that. And don't ask me why I said that about the hair in the nib, and why I didn't tell Miss Thomas all about it. I had my pride, if nothing else." She ground out her cigarette savagely in the cut-glass ashtray.

Gillian smoothed the burled walnut surface of the coffee table with her finger. "I remember your father died not long after that, didn't he?"

Vanna lit another cigarette. "He did so. He was coming home from the pub, legless as usual, and got run over by another drunk. And wasn't that the best thing that ever happened to our family at all?" She squinted narrowly at Gillian through the smoke.

Gillian felt she could hardly argue with that, especially after Vanna went on to say that her mother's father, after he heard Michael Farrell was dead, had regularly sent them enough money to live on comfortably, until he himself died, leaving her mother a fair sum. She had died happy, Vanna said, knowing that all six children were provided for.

"You never know what's round the corner, right?" She raised a sculpted eyebrow at Gillian. "As my Da must have said when he saw Dai Jones's van coming at him. God rest his poor soul, after all!"

After a light supper, they sat in Vanna's soft, grey-blue velvet armchairs while the mist came up from the sea and the foghorns moaned in the bay, until it was time for Gillian to return to Langland for the night.

IN THE STILL-MISTY MORNING, Gillian walked from the bus-stop to Saint Anne's, and smelled the salty, fishy, seaweedy tang borne on the wind from the sea. *I'm home,* she thought. *This is the smell of home.* She stopped and inhaled deeply. But what was home now, in fact? A set of lawyers' offices? An old wall? An unfamiliar bungalow on the outskirts of town? A few people who remembered her but could live perfectly well without her? With a shake of her head she walked on.

Home was Canada now. Ottawa was where she belonged, as much as she could belong anywhere. If she came back to live here now, she would be homesick for Canada. Home was her little house near the park and the river; her son and his wife, and her granddaughter, Alice; her partner Simon, and her other friends, and her spaniel, Dora. All those, along with the snow and the wide horizons had become her home.

Passing the wall of her old house, she noticed a small stout man in cap and raincoat walking briskly up the hill. Drawing level with her, he touched his cap and smiled politely, then stopped to take a second look, smiling even more broadly.

"Excuse me, lady, but does I know you?" He chuckled. "You looks very familiar. Does you come from round here, then?"

"Well, yes, I do, actually. Very much so." She pointed. "I used to live in this house."

As he peered at her, she saw something familiar about his broad, red face and bright blue eyes.

"It's never Gillian?" He burst into a high, wheezy laugh. "Well, well, well! It's Gillian Davies! There's a surprise, isn't it! I'm Robbie Bevan, Gillian. Don't you remember me? I used to bring the meat!" He seemed to find that hilarious.

She remembered him then: Robbie, the butcher's boy, in his navy and white striped apron, turning up on his ancient bicycle with shiny brown-paper packages in the front basket. A cheery, red-cheeked boy, always whistling.

"Gladys'll be amazed when I tells her!" He chuckled. "Who'd of thought it? Gillian Davies! Well I never!"

"Gladys?"

"Yes, Gladys Jones, as was." He grinned and jerked his head at the house. "Her mother worked for your mother, remember? It was after you went to Canada, I think, that we got married. Didn't you mother tell you? I always fancied Gladys, and in the end she come 'round to me, and we been very happy. Got grandchildren now, we have. Five of them!" He evidently found this side-splitting, but suddenly straightened his face. "Is you mam still alive? Last I heard she was living in Langland."

Gillian told him where her mother was presently, and learned that he and Gladys lived just down the hill from Saint

Anne's, in Number 84. Gladys would be popping in to see Mrs. Davies, he said, now that she knew where she was. He raised his cap and twinkled off, with an invitation to come and see them any time.

Curious, although not at all sure she wanted to see Gladys, or that her mother would, after what happened with Tom, Gillian made her way to Saint Anne's.

SUNITA MET HER ON THE STAIRS, carrying a tray of untouched breakfast: scrambled egg, toast, marmalade and tea. "Your mother's not eating well, Mrs. Armstrong," she said. "She didn't touch the beef jelly you brought her yesterday, and she had no dinner to speak of. I think she should go onto meal supplements just to keep her strength up until she feels better."

"Certainly. Whatever you think best, Sunita." Gillian felt a stirring of the panic she had felt on the plane. "D'you think the new antibiotic is working?

"Not yet, but it's too early to tell. We should know by tomorrow." Sunita smiled, perfect teeth in a dusky-rose face, and passed on softly down the carpeted stairs.

Her mother was sitting up, coughing. She waved her hand impatiently as if signaling Gillian to go away, but then beckoned her back. "This'll pass." She held up a finger. "Don't go. Don't leave me." She coughed again and spat a chunk of thick khaki-coloured phlegm into the stainless steel dish Gillian held for her. "That's good! I'll be all right now. I'm getting the better of this. I'll be out of here in no time."

Gillian studied her. She looked even thinner, but alert, bright almost, a faint mauve flush beneath the apricot rouge on her cheeks.

"How's my Tweetie-Pie? Did you give him a good brush as I asked you to? He needs to be brushed every day. I hope you remembered that."

Gillian forbore from showing her the scratches she had received as soon as she had laid brush on the cat. "He's fine, Mum. I did everything you asked." If she were to get anywhere with her, she would have to be patient and ignore her needling.

To soften her up she had brought along photographs of Bryn, the grandson her mother had never seen; his attractive blonde wife, Carol, the pharmacist; and Alice, Gillian's darling five-year-old granddaughter, with her *joie-de-vivre* and funny, loud laugh. Her mother would be bound to exclaim over Alice's physical resemblance to Gillian at that age: the same hair, eyes, and build, a similarity that Gillian hoped might provide a lead-in to the subject of her own evacuation at around that age and then, with luck, to the crucial disclosure.

"Oh, how unfortunate!" Her mother dropped the photograph of Alice face-down on the bedspread. She put her face in her hands for a moment and gave a little shudder, before looking up with a forced smile. "I see she has your hair." She gave a little laugh. "Although I must say, Gillian, in your case it seems to have worn well. You can hardly tell if you've gone grey or not!" She snatched up another photo. "Now this must be Bryn! He's a handsome young man, certainly. He has a look of me I think. See the eyebrows? And there's something about the mouth, don't you agree?"

Gillian gave up. There was no point in going on with her project now, since her mother seemed excited and perhaps feverish. She would try again when her mother was calmer. She gathered up the photographs and changed the subject. "Have you seen anything of the other women here, Mum?"

"There's a woman in the next room." Her mother lowered her voice. "She came in to see me last night." She leaned forward. "I think she's Jewish."

"So?" Gillian turned her head sharply, chin up.

"Oh, not that I have anything against Jewish people! I had a good friend once who was Jewish. Gilda Rosenberg. She kept the dress shop down the hill from us. Lovely woman! You probably remember her."

Gillian looked narrowly at her. "I remember Mrs. Rosenberg very well. She was indeed a lovely woman, and seemed very fond of you." She turned away, disturbed, as always, by her mother's hypocrisy and by her own memories of the end of the war.

When the victory in Europe was announced, nothing turned out the way Gillian and Tommy had hoped. Everyone who had a say in it, which, of course, did not include them, had agreed that even though there could be no more bombings, and it was indeed safe for them to come home, they should stay where they were because of Gillian's approaching Eleven-plus examination. The consolation offered was that they could go home for weekends.

Gillian tried to explain to a sulking Tommy that she could not help what they thought, and that she was every bit as fed up about it as he was. They would just have to put up with it, she said, pointing out that it was already Wednesday. In two days' time they would be home. He cheered up somewhat, but she still brooded. There were schools in Swansea, weren't there?

They adjusted, as usual, and from then on, every Friday after school, their grandfather put them on the bus for Swansea and they rode into town, jittery with excitement at the prospect of being at home. It did not matter that their parents were often busy, their father with his practice, their mother with her social life, and that they were left to their own devices. They had plenty of those, whether in the house or rambling around the neighbourhood.

One Saturday, however, Gillian was taken shopping with her mother, who had collected enough coupons to get herself a new dress. They went straight down the road to Mrs. Rosenberg's little dress shop, which had managed to stay in business all through the bombings.

Mrs. Rosenberg's sad dark eyes lit up as Gillian and her mother came into the shop. After the warm greetings and chit-chat were over, she sat Gillian in a spindly, satin-covered chair by the window, leaving a silver dish of barley-sugar sweets on the tiny table beside her. She had something especially nice put aside, she said, for "dear Iris" to try on, and they bustled into the changing room where Gillian could hear them cooing over the dress.

When they came out, Mrs. Rosenberg wrapped up the new dress in a shocking extravagance of tissue paper and placed the package reverently in a shiny white cardboard box, using an outrageous amount of pale-blue ribbon to secure and adorn it. She stroked Gillian's cheek as they left, pushing the remaining sweets into her hand.

Clipping along the pavement in her patent-leather high-heeled shoes, and holding the box flat to prevent wrinkles, Gillian's mother observed that Gilda Rosenberg had a heart of gold, and had given one hundred pounds to Swansea's newly set-up Home for Unmarried Mothers.

Gillian gasped at the huge amount. Remembering that this was her mother's favourite charity, and that she sat on its board, whatever that meant, she peered up into her mother's face to ask if Mrs. Rosenberg would be coming to the Victory cocktail party, the cause of much fuss and talk, which her parents would be giving the following Friday evening.

"No, of course not." Her mother pursed her lips.

"But why not, Mummy? I thought you were friends."

Her mother walked on faster. "We're just ... *business* friends, Gillian. We don't socialize. It would be ..." she searched for the word, "inappropriate."

Gillian stopped. "Why? Why would it be *inappropriate* if you asked Mrs. Rosenberg?"

Her mother was walking so fast, Gillian could hardly catch up. "Well, she really doesn't belong around here, you know," her mother said over her shoulder. "And, of course, there's the matter of religion to consider."

Trotting along breathlessly, Gillian said to her mother's rigid back, "But you and Daddy don't go to church, and Mrs. Rosenberg has been here much longer than Mr. and Mrs. Ashford, and I know you're asking them."

Her mother stopped and swung around. "That's enough, Gillian! You're getting above yourself! Don't talk about things you can't understand." She strode on without looking back as Gillian slipped away from her and down a narrow lane between the houses.

WEEKENDS AT HOME WERE USUALLY like that, Gillian thought, as she half-heartedly explored the lane; hardly ever as happy as she had imagined they would be. Tommy would get into trouble for being loud and thoughtless; she would be criticized for being too quiet, or reading too much, or asking too many questions; one or the other, or both of her parents might be in a bad mood, or worse still, openly quarrelling with each other, which they seemed to do more and more often lately.

One particular day, however, a Saturday in April, started as a happy one with no bad feelings on anyone's part. There was an egg each for breakfast, with the added luxury of both butter and Golden Shred marmalade for their toast. Over a cup of sweet, milky tea, Gillian watched her parents smile at each other, her mother getting up to pour her father a second cup, leaning over with her hand on his shoulder as he read out details of the victory from the morning paper. Gillian took a deep breath, the tight feeling she nearly always had in her chest relaxing. If only they could all stay like that forever! Perhaps they could. Maybe, when the war was really over, everything would be all right again, more or less.

After breakfast she and Tommy lay on their stomachs on the sunlit carpet, reading *The Beano* and *The Dandy* and giggling over the exploits of Pansy Potter, The Strong Man's Daughter, and Freddy the Fearless Fly. When Tommy pushed his comic over, pointing to the cow's tail hanging over the side of Desperate Dan's enormous pie, instead of faintly smiling in her usual superior way, she laughed with him. She noticed that he was not making that funny clicking noise in his throat that annoyed everyone.

Their mother was wearing the new dress, fawn and slightly flared, with a pattern of black V's which she said were called *chevrons*. Their father said it could be her Victory dress, since she did look rather winning in it. Savouring *chevrons* and *rather winning,* Gillian smiled to herself.

LATER IN THE MORNING, THEIR FATHER got out the little Ford Prefect and drove the family to Cefn Bryn, the ridge of hill on the common land outside Swansea. They stood on the raised centre of the Gower Peninsula and looked over at the sea on one side, bright blue, with white horses racing in, and the Burry estuary on the other, with its great stretches of mud sands on which they thought they could make out the donkey carts of cockle-gatherers. The wind, smelling of rock pools and seaweed, rushed off the sea and over the common, blowing their mother's long dark hair over her face.

The children raced each other down the path between the great stones placed there by Ancient Britons, thousands of years ago. On the way back they stopped to study the huge boulder that was Arthur's Stone. Quartz sparkled like broken glass as they looked up at the dark slit from which they agreed he must have pulled Excalibur.As they ran back to rejoin their parents, a plover appeared on the path ahead of them, dragging her pretend-broken wing to entice them away from the nest which they knew must be on the ground nearby. Tommy wanted to look for it, but their father called out to leave the poor bird alone to look after her chicks in peace. Looking back, Gillian saw her settle, wonderfully camouflaged, into a dip in the ground, safe with her babies. When she looked again after turning her eyes away for a second, they had become invisible.

The morning ended with a picnic, eaten in the car with all the doors open and the wind rushing through: fish paste sandwiches, Grandma's Victory no-egg sponge cake, and tea from the thermos. This was followed by a top-speed, roller-coaster ride over the bumps and dips on the road home over the common.

HE BEST THING OF ALL, THOUGH, was yet to come. That afternoon, her parents were taking her to the cinema, to see *The Bells of Saint Mary's;* just Gillian, since Tommy, at nine, was judged too young. Even then there was no quarrelling. The maid had been told to let Tommy have his new friend, Marcus, over to play and to give them sausage and mash for their tea.

The three of them set off for the cinema, Gillian between her parents, possibly ready to hold their hands, if they offered. They walked jauntily down the sunny side of the street, past the bombed houses, their gardens still full of rubble, and past the church where clear, diamond-shaped panes replaced the stained glass windows that had once shown Jesus performing miracles. When they came to Mrs. Rosenberg's shop, they stopped briefly for her mother to admire a dress in the window. Not far from the dress shop stood the cinema, the grandly elegant Albert Hall, somehow spared by the bombs which, according to her father, had otherwise seemed to pick on Swansea's finer buildings.

Once they had settled in the red plush seats, Gillian in the middle, her father produced with a flourish a box of six Black Magic chocolates and ceremoniously offered her the first choice. After some debate, she chose a hard, chewy caramel because it would last longer than any of the others.

The curtains opened at last on *The Bells of Saint Mary's*. Like every other film she had seen up to that point, Gillian found it totally absorbing, despite being taken aback by the Roman Catholic setting, about which her grandmother certainly would have had something to say. She fell in love with Bing Crosby, and was awed by Ingrid Bergman. She sniffled alongside her mother through the sad part, and bravely accepted the ending. When the music swelled up at the finish, and the great curtains swished together, her mother gave a satisfied sigh, and her father said cheerily, "Load of old codswallop!" and passed the chocolates around again. Gillian looked up from choosing a strawberry cream to smile at both of them, and as the cock crowed, announcing the Pathé News, she snuggled back in her seat, happy that there was more to see.

At first the News just showed soldiers marching about as usual. All seemed to be going well with the end of the war, and Gillian tuned out from the subject as she usually did, until the scene changed, and she saw that what she was looking at was not usual at all. There was no marching or cheering, no patriotic fanfares, no excited male voice talking about victories. A hushed, solemn voice was speaking; something about a camp.

And then she saw them.

Holding her breath, she pressed back in her seat. How could this be? Could skeletons be alive? Could dead bodies walk? Were those men and women she was looking at, behind barbed wire, draped in rags, with only bones for arms and legs, black eyes staring blank as stones from their skulls? Behind the walking skeletons she saw a huge pile of bones. As she stared, she saw one long bone near the top of the pile move; and then another. She closed her eyes. Who were these people? Who had done this to them? Why? She focused fiercely again on the images, the commentary unheard. She had to get this right and remember everything, always. She did not understand any of it except that it was the truth; knowledge that sank into her heart like a stone. If this was possible, and God did not prevent it, anything could happen. Anything at all.

Coming out of the cinema, that place of darkness and moving shadows, was like emerging from a cave into what you could call the light. The sun was still shining on the wide street that led back to their home, but now everywhere she looked was desolation and ruin.

For once her parents did not ask what she thought of the show. They walked home together in their separate silences. Head low, elbows clutched, she closed inward around that stone in her heart. If anyone spoke she would shatter like glass.

Gillian turned away from her mother and went to the window. How could anyone who had seen that newsreel, or read those facts, ever be the same again? And yet the world had gone on in the same old way; war after war, genocide after genocide. She stared out over the vast, restless cruelty of the sea.

When she looked back, she saw Doctor Gabriel had come into the room. He nodded at her and smiled at her mother, putting his finger to his lips before bending over to listen to her chest. He straightened up, returning his stethoscope to its place around his neck, and looked at Gillian, shaking his head. He put his hand on the old woman's shoulder. "No time to talk now, Mrs. Davies, but I'm going to put you on a stronger diuretic. There's some fluid in your chest I want to get rid of."

"Thank you for taking such good care of me, Doctor. I know we're going to beat this." She smiled up at him, and Gillian saw for a moment why people thought she was wonderful.

He smiled back. "But you must try to eat, Iris—you don't mind if I call you Iris, do you?"

"Please do!" The old woman fluttered her almost non-existent eyelashes.

"Sunita tells me you've been sending plates back untouched. At least, drink your supplements. That's doctor's orders now, Iris. You must take care of yourself." Wagging a finger at her, he turned briskly to leave, nearly colliding with Tom.

Carrying a dozen peach-coloured roses and a large plastic bag, and out of breath from hurrying up the stairs, Tom beamed at them all and rushed over to give his mother a kiss. "How are you, Mum? Are you feeling better?" He thrust the roses at her. "Look at these! Do you like them? I thought they'd remind you of Grandpa's Peace rose. Remember? He was so proud of that!"

Their mother approached her nose to one of the blooms. "No, the Peace rose was much bigger and more beautiful, and it had a wonderful smell. These have no scent at all. But they're nice. Thank you, Tom."

Gillian winked at Tom, fetching a shrug and a rueful grin.

He tried again. "Look, I've brought you some magazines, Mum: *The Tatler*, *The Lady*, *House and Garden*, and," he brought it out with a flourish, "*Royalty*! So you can keep up with the gossip."

She leaned back on the pillows. "Oh, I'm past all that sort of thing."

"I'll have them if you don't want them." Gillian reached out for *Royalty*. "This looks like fun."

Her mother smacked her hand down on the magazines. "I shall keep them, if you don't mind, so that I can pass them around to the other ladies here."

Gillian caught Tom's eye, pressing her lips together to suppress a smile.

"It's nice, though, that you're bringing me presents." Their mother picked up *Royalty,* and leafed through it, pausing to scrutinize a picture of the Queen Mother. "I used to love sending off parcels for you both when you were away at school."

Gillian and Tom opened their eyes wide at each other just as Sunita came in with medication and eyedrops. While the nurse attended to their mother, Gillian watched Tom leaning forward as he sat, his hands loosely linked between his knees, drinking in the sight of the beautiful young woman. Straightening up Sunita gave him a smile of pure friendliness, and his broad, ruddy face went slack with yearning. *Some things never change.*

Their mother turned her head to ask after Tweetie-Pie and Sylvester.

"They're fine," Tom assured her. "We're going back right after this to see to them." It was he who had given her the cat and the canary, and, unaware that she had never watched the cartoons, had suggested those names.

"That's nice. I love to see you two together. We were so rarely together, all of us, when you were growing up. It was a source of great sadness to me. Especially that you had to go away to school." She sighed wheezily. "I was so lonely while you were away, both of you."

Tom blinked and grunted. Gillian opened her mouth, but closed it on hearing her mother's wheeze get louder, and seeing her sudden pallor. "You look tired, Mum." She quickly tidied up the magazines and put the roses in water. "You need to rest. We'll be off now."

Sunita glided back in as Gillian settled her mother down.

"I NEED A DRINK!" TOM WAS breathing heavily as they went down the stairs. "Isn't she the giddy limit? Let's go to *The Cross Keys*. We can have lunch there while we're at it."

The pub was a minor miracle, famous for incorporating the remnants of a fourteenth century hospice. Despite being situated near the docks, it had remained standing, along with the ancient castle ruins, when everything else around had been flattened by bombs. Once inside, Gillian saw it now looked much like any other Tudor-style pub, apart from the stone window at the far end of the dining room.

Tom was still upset by their mother's re-writing of their boarding-school years. "I hated it there!" He gulped down half his pint of Worthington E. "After living in Tregwyr with Grandma and Grandpa, to be thrust into that brutality! I couldn't get out of there quickly enough. That's why I joined the army instead of finishing the sixth form."

"But you liked the sports, didn't you? I thought you were in all the teams and quite the star Rugby player."

"I played games to escape. It was my only pleasure."

"I can relate to that. It was the same for me, only with reading."

He ordered another pint while they waited for their platters. "How many parcels did you receive, Gill? I don't remember getting any!"

"Mum sent me knickers once because Matron said I needed new ones, but I can't remember anything else. No parcels with condensed milk, or tangerines, or hand-knitted socks in them.

Not like some girls." She laughed. "Listen to us, Tom! We sound like sulky teenagers."

"I know. But it still hurts to remember those years. And then for her to give us that scenario! *I was so lonely* indeed!" He snorted and got up. "I've got to go to the loo. And I can see my old pal, Ian Martin, over there. I'll just have a little chat with him before I come back. Pip-Pip!"

It was true, she thought, that childhood hurts could remain with you in all their intensity. So much for Time the Great Healer. Sipping her dry white wine, Gillian relived her arrival as a boarder at Deer Park School for Girls.

"I'll say again, Gillian, you're a very lucky girl to have got into such a good school!" Her mother turned around in the passenger seat as they drove across the border from Wales into England.

"I don't see why." Gillian twisted her fingers together in her lap. "My Eleven-plus marks were better than most, and so's your money I suppose. If anyone's lucky it's *you*," she burst out, reckless with anger and misery, "because you won't have to bother with us now, hardly at all. You managed to be without me and Tommy during the whole of the war," and her mind skittered back to that first year of evacuation until, wrenching her attention back to the current abandonment, she stated, "And now it's boarding school for the two of us!"

"For shame, Gillian!" Her mother turned back to face the front. "At eleven years old you should be able to understand that we're doing this for your own good. Deer Park has an excellent reputation, and you'll meet some very nice girls there."

Gillian twisted her fingers in her hair and drove an imaginary hatpin into the back of her mother's head.

In the gleaming black Rover bought to celebrate the end of the war, they drove under the thirteenth-century arched gate and up the main street of the town, her father stopping in the town square to admire the bronze statue of a man holding up a biplane. Up on the hill overlooking the town stood the imposing stone building that was Deer Park School, brownish-pink stone against the hard blue September sky.

The car nosed through the gates and up the drive to the wide parking space in front of the school. Her mother, splendid in a blue silk suit, got out, holding on to her wide-brimmed hat and gaping at the grandeur of it all. Beside her, Gillian stared up at the mullioned façade and the white clouds scudding over it, until the building seemed to be falling on top of her. Averting her eyes to the terraced lawns, flanked by cedars of Lebanon, copper beeches, and horse-chestnut trees, in front of the school, she became aware of other girls in the driveway, screaming with joy at seeing each other again, or taking tearful farewells of their parents.

"Doctor and Mrs. Davies?" A large woman, her hair swept into white wings on each side of her head, swanned up. "I am the Headmistress, Miss Campbell. So pleased to see you!" She turned to Gillian with a smile, "And this must be Gillian. Welcome to Deer Park, Gillian. I hope you'll be very happy here."

There was nothing wrong with that, Gillian supposed, but her spirits sank even lower at hearing the headmistress's accent, the same as Mrs. Macpherson's. She pretended to study the view, while her parents, after the required farewell kisses and exhortations to work hard and be a good girl, got into the car and drove off.

Standing stiff and tall, she thought of the Jolly Miller of Dee in the song they used to sing at school in Tregwyr: "I care for nobody, no, not I./ And nobody cares for me!" Clenching her teeth, she blinked at the free, racing clouds.

Miss Campbell beckoned to an older girl in a crisp, light-blue linen dress, and told her to take Gillian into the school and show her to her dormitory.

After running an eye over Gillian's ashen frizz of hair, crumpled blouse and skirt, and skinny legs, the girl led her off. "What's your name?" she asked in a plummy English accent, officiously consulting a list as they went up the wide stone steps and through the crested entrance.

"Gillian Davies. What's yours?"

"Camilla Worthington. I'm a senior prefect in my last year at school."

Sunk in misery, Gillian put her nose in the air. "Well, bully for you!"

Camilla Worthington raised her eyebrows and tossed back her golden hair. "You'd better learn some manners, Gillian Davies, if you know what's good for you!"

She shimmered along in front of Gillian, up two flights of stone stairs and down a long corridor, leaving her with an abrupt "This is it" in front of a door.

THERE WERE FIVE NARROW BEDS in the room, each with a chest of drawers and a small wooden chair beside it. Her trunk had been placed at the bottom of the bed nearest the door. The other girls had already set up home: knick-knacks and family photographs were assembled on chests of drawers, soppy toy animals lay on the pillows, and cozy dressing gowns hung behind the door. She had not thought of bringing any such homely touches, apart from the torch Tommy had given her in case she wanted to run away, but she did have the new blue woolen dressing gown her grandmother had made her.

Tommy had cried when he gave her the torch, and they had promised to write to each other, holding on to the thought of the Christmas holidays. He was going the next day to a prep school even further away from home than Deer Park, where, like her, he knew nobody.

She put the torch at the back of a drawer and hung up the dressing gown on one of the two remaining hooks, taking some comfort from how well it stood up against the others.

Another going-away present had been from Mrs. Farrell. Gillian had gone to see Vanna one last time to see if they could make up their quarrel, but Vanna had taken herself off upstairs, slamming a door. Mrs. Farrell had shaken her head sadly. She was thinner than ever, and beginning to look quite old, although she was only the same age as Gillian's mother.

"I've missed you, Gillian," she said. "I miss our talks." She turned to one of the bookcases. "I want you to have these." She handed Gillian two books: Everyman volumes of *Jane Eyre* and *Wuthering Heights*.

"These are wonderful!" Gillian opened the top one, seeing the comforting Everyman promise. "But won't Vanna want them?"

"No. Those are for you." Mrs. Farrell kissed her goodbye.

GILLIAN QUICKLY FINISHED UNPACKING her trunk. Her mother had bought her some nice clothes, she thought as she put them away, guiltily remembering how she had refused to go on the shopping expeditions her mother had said would be such fun, and how rudely she had rejected her mother's choices of "sweetly pretty" frocks. Sometimes she thought her mother had got her mixed up with some other girl, like Gladys for instance, who would have loved those bright, flowery dresses.

Propped on her elbows on the bed, she opened *Jane Eyre.* After inhaling the old book smell and flipping through for illustrations, she settled down to read. Deer Park and her parents' departure faded to nothing as she turned page after page, racked with pity and indignation for poor little orphaned Jane, and aghast at the terrors of the red-room.

The door opened with a bang against the head of her bed, jolting her back into her strange new world. Camilla Worthington appeared in the doorway, with what was obviously another new girl cowering behind her.

"You still here?" She looked at Gillian coldly. "You should be in the assembly hall. Miss Campbell expects all the new girls to wait for her there."

"How was I supposed to know that?"

"Once again, Gillian Davies, that's no way to speak to a prefect. What's more, you're not allowed to lie on your bed in the daytime."

The other girl, a dark, sallow little thing in a straight navy dress with white collar and cuffs, began to cry.

"Oh, for heaven's sake!" Camilla Worthington turned on her heel and banged the door shut on them.

The girl threw herself face-down, sobbing, on the last unclaimed bed, clutching the bedspread in her fists. "Oh, Mummy, Mummy! Why did you leave me?"

Reluctantly abandoning Jane in the red-room, Gillian sat up and studied this real-life girl. "What's your name?"

"Fiona." The girl looked up for a moment, blotched and red-eyed.

"Come on, Fiona, buck up. Let's go and find the assembly hall."

"I don't want to." She was face-down, sobbing again. "I want my Mummy!"

Gillian thought that rather childish. The last time she had cried for her mummy, she had been six years old, and a fat lot of use that had been.

"But you'll see her at half-term, won't you?" she said.

The girl wept even harder. "I won't see her for a whole year. She's going back again to India tomorrow on the boat. Now I'm all alone." She buried her face in the pillow, hiccupping with sobs, "Oh, Mummy, come back! Don't leave me!"

"What about your father?"

She looked up at Gillian, her eyes brimming. "He died." The tears rolled down. "Last Christmas. There's only me and Mummy now," she sobbed. "I want to go home!"

Well that *was* tough, Gillian thought, but she would just have to get on with it, like the rest of them. "Look here, Fiona." She stood up and straightened her skirt. "I really think we'd better go to the assembly hall. The headmistress probably wants to tell us all the rules. Maybe take attendance. You'd better come, or you might get into trouble."

Blowing her nose and catching her breath in little sobs, Fiona followed like a new-hatched chick as Gillian went down to look for the hall.

MISS CAMPBELL LOOKED DOWN FROM the podium at the new girls gathered before her. She welcomed them all and spoke in a generally encouraging sort of way before going on to explain not only the rules, but also the reasons for the rules. She followed that with a description of the boarders' daily and weekly schedules.

With Fiona sniffling beside her, Gillian listened carefully, her head sinking lower and lower. When the headmistress came to the weekend routine, Gillian realized the problem: there was no spare time. Not anywhere. Not in the day, not in the week, not even at the weekend. There would be no time in which to read *Jane Eyre*. As long as she could read, she had told herself, she could get through anything, but evidently it was not going to be so easy.

When she tuned back into the talk, she heard Miss Campbell explaining the significance of the school motto: *Servate Honorem*, 'Preserve your Honour'. Apparently it meant that all of them should, and could, live their lives so that they need never, ever, feel ashamed of themselves in any way. Gillian glanced furtively around at all the open faces staring up innocently at the headmistress. She looked down at the laces coming undone in her stiff new black shoes, a hard ache in her stomach.

"STONE WALLS DO NOT A PRISON MAKE," her grandmother would say, quoting as usual, "Nor iron bars, a cage." Gillian had not seen any iron bars during her first week, apart from the entrance gates, but there were plenty of stone walls, and as far as she was concerned, they jolly well did a prison make. Sitting down at one of the long tables to chunks of tube-filled liver with lumpy mashed potatoes and soggy cabbage, or stinky boiled cod with wallpaper-paste sauce and grey leather-skinned broad beans, she thought longingly of her grandmother's clever ways with rations and homegrown vegetables.

As she had foreseen, the lack of privacy and spare time was even harder to bear. The only spot of time the boarders had to themselves, between the end of 'prep', the time to be spent on homework, and bedtime, provided nothing else had been organized, had to be spent in the din of the Junior Common Room, with its sagging sofas and odours of sweat and digestive biscuits and ink. This was the time for the hazing of new girls, the other girls discussing them as if they were not in the room.

On her third day there, Gillian surfaced from *Jane Eyre* at the sound of her name.

"She's never got her nose out of that stupid book." Pamela Bingham, a chunky Upper Fourth girl, was exclaiming. "And did you ever see such hair? Like Harpo Marx! Touch of the old tar brush, if you ask me!" This raised snickers, and a remark about gooseberry eyes. "And those legs! Like broomsticks! But it's her parents I feel sorry for. I mean, wouldn't it be absolutely the pits to have a drippy daughter like that! But I expect the Welsh aren't so fussy."

Gillian looked up to see a semicircle of fourth-formers staring at her, shaking their heads.

She stood up. "I'm sure my parents would prefer it to having a greasy-haired, pimply-faced daughter, with legs like tree trunks, who can only read things like," she picked a dog-eared book off the table, "*Mad-cap Moll of the Lower Fourth.*" She dropped the book, brushing her fingers together, and left the room.

Life was more tolerable in the dormitory. The other girls: Anita, with her blonde curls and dimples, sturdy, athletic Diana, her short black hair cut in a dead-straight line above her equally straight eyebrows, and lanky, round-shouldered Chris, the obsessive piano player, her hair dangling in thin brown plaits, all seemed to know each other and get on well, leaving the two new girls alone; Gillian to read, and Fiona to cry. Chris and Anita arranged each other's hair, and Diana talked non-stop about games. All three of them discussed the teachers and prefects, at which times Gillian gathered they did not like Camilla Worthington any more than she did. They politely tried to include her in their conversation a few times, but finding they were no competition for *Jane Eyre* they soon gave up the effort.

DURING HER FIRST TWO WEEKS AT SCHOOL, Gillian hid in the library during break, tried unsuccessfully to persuade Matron she was sick, and even managed, with a little help from Anita, to conceal herself inside the vaulting horse in the gym in order to be left alone with her book, but nothing worked. Finally she decided she would have to read in bed, after lights out, using Tommy's torch.

Bed was the one place in all this whirling commotion where she felt safe in her own space, and where she did not have to do anything, or answer to anyone.

That night, snuggled into the coarse sheets, heavy blankets pulled over her head to conceal the torchlight and shut out the sound of Fiona's sobbing, she was riveted by the approaching death of Helen, Jane's saintly friend, at terrible Lowood School.

"Are you going somewhere, Helen? Are you going home?" Jane was asking.

Gillian turned the page, her heart beating fast in grief and dread.

"Yes; to my long home—my last home."

Gillian felt the shock of bedclothes being pulled away. Back for a moment at Maenordy, she put her arms around her head, waiting for the slaps.

"No reading after lights out, Gillian. You need your sleep." Matron spoke softly so as not to wake the others. "I'm sorry, but I'm confiscating these." After a few quiet words with Fiona, she slipped away with the book and the torch.

Covering her head, Gillian began to weep quietly, not for her home, or her parents, or even for Tommy, but for her lost world: for Jane, for Helen, and for all the poor, unwanted girls at Lowood School.

"Are you crying for your mummy?" a voice whispered by her ear.

"I am *not* crying for my mummy! I'm crying for my *book*. Matron took it away."

"How can you cry for a book? It's just a story. It isn't real. Don't cry!"

After sending Fiona back to bed, Gillian stared into the darkness, thinking about what she had just said. Truly it was strange that Lowood seemed so real to her; more real than

Deer Park. And how was it, she wondered, that she understood so well what people in books were feeling? She knew as if they were her own, Jane's loneliness and anger, Pip's shame and sense of inferiority in *Great Expectations*, the longing of the Forsaken Merman for his mortal wife in the poem they had read that day in English class, and the yearning, too, of the merman's wife after she had returned home, for the little mermaiden she had left behind. She had never been in any of their situations, and yet she knew their inmost feelings. Why was that?

THE NEXT MORNING, WHEN THEY were up and dressed, and the other girls had gone chattering off, Gillian saw that Fiona's thin face, behind its curtain of stringy dark hair, was the colour of green olives, with purple shadows under her eyes. Her tie was crooked and her tunic on back-to-front. She drooped on her bed, sniffing and fiddling with her sash. To keep her out of trouble, Gillian persuaded her to come down to breakfast even though she knew she wouldn't eat anything. She never did.

Later that morning, Miss Lamb, the English teacher, elegant in a chignon and a long black cloak, read aloud from a poem called "Pippa Passes."

God's in his heaven.
All's right with the world!

she concluded with an airy wave of her hand, followed by a thud from the back of the class as Fiona fell off her chair in a dead faint.

AT BEDTIME GILLIAN WENT TO THE SICK BAY.

"Ah, Gillian, the reading girl," Matron looked up from her logbook. "I want to talk to you, dear. That poor little thing from your dormitory is breaking her heart. She's not sleeping, and she won't eat a thing. She's just pining away for her mother."

"Yes I know. Can I have my book back, please, Matron?"

Matron looked at her for a long moment over her glasses, sighed, and shook her head. "You may. I'm keeping the torch, though." She handed the book to Gillian who stuffed it down the front of her box-pleated tunic, tying the sash tightly.

A few nights later, just before lights out, Gillian looked up in a daze from *Jane Eyre*, her eyes resting on Fiona's empty bed. She wondered for a moment what was happening to her tearful little roommate, until the mystery of the demonic laugh through the keyhole of Jane's bedroom door reclaimed her attention and she sank back into her book for the last precious minutes of reading time.

The next day she was summoned after classes to the sick bay. Matron was all starched up as usual in her white uniform, but she did not have her cheerful "How-are-we-today?" face on.

"Poor Fiona isn't doing well at all," she said. "She's just breaking her heart. She still won't eat or sleep, and I'm very worried about her." She looked at Gillian with her head on one side, her soft dark eyes reminding Gillian of Mrs. Rosenberg. "Now then, Gillian, Fiona says the closest she has to a friend here is you, poor little thing, so I want you to go in and talk to her, and see if you can cheer her up a bit."

Stung by that "poor little thing", and resolving to try harder for Matron's good opinion, Gillian nodded.

Fiona was lying back in a chintz armchair by the electric fire in Matron's cozy sitting room, her eyes sunk in dark hollows and her cheekbones jutting out. She looked worse than ever.

"Hello, Fiona." Gillian put on a fake, cheery smile. "When are you coming back to the dorm?" Making a big effort before Matron left the two of them together, she added, "I miss you."

"Do you?" Fiona looked at her with lacklustre eyes that straightaway overflowed. "I don't know why you would. Why would anyone miss *me*?"

Good question, Gillian thought, at least as far as school was concerned, but she found what seemed to be a good answer: "Well, your mother cares about you, doesn't she?" From the way Fiona had carried on, it appeared the two of them must have been close in a way that Gillian could hardly imagine.

Tears gathered, trembled, and flowed again down the sunken, yellow cheeks. "She used to, but she doesn't any more. She could've stayed with me, or she could've taken me back home with her, and we'd have managed somehow, but she said she'd got to go back by herself," she began to sob loudly, "to get more money."

"But perhaps she went to get more money for your sake?"

Fiona leaned forward urgently, pushing rat-tails of hair off her face. "How could she leave me all alone for a *year*? I think she wanted to see more of Uncle Rodney without me hanging around all the time. She doesn't want *me*." She put her head in her hands and began to cry. "Nobody wants me."

"Who's Uncle Rodney?"

Fiona took a shuddering breath. "He was a friend of Daddy's. He lives in Delhi and he's very rich. I hate him." The sobs became desperate as she turned to hide her face in a blue velvet cushion.

Matron came back in, bringing Fiona's medication. "Thank you, Gillian." She put her arms around Fiona. "Wait for me in the sick bay."

Gillian was beginning to feel like crying herself as she sat on the hard chair by Matron's tidy desk. All that about Fiona's mother not caring had been very upsetting, and her efforts to cheer her up seemed to have made things even worse. Matron would be disappointed in her.

Matron came out of her room, shutting the door behind her. "I'm sorry, Gillian dear, I know you really tried, but Fiona is quite inconsolable. I'm at my wit's end. I can't reach her mother of course, and there's only a solicitor for contact." She pursed her mouth and looked seriously at Gillian. "Can you, by any chance, think of anything, Gillian? Anything at all that might make a difference to her?"

Gillian tried hard to think of a remedy. What would she herself do in this situation? "I know, Matron! I've got it!" She leapt to her feet. "I could lend her *Jane Eyre*!" It would be a wrench, but to be honest, she was getting a bit bored with that St. Jean Rivers man, and she could take a break from the book. She would start on *Wuthering Heights* while she waited to get it back.

Matron smiled and actually gave her a quick hug. "That's really very kind of you, Gillian. I know how much that book means to you, and I remember how I felt when I read it myself, at about your age. But you know, dear, I don't think the subject matter would help Fiona. As I recall, it's about a poor little orphan girl who has to struggle to make her own way through a hard, cruel world, and then marries that awful Mr. Rochester."

"Oh … right. But Matron, Jane manages really well, doesn't she? And perhaps Fiona would see that if Jane managed, she could too."

"Well, that's a thought. We could give it a try, I suppose. Why don't you pop down and get it while I go and have a quick word with Miss Campbell about calling the doctor again?"

She locked the medicine cabinet and put the keys in the bottom drawer.

Camilla was patrolling the silent corridor as Gillian scurried along to the dormitory, mentally arguing with Matron about Mr. Rochester.

"You're not allowed on this floor at this time, Gillian Davies," she hooted down the hall, "You should be in prep. *And* you were running down the corridor. I'll have to report you."

Gillian kept going. "I'm on an important errand for Matron, Camilla, and if you'll excuse me, I'm in rather a hurry. You can check with Matron if you like."

When she got back to the sick bay, book in hand, she was surprised to find Fiona already in bed, a patch of pink on each cheek. There had been a rustle of bedclothes as she reached the door, and something pushed under the pillow before Fiona turned to face her. Fiona took the book with limp hands, and without even opening it, put it down behind the half-empty glass of water on the bedside table. She thanked Gillian but seemed even more tired and distant than usual and turned her eyes back to the rain running down the darkening window. Still, Gillian thought, once she opened the book and read about how horrible the Reed family was to Jane, she would have to read on to see what happened to her, and then, once she got to the red-room bit, she would not be able to put it down. It would change her life.

"I'll come back this evening, if you like," she offered nobly.

"No thanks. I'm awfully tired. I'm going to sleep."

"Well that's great, Fiona! You'll feel much better tomorrow. I'll come and see you after school."

Fiona smiled faintly but made no reply.

THE NEXT DAY, HOWEVER, WHEN GILLIAN went up to the sick bay after netball, Fiona was not there, and neither was Matron. The bright overhead light was turned off, and Matron's chatty radio was silent. Fiona's bed was newly made up, and all her things were gone. On the taut white chenille bedspread Gillian saw *Jane Eyre,* together with the torch and a note saying, "For

Gillian Davies," in Matron's handwriting. She picked them up, wondering what could have happened. Had Matron taken Fiona to the cottage hospital?

THE WHOLE SCHOOL WAS AGOG. Fiona had disappeared, and Matron seemed to have gone too. Rumours were flying: Fiona was hiding somewhere in the building; she had run away; her mother had mysteriously reappeared and taken her away, threatening to have the law on the school for starving her. Gillian was in demand for once, since she had been one of the last people to have seen Fiona, but she could throw no light on her disappearance except to say that she did not think she would have had the strength or the gumption to run away, and that she had nowhere to run to anyway.

That evening Miss Campbell summoned the boarders to the main hall, where they assembled quietly to wait for her, the teachers and prefects on chairs, and the rest of the girls sitting cross-legged on the polished wood floor. Finally the headmistress appeared on the platform by herself, looking pale and shaken, the white wings of her hair drooping. She regarded the assembly for a long minute before beginning to speak.

"Girls," her voice was deep and slow. "Something terribly sad has happened." In the silence that followed, Gillian held her breath and stared at the floorboards, frozen with apprehension.

Miss Campbell looked around the gathering. "I'm giving you the whole story, girls, so that you'll know the truth and won't invent, or believe, rumours." She took a deep breath and gripped the lectern. "Fiona was a heartbroken little girl who was very weak and tired from three weeks of not being able to eat or sleep. Matron and I decided last night, therefore, that she should be taken to the hospital for a thorough examination." She stopped to clear her throat. "The doctor there discovered that in fact, unbeknownst to us, Fiona had a serious heart problem. Apparently the stress of separation from her mother had aggravated her condition to a point where, I'm desperately sorry to say, girls, despite all their, *and our*, efforts to save her, her heart gave out." She paused and raised her face to the ceiling. "Fiona died early this morning in the hospital." She held on to the lectern and then bowed her head as if praying.

There was a stir throughout the hall and gasps of horror. Some of the girls began to cry. Gillian felt sick and realized she had to breathe deeply if she were not to faint. Through a feathery white fog she heard her name, and then the headmistress's voice.

"Matron, who, I'm sorry to say, has left us, told me that Gillian tried to show some friendship towards Fiona, and did her best to help her."

Gillian was aware of the other girls looking around at her in disbelief. She knew she was not exactly famous for her friendliness and was generally held to be a nasty sarcastic thing, best left alone. She looked down into her lap, seeing the fringe of her sash in sharp detail as if for the first time. She could not swallow for the jagged pain in her throat.

IN THE DORMITORY THAT NIGHT, the four girls huddled together in their dressing gowns on Anita and Diana's beds, trying to come to grips with what had happened.

"At least you tried to help Fiona." Anita looked at Gillian. "The rest of us tried for a couple of days and then gave up and just ignored her until she *died of a broken heart*." She dabbed at her red eyes. "I feel terrible."

The others agreed tearfully. The pain was back in Gillian's throat. "I ignored her too. I didn't do my best to help her at all. I shut my ears to all that crying at night, and sometimes I tried to avoid sitting next to her at meals or in the common room. I wasn't any better than anyone else. I only tried to help because Matron asked me to. The only thing I wanted to do was to read my book. I couldn't see … I didn't think … I didn't know … And now Fiona's dead! And Matron's gone too!" She gave way to sobs such as she had not uttered since she had first been sent away from home at the beginning of the war. She shrugged off the arm that Anita put around her, and ignored Chris's offer of a handkerchief.

"Would this help?" Diana fetched *Jane Eyre* from Gillian's chest of drawers and put it into her hands. Gillian was about to push the book away, when she noticed a small white triangle poking out from behind the front cover. Turning her back, she removed the envelope before dropping the book on the bed, to be picked up and leafed through by the other girls.

"Dear Gillian," Matron had written, "I don't want to leave without telling you that I won't forget you. I can see that you have had your own troubles, but always remember, dear, you have a kind heart. Goodbye and God bless, Rose Solomon."

Gillian's shoulders dropped down and back as she took a deep breath, the pain in her throat subsiding. Matron would not forget her. Matron had called her 'dear', and said she had a kind heart. She could feel that organ warming and expanding in her chest as she reread the words.

"What's so terrific about this book, Gill?" Diana held it out towards her. "You always act like it's the best thing in the world."

The other girls looked at Gillian expectantly.

"Nothing." Wiping her eyes, Gillian looked over at Fiona's empty bed. "Nothing at all. It's just a story."

Tom rolled up, a fresh pint in his hand, just as the waiter arrived with their orders.

"Hadn't you better take it easy?" Gillian raised an eyebrow. "You've got to drive to Langland after this."

"You're right. This is my last. But Mum upsets me. Nothing pleases her, however hard I try. There's no doing anything with her!" He took a long swallow and set his tankard down. "But the thing is, Gill," he looked hard at her, "I don't want her to die without sort of giving me her blessing, if you know what I mean."

Gillian sat back, tears in her eyes. "I do know what you mean, Tom! That's what I want too. I thought I came because I wanted to tell her about Angus, and so I do, but this goes even deeper." She leaned forward. "But why should we be asking for her blessing, Tom? Isn't it she who should blessing beg of us?"

"Where's that from?"

"King Lear."

"Ha! Well let's not exaggerate, but I think you're right."

"In the play it goes both ways: Lear and Cordelia open their hearts completely to each other before they meet their deaths."

"Well, this is small potatoes compared to that I suppose, but still . . ." He picked up his knife and fork and set about his steak and chips.

AT THE BUNGALOW TWEETIE-PIE lumbered to meet them, tail erect.

"How's my big boy?' Tom swept him up to ride on his shoulder. As they entered the sunlit living room, Sylvester let loose a trill of joy, or, for all Gillian knew, anger.

"What will become of these two if . . . ?"

"Oh, I'll take them myself. I promised her that when I gave them to her. You know, I think I'll have a bit of a nap, Gill, if that's okay. And then maybe we'll have a cup of tea and go for a walk on the beach."

He and Tweetie-Pie ambled off to the spare room, while Gillian settled into the cushioned rocking chair from the old home in Tregwyr, to look out over the calm sea until she too fell asleep.

TWO HOURS LATER, THEY WERE WALKING along hard, damp sand, dotted with shells, pebbles, clumps of seaweed, pieces of driftwood, and stranded starfish; a cracked Frisbee here, a small red spade there, the dried remains of a seagull scrunched under a log a few steps ahead. Gillian picked up a piece of bladderwort and popped its bubbles, getting slime on her fingers. Squinting into the sun, she pulled a strand of hair off her salty lower lip. “I bumped into Robbie, the butcher’s boy, this morning. Did you know he married Gladys?”

“Yes, of course I knew. She married him straight after our divorce. Bit of luck for me, that. Almost as good as her flying off, literally, ha, ha, with that fellow who owned an airplane!”

“Bit of luck for her, too. Robbie seems devoted to her, God knows why.”

Tom slouched along beside her, shoulders hunched, hands in his jeans pockets. He stopped and faced her. “Have you seen Vanna?”

Gillian nodded.

“Did she say anything about me?”

“Actually, she did. She asked after you quite particularly. She seems to be pretty up-to-date on your affairs, so to speak. Have you been seeing her at all?”

“Oh, now and then, off and on, you know.” He looked out over the sea. “But I don’t think she’ll ever return my feelings. Nobody ever has, really, come to think of it.” He turned to her. “What’s the matter with me, Gill? I mean, I’m not bad-looking. I’m not poor, or weird, or anything. All I want is to settle down happily with someone, but it never works out.”

Gillian put her arm in his. “Well, I love you.”

He hugged her arm into his side. "I know. You're a rock." He picked up a stick and threw it for a Jack Russell terrier which had appeared out of nowhere. "That was a bad business about that creep, Stan. Remember? I think Vanna always saw me as a bumbling fool after that."

"I don't think she knew you told Gladys where he could find her, Tom. How could she? I think she might have suspected me, though. She turned cold towards me again for years after that, until just before I went away."

They walked along in silence for a while, Tom obliging the fanatical dog, and Gillian thinking about the uncomfortable events of that summer holiday more than fifty years ago.

Home for the summer holidays, alone for once, since their father was giving Tom his Saturday morning tennis lesson, and their mother was meeting friends for coffee, Gillian sat on the couch in the sunlit living room. In her hand were her General Certificate results, just received in the post, all of them even better than she had hoped. So it was on to A levels in English, French, and Latin, and in two years' time, university; a lifetime of freedom and reading opening up for her.

Two more years before she got out of prison! School had become more bearable as the years had passed, but she had never been one of those girls, and there were surprisingly many of them, who loved being at boarding school, and probably *would* say in their old age, that those really had been the happiest days of their lives. She herself was just getting through it as best she could, doing her work, and waiting for her happy life, broken off at six years old, to begin again somehow, when she got out into the world.

Fortunately, the housemistress had stopped writing comments like "Gillian should participate more enthusiastically," and "Gillian gives the impression of living in a cage," which had caused a bit of an uproar, with her parents insisting that she stop embarrassing them and start joining clubs and trying out for teams.

That bit about living in a cage had been true though, in more senses than one. In the first months she had struggled, first to adjust to that new, regimented life, and then to deal with the death of Fiona. Things became even worse when her periods started. Even though she had vaguely known in theory what would happen, she had turned in on herself, shocked at her body's gross betrayal. Profoundly embarrassed by the whole thing, she would withdraw into a book whenever the talk in the dorm turned, as it did more and more often, to the excruciating subject of boys, and making babies and what went where and how.

"I've seen my brother with nothing on," she heard Chris say, "and it beats me how that little floppy thing can get into anything, let alone in *there?*"

"Oh, I think something happens to it," Anita said, and blushed.

"What d'you mean? What happens to it?" Diana and Chris stared at her, fascinated.

Silent and appalled, Gillian tried to suppress the images that arose unbidden: the winking eye of that thing, stiff as a policeman's truncheon; Angus's demands on its behalf; and the eventual milky fountain, like a whale spouting. Floppiness would not be a problem, she thought, though size certainly would be. Angus had said he was going to get it right in her next time, and she had been terrified at the thought of what would happen to her if he finally succeeded. Thank God Grandma and Grandpa had sent for them when they did!

Even more excruciating than the dorm discussions had been the time when the biology teacher had given the Upper Fourth a lesson on the mechanics of human reproduction, using unspeakable words like *engorgement* and *ejaculation.* As

Miss Sinclair, glaring over her shoulder, wrote and even drew on the board Gillian had wished she could be anywhere but there, or that she could—perhaps not die, because that would attract too much attention—but just cease to exist, right there in the smell of formaldehyde, amongst the test tubes and Bunsen burners and stained sinks.

In time however, she had roused herself and managed some success at taking part in school life. She had begun by joining the knitting circle, where she made Tom a pair of too-small socks, and had gone on to help Miss Lamb with the organization of a junior poetry competition. To the delight of her father she had been selected for the junior tennis team, but it turned out that while she could be a competent player if merely enjoying the game or bringing up the score, whenever a game reached a critical point, in an interschool match for instance, she could never hit a winner. This, no doubt, was why she had never made it to the senior team.

She was on the senior hockey team, though, playing defense; always and only defense, but nevertheless definitely participating. When school started again, she would be in the sixth form and had agreed to work behind the scenes on the senior school production of *Twelfth Night.* What was more, she would be a junior prefect, and had been asked to join the editorial board of the school newspaper. She was playing her part as well as she knew how. What more could they ask?

THE SIDE DOOR SLAMMED AND TOM burst into the room, dropping his tennis racket with a clatter on the parquet floor, and throwing himself sideways into an armchair. High colour burned on his cheeks as he fixed the blue blaze of his eyes on her. "You'll never guess who I saw in Woolworth's earlier this morning, Gill! Go on. Guess!"

She sighed. "Just tell me, Tom."

"I saw Vanna! Vanna Farrell!"

Gillian sat up. "Vanna? You saw her here in town?"

"Yes. And she's absolutely gorgeous, Gill! She's the most beautiful girl I ever saw in my whole life!" He grabbed the quiff of dark hair on top of his head in both fists.

"I see. And is she still covered with freckles?"

"Yes, but her freckles are gorgeous too! And you should see her hair! She's cut off her plaits, and it's all long and loose and curly. She's absolutely stunning!"

Remembering her first sight of Vanna's mother, Gillian knew what he meant. "Did you talk to her?"

"No, she was busy serving someone. She didn't see me."

"Serving someone?"

"Yes, she was behind the counter in the women's bit; jewelry 'n stuff."

Gillian put the letter from school down on a side table, her self-satisfaction draining away. Instead of being behind the counter in Woolworth's, Vanna too, should have been getting excellent G.C. results at this point, with a good chance of being able to go to university in a couple of years on a scholarship.

"Could you go and see her, Gill?" Tom fixed pleading eyes on her. "Maybe get her to meet you after work? And then, maybe I . . ."

"Don't be daft, Tom. Vanna's two years older than you, and if she's as gorgeous as you say, she probably has a boyfriend already."

Tom pouted and kicked at the coffee table with a hefty tennis shoe. He was awfully big for fourteen, she thought; strong enough to have beaten their father at tennis the day before, and with the makings of a mustache showing on his upper lip.

"You could go and see her anyway," he suggested, leaning forward. She could tell Vanna that he, Tom, wanted news of Francis.

"Why don't you ask her yourself?"

He flung himself back. "Oh I couldn't! I'd be terrified to go up and talk to her just like that. Please, Gill, go to see her. Just to say hello?"

"Oh, I don't know, Tom. It's sort of awkward." Gillian was remembering her last face-to-face encounter with Vanna after the Eleven Plus exam.

"Listen." Elbows on knees, chin in hands, he fixed his eyes on her. "I'll tell you something. For years now, ever since we left Tregwyr, I've had this dream about Vanna. Don't laugh, Gill. We're at Grandma's having tea, and Vanna eats a whole sponge cake."

Gillian laughed. "And are you angry in the dream? You certainly wouldn't like it in real life."

"No. I'm giving it to her, slice after slice."

Gillian studied his flushed face. "Crikey, Tom, I'd no idea it was as bad as that."

"Neither had I, not really, not 'til I saw her today. Well, some idea, of course. I always thought she was fabulous, but this, today… It was like a bolt from the blue!" He propped an ankle across a tanned knee, the hairs on his leg much more noticeable than she remembered. "You know, maybe I'm not too young, Gill. Old Glad Eyes doesn't seem to mind."

"What? What do you mean? Are you saying *Gladys* fancies you?"

"Yeah, well. Me and whoever."

Gillian and Tom saw Gladys from time to time during school holidays when she came in to collect her mother. Dark-haired and fine-boned, she had cultivated the Audrey Hepburn look with more success than many, despite her lack of height. She would tease Tom, flirting with him shamelessly, and to Gillian's disgust, act towards her as if they had always been the best of friends.

Earlier in the holiday, she had casually let drop that she sometimes visited her mother's cousin, Auntie Blodwen, in Croesffordd. "I seen Angus there one time." She smiled up at Gillian, batting her long eyelashes. "He've got ever such a posh girlfriend now. All tall and blonde she is, and la-di-dah English."

Gillian could not have cared less about the girlfriend, but the mention of Angus had sent her into a flat spin for days, and she had avoided Gladys ever since. Why couldn't he just stay in the deep, dark cellar she had assigned him to? Why did he keep popping up when she had forgotten all about him, like some monstrous Jack-in-the-box?

"What about it, Gill? Will you go? Please!" Tom often got his way through sheer persistence.

"I'll think about it." She was distracted by her unwelcome memories, the multiple shock of the Vanna sighting, and the glimpse into the secret lives of Tom and Gladys.

TWO DAYS LATER, SHE ENTERED Woolworth's. Vanna was leaning over the jewelry counter, sorting cardboard boxes of earrings. Even taller than Gillian, she not only looked like her mother, but moved as gracefully. Holding back their glittering contents with a long, white finger, she was turning over the boxes to check the price sticker underneath. Absorbed in her task, she did not look up until Gillian stood across the counter from her.

"Can I help you?" She raised her head, a mechanical smile on her rose-tinted lips. At the sight of Gillian, she dropped the box she was holding, her face flooding with the deep colour Gillian remembered. "What do *you* want? Buying Woolworth's earrings are you? You must've come down in the world!"

"Vanna," Gillian faced her, "couldn't we be friends now? I know what happened was terrible for you, but none of it was actually my fault."

Vanna ducked down to see to something under the counter, muttering something that sounded like "You could've tried to help."

Gillian was taken aback. She couldn't have known Vanna needed help, could she? If she had been another sort of girl perhaps, a generous, sensitive, thoughtful girl, she might have thought to ask, but she was not, and had not. She ran her fingers through the pink and blue pearls hanging from a hook and pooling on the counter beside her, trying to think what to say.

Vanna resurfaced, darkened lashes blinking away tears. "I'm sorry. That wasn't fair. But I've always been so jealous of you. And that damned exam ruined my life. Totally destroyed it! I'm doomed to stay in jobs like this, if I'm lucky, and live in poverty forever!"

If she still had plaits, Gillian thought, she would be wringing them. "You don't *know* that, Vanna. You never know what's round the corner. Things might turn out all right in the end. After all," she ventured a smile, "we found the baby Jesus. Remember?" They had fished the tiny doll out of the rubbish bin by the back door of the school, together with the rest of their treasured, hole-in-the-wall home furnishings.

"I'm glad you're amused." Vanna had gone back to her checking.

"No, I wasn't laughing at you. I just remembered Tommy and Francis running ahead to your house shouting out the good news to your mother that we'd found Jesus, and the old woman next door to you screeching, 'Glory be! Praise the Lord!' Do you remember?"

The corner of Vanna's mouth tweaked. "Yes, poor old Mrs. Lloyd. I'd forgotten that."

"How is Francis, anyway? Tom was wondering about him. And your mother? And all your family?"

A large shiny dress of navy and red vertical stripes loomed up beside her as its occupant rapped on the jewelry counter and glared at the two girls.

Gillian persisted. "Look, why don't we meet for a chat. How about at the Kardomah after you get off work today?"

"Wednesday, maybe," Vanna said after a pause before turning her attention to the customer.

AT THE KARDOMAH CAFÉ, Gillian took a table for four near the window and facing the door. Waiting for her pot of tea, she thought about Vanna's likeness to her mother. She knew that girls sometimes did look very like their mothers—there were a couple of girls at school like that—but this was almost uncanny: the height, the poise, and every detail of build, feature, and colouring.

Unlike Tom, she herself did not take after their well-built, dark-haired, blue-eyed mother in the least, and despite the head-shaking on the subject on the part of her mother's friends, she was glad of it. Nobody quite knew whom she did look like, apparently, with her tall thin build, strange hair, and green eyes. "She's one of a kind," her father would say. "One in a million is our Gillian."

Her mother said she was a throwback to an ancestor on their grandmother's side, one Great-Uncle Theophilos, who had gone out to Patagonia and become a famous preacher.

The Kardomah was noisy and bright with the clatter and sparkle of crockery and cutlery, the aroma and roar of the huge, stainless-steel coffee machine, and the babble of gossip. Gillian worried about what to order. Would Vanna be hungry and want her tea? Would she have to catch the bus to Tregwyr, or did she live in town now? Should she treat her to tea, or would that enrage her? Twiddling her hair, she realized she was getting in a state, almost as bad as Tom who had said he intended to bump into them accidentally.

He had spent an hour in the bathroom before she left, probably squeezing his spots and shaving off his moustache, and sloshing on their father's Imperial Leather aftershave. She had advised him not to wear his suit; "Just wear those tan linen trousers and a clean white shirt. Try to look normal."

At ten past five she was surprised to see Gladys, heavily made up, her hair in a pixie cut, teetering into the café on the arm of a short, thin man. She was wearing a red dress with the plunging neckline, tight bodice, and voluminous skirt that was the latest fashion. Large gold hoops dangled from her small ears. Seeing Gillian, she gave a shriek of delighted recognition. "Cooee!" she called, waving across the crowded restaurant, "Cooee, Gillian!" and made her way over, dragging the man with her.

The man wore a pinstriped brown suit. He had a narrow moustache and was holding a fedora.

"Pleased to meet you," he said, as Gladys introduced "my friend, Gillian Davies, the *doctor's* daughter, you know." His name was Stan.

Gillian realized with alarm that he was staring at her intently, a slight smile on his thin lips. *I know you*, his little dark eyes seemed to be saying, *I know everything about you.* His eyes roved down to linger on her blouse, then slid back up to meet hers. *I know your secret.*

Her mouth dry, Gillian turned to Gladys. "Tom will be here in a minute. He'll be pleased to meet your friend."

"Got to go now!" Gladys led Stan off, past the plump matrons with their perms and their diamonds, who looked them up and down over forkfuls of chocolate cake. "Lovely to see you!" she fluted over her shoulder.

He couldn't know. How could he? But she felt that he did, and that he could have power over her somehow, like Angus.

She gave herself a shake. She would not think about Stan. She would relegate him to the place where she kept Angus: throw him down into everlasting darkness and bolt the trapdoor over him. She sat up straight and shakily poured herself another cup of tea.

A few minutes later she looked at her watch. Half past five. Vanna would not come now. But as she looked, first through the window, and then down to the front of the café to see if Tom was in sight, the revolving glass door swung around, and Vanna made her entrance. The sun blazing on her hair, she surveyed the populace. Heads turned to follow her progress towards Gillian's table. A young man sat up straight and smoothed back his Brilliantined hair, openly staring. A solitary, middle-aged man watched furtively from behind his newspaper as she swept past. Across the café, Gillian saw Gladys and her loathsome companion crane their necks and gape as Vanna arrived at her table.

"Sorry I'm late." Vanna took the chair opposite Gillian, ordered a pot of tea from the waitress, and accepted a Cherry Danish from the plate of pastries Gillian had ordered. "Had to help with inventory. Can't stay long. Got to catch the Tregwyr bus at six."

"I'm glad you came, anyway." The two girls looked warily at each other as the waitress appeared with the tea.

Vanna picked up her teapot and put it down again. "I'm sorry about the other day, Gill. Of course you're absolutely right. None of that was your fault. I'm ashamed that I was so horrible to you, and that I sulked like that for *five years*. Can I ever hope to be forgiven?" She raised her eyebrows, her mouth turned down in a tragic mask.

"Of course!" A hard little pain dissolved. "Forget about it."

Vanna smiled and sat up, filling her cup. "How's boarding school? I suppose you're carrying all before you?"

Tea sloshed into their saucers. "Sorry! Sorry!" Apologizing for his clumsiness, and declaring his amazement at seeing them, Tom, pale for once, except for his spots and a gash on his chin, stood gawking at Vanna.

"Sit down, Tom." Gillian patted a chair. "D'you remember Vanna?"

"This is Tommy?" Vanna opened her eyes wide as Tom folded himself into the chair. "My, what a big boy!"

Tom blushed up from his throat, and seized a Chelsea bun. "Hello, Vanna," he said in a sepulchral voice. "Long time no see!"

Vanna grinned, "You speak the truth, my noble Indian friend," and Gillian saw them all as children, crowded around the radio in the back room of her grandparents' house, listening to *The Lone Ranger*.

Tom looked over his bun at Vanna with drowning eyes, his mouth open. Gillian kicked his ankle. "Tom was asking after Francis, Vanna."

Vanna drained her cup. "He's fine thanks, Tom. Doing well in the grammar school. As is Bridie. Listen, I'm sorry to rush off. I'd love to stay and talk to you both and get all the news, but I've really got to go now." She stood up, people turning again to look. "Tell you what. Why don't you both come out on Sunday afternoon? Mama'd love to see you, and so would the others. Francis was so excited when he heard that I'd seen Gillian!"

Tom swung his eyes round to Gillian.

"That would be lovely," she said.

THE NEXT DAY GLADYS CAME to the back door asking if she could see Gillian. Gillian's mother, who, to Gillian's disgust, always had a soft spot for Gladys, had called Gillian down to the kitchen. "She's a sweet little girl," she would say about Gladys, "Always so bright and chatty."

Not like some, Gillian would think, hating the two of them.

"Hello Gillian." Gladys put her head on one side and smiled up at Gillian as her mother went back to the living room. "There's a nice surprise, isn't it, seeing you in the Kardomah yesterday!" She fiddled with the clasp of her patent-leather handbag and fluttered her eyelashes. "Um, I was just wonderin', Gillian, who was that girl you was talking to? The thing is, see, Stan thought she looked like a model, and he wondered what her name is, and if she do live round here. Is she a friend of yours? I never seen her before." She looked up, wide-eyed.

Remembering with a shudder the way that man had looked at her, Gillian thought of saying that Vanna was a friend from school, but knew that would not work in the long run.

"Why does he want to know?"

"Oh, well, he just might be able to put a bit of modeling work her way, he says. He've got connections in the business, you know. He says she's just the type they're looking for."

"Has he found anything for you then, Gladys?"

Gladys pursed her lips and batted her eyelashes again. "I'm pretty enough, he says, but I'm not tall enough for most of the work in that line. But he says he got another idea for me."

A horrible thought struck Gillian; so horrible that she could not look at Gladys. "Gladys, what does Stan do? Where does he work?"

"I dunno really. A bit of this and a bit of that, you know. He makes a lotta money, whatever it is, and he's ever so good to me. He takes me to posh restaurants, and he buys me things. He bought me that dress I was wearing yesterday, and this handbag." She heaved up the gleaming object.

"Does your mother know he does that?"

Gladys flushed, clutching the handbag to her chest. "'Oo d'you think you are, asking me questions like that? Mind you own bloody business!" About to flounce out, she turned around, suddenly crestfallen. "Oh, I nearly forgot. You never told us who that girl is. Stan's ever so keen on signin' her up. What's her name then, Gillian? Go on, be a sport. You can tell me."

"Why don't *you* mind your own bloody business, Gladys?"

Gladys hung onto the door knob like a frightened elf. "Oh come on, Gillian. Give us a clue. Stan asked me particular to ask you. Tell us her name, or at least where she do live. Go on! Please!"

"Go away!" Gillian said. "And stay away!"

"Stuck-up bloody cow!" Gladys slammed the door behind her.

"What was that all about?" Gillian's mother came into the kitchen, "Did I hear you quarrelling with Gladys?"

Gillian had never exactly wished Gladys well, but the suspicion she had formed was too serious to be ignored. Against her usual instincts, she told her mother about the man.

Her mother's eyes grew round as she listened. She put on her Chairman of the Board face. "I'm going to drive over to Mrs. Jones's right now," she said. "I think Gladys is in danger. She's barely seventeen, and her mother should know about this man. You did right to tell me, Gillian."

It felt good to have actually managed to do something right for once. She almost relayed this achievement to Tom, who came in soon after, looking excited as usual and going on about how the butcher's boy had tried to run him over with his bicycle, but decided he was too young to understand the implications of the situation.

SHE WOULD HARDLY HAVE recognized the Farrells' house. The front door and window frames had been painted grey-blue. The hall had been repapered and painted, as had the rest of the house. Rugs lay on the polished floorboards, an embroidered cushion adorned a green brocade armchair, and every available bit of wall space in the living room was taken up with well-filled bookshelves. There was a fresh smell of baking in the air. In the middle of the table sat a sponge layer-cake, oozing jam and cream and surrounded by sandwiches, scones, and homemade biscuits.

Mrs. Farrell welcomed them in off the three-o'clock bus, kissing them both and exclaiming how wonderful they both looked. She looked very good herself, Gillian thought, elegant actually, in a cream silk blouse and charcoal skirt. Francis and Tom grinned awkwardly at each other while Bridie, Patrick, Kathleen and red-headed Devlin, the youngest, shyly examined the visitors. Tom, who had been brimming over with excitement on the bus, and pestering Gillian for suitable conversational openings, kept looking around while he talked to Francis, until she realized that Vanna was not there.

"Vanna says she's sorry not to be here to meet you." Mrs. Farrell looked at the brass carriage clock on the mantelpiece. "She should be here any minute now though, off the next bus. It's quite exciting, Gillian! She had an interview yesterday with a representative from a modeling agency and had to go back for trial photographs today. Strange on a Sunday, wouldn't you think? But those people are different I suppose."

It had to be him! Remembering Stan's eyes, Gillian felt her stomach clench. Should she tell Mrs. Farrell what she knew, and what her mother had said? Or should she wait to find out more? If Vanna was not on the bus, she decided, she would have to say something.

The front door burst open and slammed shut as Vanna stormed into the room. "Sweet Mother of Christ!" She hurled her handbag onto a chair. "You wouldn't believe, Mama, what that man wanted me to do! I'm not stupid. I could see right away what he was after, and I told him to go to hell, and walked out."

"Praise be to God! That's my fighting girl!"

"What did he look like?" Thankful that Vanna had her mother's brains and some of her father's temper, Gillian waited, fearing the answer, while Vanna slung her coat on a hook.

"Sleazy. He had black hair, little dark eyes, and a nasty thin moustache."

Gillian winced. "How did he find you?"

"He walked into the shop on Thursday morning and said he'd been told a real knockout was serving behind the jewelry counter in Woolworth's." She glanced at Gillian. "I wonder who told him that."

Tom made a noise in his throat and closed his eyes.

Gladys! That little bitch! She must have nobbled him the other day as she was leaving the kitchen after their quarrel and he was coming in.

They sat around the table, drinking tea and handing around sandwiches and scones, Tom passing wanly on every plate, until the time came for the sponge-cake. After she and Mrs. Farrell had been served, Gillian saw Vanna cut a large slice and offer it to Tom with a smile. His lips pressed tight, he swallowed and blinked hard. "No, I couldn't, thank you, Vanna."

"Here's someone who wants it I think." Gillian diverted attention to little Devlin who was holding out his plate, and the chatter rose again.

BEFORE RETURNING HOME, they made a quick visit to their grandparents' house. Since their grandfather was at a chapel meeting, Tom went outside, hands in pockets, kicking a stone down the garden path while Gillian told their fascinated grandmother about the improvements at the Farrell's house.

Her grandmother had a cold and dabbed at her nose. "Run up and fetch me a clean hanky, would you, Gillian, there's a good girl? They're in my dressing table, top drawer."

Lifting the delicately embroidered handkerchief sachet, Gillian found a small brown photograph album with

"Porthcawl, May, 1932. Bethesda Outing" written on the cover. Inside were tissue-covered sepia snapshots, first of the whole group of merrymaking chapel-goers enjoying themselves at the seaside, and then of just her grandparents: Grandpa in a silly hat, although still wearing his dark suit; Grandma, in a flowered dress and button shoes, smiling as she sat on a donkey. At the back of the book she found a photograph of her mother, arm in arm with a barefoot young man in an open-necked shirt and rolled-up trousers. They were laughing into the camera.

She examined her young mother's face. Except for the long hair and radiantly happy expression, she could have been looking at Tom; the same wide-winged eyebrows, high cheekbones, and full mouth. The young man was tall and thin, his light hair cut very short, a faint squiggle discernable on his forehead. He looked familiar but she could not place him.

Handkerchief and album in hand, she went downstairs to ask her grandmother who he was.

The smile faded from her grandmother's face. "Oh that's Ieuan, my second cousin Dewi's son, same age as your mother. Thick as thieves they were, those two, since they were little." She pressed her lips together. "And then your mam met your father, and that was the end of that. He came to see her though; Ieuan did, the night before the wedding, to … But I shouldn't be going into all that with you. Here, let me put that away."

"What happened to him?" Gillian looked with even more interest at the laughing young man.

Her grandmother took the book from her hands. "He died." She pulled opened a drawer in the Welsh dresser to put the book under a set of napkins. "In Australia. Twenty-five years old he was." She slammed the drawer shut.

Died? That laughing face? That joie de vivre? "How did he die, Grandma?"

Her grandmother looked out of the window. "That's all water under the bridge now. Here comes the rain, and you're going to miss the bus, you two, if you don't hurry. Come along now. Call Tom, and off you go!"

Rain slashed the windows of the bus as they traveled home, each lost in their own thoughts. Gillian saw again the euphoric face of the young man, and longed to know more. She could not, she felt, ask her mother about him. Tom had hardly said a word since Vanna's question at the Farrells' table. He had turned in on himself, his eyes burning with anguish.

THE DOG SHOOK ITSELF over Gillian's legs and feet as she turned to face Tom. "Vanna doesn't think you're a bumbling fool, Tom. I can tell she's fond of you from the way she asked after you. And she does see you from time to time, doesn't she? She wouldn't bother if she didn't like you. She's always had plenty of men to choose from after all."

"Tell me about it!"

"Why don't you go and see her while you're here? You don't have to spend all your time with Mum and me."

"Perhaps I will. But I want to see as much of you as I can. We haven't spent much of our lives together, have we?"

"When this is over, you've got to come to visit me again in Ottawa. You only came that once, about twenty-five years ago. You could get time off from work, couldn't you?"

"I bet I could. I'd love to come." He threw the stick into the sea for the indefatigable dog. "I will. I promise. I'll do it as soon as I can."

"DROP ME OFF HERE, TOM," Gillian said the next morning, as they neared the university entrance in their drive along the coast road into Swansea. "I'll walk over to Saint Anne's in an hour or so. I just want to look around at all the changes in the campus and walk through the park."

The university was indeed greatly changed. In her time it had been a jarring juxtaposition of prefabricated lecture rooms and the venerable stone buildings that had once comprised the home of the Vivian family. The old buildings were still there she saw, as she walked through the campus to the park, but the university had grown enormously. Multiple impressive structures had more than replaced the prefabs. After walking around, wondering at the changes, she passed through the old stone entrance building and into the great park which had once been the Vivian family estate.

The park had not changed much. Smooth lawns still stretched away into the distance, shaded by chestnut trees, beeches, and oaks. She walked through the glossy foliage and lush blooms of the rhododendron garden. Averting her eyes from a monkey puzzle tree, new since her time, she passed the familiar fountain, surrounded by trellised wisteria, and the grotto where as a child she used to play at being a little cave-girl. The Swiss chalet was still there, she noticed, and the boundary wall at the far end of the park was still covered with shining, dark-berried ivy.

It was hard to believe that thirty-seven years had passed since she first walked through that park as a university student, about to meet Gordon, James, and Llewellyn, and the rest of them.

"AND WHAT HAVE YOU BEEN reading this summer?" At the end of the assessment interview, Professor James Falconer leaned back in the swivel chair in his book-lined office, swept his fingers through his bronze waves, and looked sternly at Gillian over non-existent glasses.

"Well, I read *Middlemarch,*" she glanced shyly at him, "and the poetry of William Blake."

"Really?" He raised his eyebrows. "Why?"

She twisted her fingers in her lap. "Shouldn't I have?"

"Certainly not! Where's the fun in that? But never mind." He stood up and shook her hand. "Welcome to the English department."

As she reached the door, he looked her up and down. "And remember, er, Gillian, any time you have a problem, anything at all, you must come and see me."

In her gauzy white sundress she walked away from his office, past the drifts of honey-scented alyssum that softened the hard edges of the new classrooms, and back to the coolness of the old stone building that housed the main entrance.

On their last night at school, she and her friends had discussed what sort of men they would marry. Anita would marry her farmer boyfriend and have lots of babies; Chris would marry a saxophonist; and Diana, when she had quite finished exploring the world, might consider finding herself a filthy-rich businessman, preferably not long for this world. Gillian had declared that she would marry an English professor. The two of them would discuss literature all the time, and read poetry to each other before going to sleep. She left the university grounds deciding for about the fifth time that day that she had a great deal to learn.

THREE WEEKS LATER, SHE ENTERED The Uplands Pub, her first act of defiance against her parents' ban on such places. With her newly-acquired boyfriend, Gordon, a lanky, bespectacled, third-year philosophy student, she joined a group of his friends sitting around a table with Professor Falconer who was entertaining them by reciting lines from *Under Milk Wood*, by Swansea's own poet, Dylan Thomas, born just around the corner from where they sat. "*Call me Dolores, like they do in the stories,*" he whined girlishly in a stage Welsh accent, to appreciative guffaws.

He quirked an eyebrow and raised his pint to Gillian as she and Gordon seated themselves. Oppressed by the noise and smoke, and uneasy at the hilarity, she sipped her warm, sticky gin and orange and tried to ignore the glances he kept flicking her way.

A week or so later he stopped to talk to her after an afternoon class, casually observing that as they lived in the same direction from the university, they might as well walk home together through the park. Alarmed by his reputation as a hard-drinking ladies' man, she scurried along beside him, clutching her books to her chest and replying to his conversational overtures as minimally as possible. His questions about how she was getting along in her classes seemed harmless enough, however, as did his explanations about the point of learning Anglo-Saxon and about the subtleties of a Shakespearian sonnet, and she gradually relaxed her guard somewhat. After several such walks and talks, much insistence on his part, and many lapses on hers, she was finally prevailed upon to call him James.

One November afternoon, he suggested a detour past the rhododendron gardens to a path that ran along under the wall enclosing the park. They were alone on the path when he stopped and leaned against the wall. A loose spray of ivy detached itself from the mass of leaves and dark berries that surrounded him and draped itself over his shoulder. The bruised foliage gave off a dull bitter smell.

"Do you like me, Gillian?" He took hold of the spray and twisted it this way and that, as if to break it off.

"Er, yes. Yes I do." She wished he would leave the ivy alone and get back to explaining Donne's image comparing two lovers to a mathematical compass.

"Why do you like me?" He abandoned the spray and looked into her eyes. "Tell me, what it is about me that you find most attractive?"

There was no getting out of it, even though she had never actually said, or felt for that matter, that she *was* attracted to him. She analyzed his appearance. He was rather old, at least twelve years older than she was, but not bad-looking she supposed: tall and rangy, his rich-coloured, poetically long waves framing a round face in which the features, while regular enough, were somewhat crowded into the middle, like those of the sun in ancient pictures. His blue eyes twinkled encouragingly at her from under heavy lids and arched eyebrows that seemed permanently raised. His wide, thin-lipped mouth was winsomely pursed. She rummaged around for an honest answer. She could not fool him she knew, nor did she want to.

"I'm not sure," she said finally, "but I think it's that you're cleverer than I am."

The brightness fell from his eyes, and the shoulders of his green corduroy jacket drooped as he detached himself from the wall and turned away. What did he expect her to say? That it was his animal magnetism? To her surprise, she had experienced that phenomenon recently and knew that, as far as she was concerned anyway, neither he nor Gordon had it.

"Seriously though," he said, as they neared the iron gates of the park. "Have you never thought of setting your sights on, um, somewhat older men instead of those callow youths that surround you?" He stopped and looked at her with his head on one side. "You're wasted on them, you know. You could get yourself something really worthwhile."

"But wouldn't that cause a great deal of trouble?" Gillian cast her mind over the older men she knew, all of them married, and failed to come up with a catch. "It probably wouldn't be worth all the fuss." It struck her that the professor pursed his lips rather disagreeably as he nodded goodbye and struck off in a different direction.

THE POSSESSOR OF ANIMAL MAGNETISM had appeared in the refectory about a week before that conversation. He had been sitting on a table, swinging his feet and waving his hands, and talking in rapid-fire Welsh to a group of five or six nationalists. She asked her friend Eleri, a fringe member of the *Plaid Cymru*, the Welsh Nationalist Party, who he was.

"Oh, that's Aneurin Llewellyn Caradoc Parry-Jones," Eleri said. "Lew or Llewellyn to his family; Aneurin when he preaches; Caradoc in the Plaid; and in BBC Wales, where he works, they call him Dewi, don't ask me why. Dunno what his associates in the Taffia call him."

"What's the Taffia?"

"You know, the Welsh Mafia. He's got many fingers in many pies, does our Lew."

"Is he related to you then, Eleri?"

"He's the son of my mother's cousin, my Aunty Dilys. The apple of her eye!"

"What did you mean, 'when he preaches'? Is he a minister?"

"He's a lay-preacher in the chapels. Preaches up a storm he does."

Eleri seemed to have a bit of an edge on her, Gillian thought, as she went back to studying the young man. What Eleri had told her was interesting, but it was his appearance that fascinated Gillian. She thought it was extraordinary, the way his short, curly hair and his skin were exactly the same colour, a light golden fawn. His eyes were an unusually pale blue-grey, and his features were clear-cut and regular, everything just so. He was well made, and moved fluidly she saw as he went to the drinks counter. Like Chaucer's squire, neither short nor tall, nor thin nor fat, "of his stature he was of evene lengthe." She kept sneaking glances over her coffee mug at this wonderfully indeterminate-looking man until Eleri said sharply, "He's definitely not your sort, Gill. Don't even think of it."

She was probably right. Gillian had never thought of associating with the *Plaid Cymru*, and even though she did not think of herself as English in any way, she had not been brought up speaking Welsh, and had been educated outside Wales. Moreover, she disapproved of stuffing bombs into postboxes. Despite that, she could not get him out of her head. She kept seeing his even skin, light hair, and clear, pale eyes. He flitted in and out of her dreams. Every morning she woke up wondering if she would see him that day. Instead of studying at home for the end-of-term exams, she made a daily trip to the university, ostensibly to work in the library, in fact to check the refectory board for a notice of a *Plaid Cymru* meeting. Finally she saw one posted, to be held in three days' time.

As she had hoped, the members of the *Plaid*, including the man of many names, who was chatting to a dark-haired, black-eyed girl with a bosom rightly belonging to someone twice her size, came into the refectory after the meeting, probably to continue their scheming. She sat at the worn wooden table, sipping the pallid coffee and pretending to read, while glancing over her book at their nearby table.

He was wearing a finely cabled wool pullover that looked hand-knitted and was the exact colour of his eyes. Its pushed-up sleeves showed muscular forearms, covered with a fine pelt of fawn hair. She had not thought he had noticed her, but at the break-up of the group, he came over to her table.

"I think you're a friend of our Eleri," he said. Like hers, his accent was barely perceptible. "I've seen you in here with her. May I join you, or are you just off?"

Gillian gestured to the chair opposite. He sat down staring at her hair, which she had let loose that day, and which surrounded her head and neck in a cloud. His pale irises, she saw when his eyes met and held hers, were finely ringed with dark blue.

"Gillian Davies, isn't it? Doctor Roy Davies's daughter? I'm Llewellyn Parry-Jones, Eleri's cousin. What's that you were reading?"

She indicated the volume of poetry beside her.

"Ah, Matthew Arnold! A favourite of mine." He smiled, showing teeth as purely white as the whites of his eyes, a slight chip off the inside corner of a centre one. "I've always identified with the Scholar Gypsy. Like him, I'm 'waiting for the spark from heaven to fall'."

"Isn't the *Plaid Cymru* your spark from heaven?" Gillian asked, her breathing becoming regular again.

He smiled. "Oh I've had a shower of little sparks in my time, but I'm waiting for the big one."

"And what will that be, do you think?"

"I don't know. Just as long as it isn't The Call!" He laughed and looked at her, and his face went still. "Your eyes are sea-green," he said. "'The cold strange eyes of a little mermaiden.'"

He put out a hand and touched her hair, and as easily as that, she was lost. Cold strange eyes or not, she was totally in love. When he suggested they walk part of the way home together, she feared her legs would not hold her, she had such an urge to lie down.

"IT'S A FIRE OF STRAW." ELERI PULLED a long face. "It won't last. Never does with him." But it did, for over two years. Her parents did not know what to think. On the one hand they seemed to be quite impressed with Llewellyn; first-class degrees from Swansea and from Cambridge went a long way with them, as with almost everyone else in town. On the other hand, he was a Welsh Nationalist, a preacher, and apparently, by some accounts, not altogether respectable; not good enough, they said, for their now strangely beautiful daughter.

Llewellyn was a busy man. He drove his MG sports car around South Wales, interviewing and researching for the BBC. He translated material for the Plaid Cymru. He cultivated political connections, and dealt in mysterious secret matters, some political, some not, Gillian gathered.

He also seemed to be in demand as a preacher. At first she wanted to go to meetings with him despite her lack of Welsh, or, better still, to hear him preach, but apparently he preferred to keep his complicated life compartmentalized. As long as she had sole occupation of the girlfriend compartment, she decided, she could live with that.

He would make time for them to go on their own outings, however; just the two of them, usually to the remoter beaches of the Gower coast, where alone together, they would walk hand in hand across the hard, damp sands, or curl into the soft secrecy of the dunes, or lie, stretched out like lizards on the warmth of sun-baked rocks.

At first, although fascinated by him, she had been repelled and frightened by the slightest suggestion of sexual intimacy. Llewellyn, however, who enjoyed a challenge, had been patient. She had been brainwashed, he said, into an excess of purity and needed to be deprogrammed, and he was the man to do it.

Despite this misreading of the situation, his tactics and technique, along with her intense attraction to him, eventually brought success. Everything was new and thrilling to her: his crisp hair; his voice, especially when speaking Welsh; the unexpected softness and salty taste of his skin; its smell, like fresh-baked bread.

He, on the other hand, having overcome that particular hurdle, forever seemed to be seeking new sensations and further adventure. At his urging they made love on the crumbling battlements of a ruined castle, loose stones rattling down beneath them; over the prone effigies of a knight and his lady in an ancient church, tourists approaching in the near distance, cameras at the ready; and, at the back of a narrow cave, with the tide coming in fast, reaching their climax just as a huge breaker rushed through the narrow opening and dragged them out in its undertow.

"We could've drowned!" Gillian gasped, laughing after the cold wave flung them up on the hard sand.

Llewellyn, spread-eagled on his back, turned his head, "I've always dreamed of doing that!"

"You have? You mean you knew what would happen?"

"I did." He rolled over and kissed her. "That was the best fuck of my life!"

ONE EARLY SUMMER AFTERNOON, they sat in a sheep-bitten hollow at the very end of the Worm's Head promontory. Buffeted by the wind off the sea, and deafened by the screaming of gulls and the roar of breakers channeling through the hollow rocks below, they exchanged cold salty kisses and cuddled together, looking out over the green, white-crested ocean.

"Next stop, America!" Llewellyn shouted over the wind.

"Canada, actually, as the bird flies." Gillian had often studied Canada in her school atlas, having thrilled as a child to tales of the Frozen North in Tom's *Chums* annuals: *"Back, you brutes! Back!" cried the trapper, snatching up the last burning brand, as the gleaming circle of green eyes drew ever nearer…*

Diana, who had been in Vancouver for a year, had written of spectacular winters and gorgeous summers and opportunities for work of all kinds. She should come, Diana had written. It was a whole different life.

"Time to go home now." Llewellyn spoke through the last piece of his mother's excellent fruitcake. "I'm covering a meeting in the Town Hall tonight about the future of the docks. And your mummy'll be worrying about you."

WHEN SHE TURNED TWENTY-ONE, and had graduated, and was studying for her teaching certificate, Gillian thought she would be allowed more freedom, to be at least as free as Tom was when he came home on leave from the army, but as long as she lived in her parents' house, they said, she lived by their rules. There could be no question, for example, of her going away with Llewellyn, a restriction that caused considerable tension between the two of them until eventually, he forced the issue by asking her to come with him on a trip in May, to Bangor in North Wales, to cover a conference on a proposed new reservoir. They would be away for two nights and three days, he said. It would be wonderful.

Her mother's subsequent tirade, no doubt exacerbated by Gillian's indifference to the eligible youngish surgeon her parents had recently invited to dinner, culminated in the declaration, made with flashing eyes and wagging forefinger, "You're making yourself cheap, my girl!"

Frustration and anger made Gillian bold: "Oh, really? How much do you think I should charge?"

Her mother clapped both hands to her cheeks. "Oh! To speak to me like that! You should be ashamed of yourself!" She shook her finger at Gillian. "After all your father and I have done for you! After all the money we've spent on your education! All the sacrifices we've made for you! And now you want to disgrace us like this!" She cast her eyes up to the ceiling. "What have I done to deserve such an unkind, thankless daughter?" She turned her head as she swept out of the room. "You've turned out to be a great disappointment to your father and I, Gillian."

"Me."

"What?"

"It's 'Your father and *me.*'"

Her mother slammed the door.

"COME ANYWAY," LLEWELLYN SAID as they drove back from a Gower pub that evening. "They'll get over it. We'll just sort of elope."

Gillian turned to face his profile. "But don't you have to be getting married to elope?" There had been no previous suggestion of any such development.

He glanced at her for a moment. "We could get married, you know." He grinned. "I know how to fix it. There's just enough time. I could set it up, and we could get married in Bangor." His eyes were glinting with mischief. She knew he was thinking how they would be putting one over on her mother and father, and causing a stir amongst their friends, not to mention upsetting his own perfectly nice parents.

"No, Lew, we can't do it that way."

He stopped the car and turned on her. "What d'you mean? Are you saying you don't want to marry me?" His eyes were like ice-picks. "The idea does not appeal to you, perhaps?" He seemed to be working himself up into a temper.

"I didn't say that, Lew. I'd love to marry you, although I don't actually remember you asking me. It just doesn't feel right to do it like this. It's … it's sort of perverse."

"*Perverse* is it? You think I'm *perverse*?" He shook out a cigarette while still looking at her. Rare spots of colour appeared on his cheeks. "I'll tell you what, Gillian. That's the trouble with you. You never do things spontaneously. You're so *cool-hearted*, always watching, always thinking. You never just throw yourself into something; there's always part of you holding back. You never give your all." He turned away to stare out of the side window.

I never give my all? Gillian began to shake. She could hardly breathe for the tightness in her throat. "How can you say that, Lew? Do you really think that?"

"Yes I do. And you can forget about coming to Bangor. I'll go by myself. Or maybe," he kept his head turned away, "I know someone else who'd like to go."

Gillian closed her eyes. She knew at once who that would be. Angharad, the girl she had seen him with that first day in the refectory; she, whose very name meant 'beloved'; a friend of Eleri's, and a staunch member of the Plaid Cymru. That rosy, dark-eyed girl, with her lustrous black curls, wide red mouth, and loud free laugh, the very antithesis of herself; the reserved, no-fun, pusillanimous one, thin and pale, with ash-coloured hair, and cold strange eyes. Angharad would have no trouble giving her all, whatever that was, Gillian thought. Probably gave it all the time.

She got out of the car on trembling legs, saying she wanted to walk home.

"That's it?" He was standing on his side of the low car. "You're not even going to discuss it?"

"What's the point?" Gillian managed not to give way to tears. "Now that I know how you feel. You'll do what you want to sooner or later anyway."

She succeeded in getting into the house without anyone seeing her, but before she could flee upstairs to her bedroom, she heard her mother's voice. She turned quickly into the cloakroom, full of winter coats, and pulled the door shut. In the mothball-smelling darkness, half-covered by her father's heavy, tobacco-scented, Melton overcoat, she succumbed. "Don't leave me! Don't leave me!" she sobbed into her mother's perfumed fox-fur cape. After a while she looked up, her eyes searching the darkness. Was it really all over? Was it already too late? Or should she try to make up the quarrel and win him back? A voice rose up from her childhood: *You can fight if you like, but you can't win.* She hid her face again in the wet fur.

TWO MONTHS LATER, IN HIGH SUMMER, she went to a party at a senior English professor's cottage on the north coast of the Gower peninsula. Her father, much more indulgent since a recent heart scare, had lent her the car so that she could leave early if she wanted, as likely she would.

James was there of course, not being the man to miss a well-heeled party. He had been on leave the previous semester, working on a book about Dylan Thomas, recently dead of "a massive insult to the brain" after a drinking binge in New York. James was onto a good thing there, she thought, considering the market for anything related to the dead poet.

She was pleased to see Gordon, still a good friend, at the party. Eleri was there too, not unexpectedly since she was an enthusiastic partygoer and knew the hosts. Less welcome was the sight of Angharad, resplendent in a red silk blouse and demonstrating considerable vivacity. According to Eleri, she had come to have some fun since Llewelyn was away, covering a trade conference in Cardiff.

Gillian and James had crossed paths several times during the previous two years, mostly at parties or in pubs, where he would fetch her drinks, smile at her offbeat comments, and make cracks about Welsh nationalists. He registered her presence with a long, meaningful look across the smoke-filled room, and a lift of his glass.

The noise and smoke, along with unremitting peals of laughter from Angharad, drove Gillian to leave the room and retreat down the rocky path behind the cottage. Seated on the low, whitewashed stone wall overlooking the water, she took from her pocket the brochure of the Canadian Rocky Mountains she had received that morning from Diana. For a moment her heart lifted at their splendour, until she sank back into brooding, as so often those days, over what Llewelyn had said. Had he really meant it? Was she, in some way she couldn't grasp, essentially cold? Was she all that different from other women? What did they have to give that she did not? She shivered and looked again at the brochure.

A rattle of stones announced the arrival of James. In a new corduroy jacket the same colour as his hair and accessorized by a paisley cravat, he was making his unsteady way down the path. Managing, after a few tries, to find a safe place on the uneven surface of the wall for his whisky glass and to light a cigarette, he went straight to the point. Now that now she'd been knocked about a bit, so to speak, might she not be kinder to a faithful admirer? "How about it, Gillian?" He cocked his head at her, blowing out smoke. "It could be just what we both need."

"I don't think so." Gillian looked out across the sands, wet from the retreating tide. "After you get what you want, you don't want it."

"Nonsense! You don't know what you're missing." He sat down beside her on the wall and took her hand. "But I think you do know that we're two of a kind in a way, you and I. We could be great together; I with my superior brain, ha, ha, and you with your not altogether disagreeable looks. Come on, what d'you say?" He held out his arms. "Be a sport."

Be a sport? She shook her head. "I'm sorry, James, but I'm not much of a one for the sporting life." *Llewellyn would certainly agree with that.*

He sighed gustily and crushed his cigarette out on the wall, flipping the stub onto the bushes below. "You'll be sorry one day, my girl." He got up, raising his eyebrows admonishingly at her. "Chances like this are hard to come by." She watched him stumble back up the path.

Wouldn't it be funny if it were true! Despite his crassness just now, probably due to the whisky, he was the only person she had ever met who always recognized her allusions, capped her quotations, and laughed at her jokes. He made her laugh in turn, never bored her, and seemed to find her attractive. Maybe he was right: perhaps he could help lessen this hollow ache, this ghost-like feeling.

She sat for a while, thinking about what he had said and watching the black and white oyster-catchers running along the sands below, digging after their prey with long, curved, orange beaks. Although it was mid-July, she shivered when a cloud covered the sun.

Back at the cottage, she looked around. The party, which had spilled out-of-doors, looked far from festive. The mostly middle-aged guests, many of whom she did not know, seemed both staid and drunk at the same time. The cottage was smaller and shabbier than she had thought, while the formerly gleaming beach had become a mud-flat. There was no sign of James. Still shivering, she went in to collect her cardigan from the little bedroom where she had left it.

In the living room, Gordon was putting on a '78 record. "Just a minute, Gill!" he said sharply as she went towards the bedroom.

"Be with you in a sec." Pushing open the door she heard scuffle and a throaty giggle and saw in the half-light from the small, ivy-shaded window, tousled dark hair and a rosy face half-hidden by a corduroy shoulder. Angharad, her mouth loose as an overblown peony, and her crimson blouse rumpled and unbuttoned, was looking up at James, clearly willing to give her all, if she had not already. Turning his head and seeing Gillian, James grimaced like a man experiencing severe acid-reflux.

Keeping her eyes down, Gillian snatched her cardigan from the back of a chair and retreated into the living room, shutting the door smartly behind her. Gordon grinned and jerking his head at the bedroom, rolled his eyes. Looking from the gramophone to her, he held up a long forefinger.

The music filled the gloomy, black-beamed room.

Love, oh love, oh careless love! the voice sang with full heart, bittersweet and dark.

Overwhelmed, Gillian held her breath, until, seeing Gordon's face, she burst out laughing.

> *"You go to my head like wi-ine,"* they sang along,
> *"You ruined the life of many a poor girl,*
> *And you ver' near ruined this life of mine."*

GORDON DANCED AROUND the scruffy room, waving his wine glass, his dark hair flopping on his forehead.

Dear Gordon. Why couldn't it have been you? Giving him a quick goodbye kiss, and asking him to thank the hosts for her, Gillian stuffed Diana's brochure into her handbag, stepped over a recumbent junior lecturer by the front door, and left the cottage to follow the winding stony path to the car.

AS SHE SAT BY HER SLEEPING mother later that morning, Gillian thought how those events during that long-ago summer had all pointed in the same direction: away from Llewellyn, and away from her mother. Canada would offer a fresh start, new possibilities. And so it had, even if it had not created a new Gillian.

The room was quiet, apart from the rasp of laboured breathing. Her mother's dentures grinned from a glass of water on the bedside table. Stripped of her feistiness and make-up, she was fearfully diminished. Taking in the pallor of the sunken cheeks, the hollowness of the eye sockets, and the collapse of the half-open mouth, Gillian saw 'the skull beneath the skin'. The eyes opened to drift unseeingly around the room until they lit on her, stilled, widened for a long moment, and then with a wince closed tight, her mother seeming to shrink even further.

"What's wrong, Mum?" Gillian leaned over to stroke the hot, dry forehead.

"Nothing. Why d'you ask?" With an obvious effort, her mother roused herself. "Give me my glasses, would you, and my dentures. I wasn't expecting you today."

"But I said I'd be coming. I come to see you every day."

"Yes, *now* you do." She strained to sit forward as Gillian placed an extra pillow behind her back, and supplied the missing items. Settling back against the pillows, she added, "After over thirty years." With her teeth in, and her glasses on, she was back in the world of the living.

Gillian straightened the bed, pulling the sheet tight and refastening it with 'hospital corners' as she had been taught long ago at school. She shook out the cotton blanket with a snap. "Has Tom been in?"

"Yes he has, but he was so noisy and made so much fuss, I told him to go away."

Gillian threw the blanket down on the bed. "Tom loves you, Mum, and he tries hard to please you. Why are you so harsh?" In her anger on her brother's behalf she pushed the question further, surprising herself. "Why have you always been so cold and hard towards both of us, all our lives, even when we were little children?"

Her mother's fingers flew to the base of her throat, her rheumy eyes wide. "*Me*? Cold and hard towards *you*? Oh, Gillian! If you only knew what a sacrifice I made for you both, so that you could have every advantage and never go without." She closed her eyes. "What happiness I gave up for your sakes."

Gillian stepped back, colliding with the chair, "What? What are you talking about? What sacrifice? What happiness?"

Her mother kept her eyes closed and waved a hand. "Water under the bridge, Gillian! Water under the bridge!"

"'Water under the bridge' my foot! Bloody great dam more likely! What's this all about, Mum?" She gripped the frail shoulder, close to giving it a shake. "Tell me!"

"Don't you bully me, my girl! It's none of your business."

"It damn well is my business, if it has anything to do with what came between us." Gillian sat down, trying to breathe slowly. After a moment she took her mother's hand. "I'm sorry I was cross, Mum, but what you said about sacrifices and lost happiness shook me. Will you tell me what you meant?"

Her mother looked away, coughing. "I was very hurt to hear you say I was cold to you," she wheezed, "I did my best, you know."

A straight answer would be nice. "I know you loved me when I was very little." With a sigh, Gillian stroked the translucent skin on the back of her mother's hand. "I remember going through scraps of cloth in your rag bag, feeling the textures while you told me the words for them: *crepe de Chine, taffeta, bombazine*; and the names of colours I didn't know: *heliotrope, crimson, Nile green*... you said that was the colour of my eyes. There was tenderness and closeness between us then, I'm sure of it. But something changed." She looked up. "What happened, Mum?"

"I've always loved you, Gillian, despite your difficult nature, but … things got complicated." She glanced at Gillian out of the corner of her eye, pleating the sheet between her fingers and clearing her throat. "Do you, by any chance, remember a man coming to visit us when you were four years old? A tall man, very tanned? He brought you a stuffed toy—a Koala bear."

"I remember the bear, Ozzie. Tommy threw him into the duck pond in Brynmill Park." She looked sharply at her mother. "Why? What about him? That man?"

"Well he …" Her mother took a deep breath, setting off a fit of coughing that left her ashen and gasping. "He was …" Another paroxysm gripped her. "I'm sorry, Gillian," she gasped, "I can't talk now." She lay back, deathly pale, her chest crackling and her eyes closed.

Hardly able to breathe herself, Gillian watched her mother struggle for breath as something rolled, clanking, down the hallway. Hoping to find Sunita, she went to the door, but found the passage silent and empty.

A minute later her mother looked up with a start and seized Gillian's wrist.

"That time …" she whispered hoarsely, "… that time when you were at Croesffordd." She pulled on the wrist. "Was it all right, Gillian? With that boy, Angus, I mean?"

Gillian stared at her, the blood pounding in her head.

Is this it? Now?

Her mother tugged again, nodding encouragingly. "Tell me it was all right!" The wheezing grew louder. "I've always been a bit worried …" She fell back, seized by another fit of coughing.

Gillian pulled her hand away. At the window she laid her forehead against the cool glass.

She knew!

Outside, gulls screamed and wheeled in the wind.

She has always been "a bit" worried? Gillian clenched her teeth, her eyes squeezed shut.

And now, when she's at death's door, and I can't tell her, she needs to know it was "all right"?

After a long pause, filled with the thump of her own heartbeat, her mother's wheezing, and the shrieks of gulls, she opened her eyes and said, still facing the window, "Yes, it was all right."

"You're sure?"

For a moment she wavered, but made herself turn back to the bed. "It was all right, Mum."

Her mother put her head back, closing her eyes. Gillian let out a long breath and tidied up the bedside table.

WITH A CLATTER AT THE DOOR, Sunita came in, carrying a loaded, stainless-steel tray. "It's time for your Lasix injection, Iris, and for your sponge bath, and your pills." She turned to Gillian. "Mrs. Davies asked me to call her Iris. She said it made her feel more at home."

"It'd make me feel the same, Sunita, if you'd call me Gillian."

Sunita smiled and turned back to her patient, her face becoming serious. "How are you feeling, Iris?" She looked at the water glass. "Oh dear, you haven't drunk any of your water! Remember Dr. Gabriel said it was very important for you to drink plenty of fluids." She felt her patient's pulse. "Is there anything you'd like to drink? Does something tempt you in particular?"

Gillian's mother made a big effort. "That stuff you found for me the other day, Gillian, what was that called now? I liked that."

"Lucozade. I'll get you some more right now, Mum. What about a bottle of Ribena too? I know where I can get that."

"Thank you, darling. That would be lovely."

So that was that. It had been close, but there would be no revelation, no heart-to-heart reconciliation, and no closure. Holding onto that 'darling', Gillian left her mother to Sunita's care.

WALKING UP TO THE SHOPS, she searched for memories of Ozzie, and fetched up an image of the little bear with the funny face being held out to her in the thin, brown hands of a tall stranger smiling down at her. Something stirred in the back of her mind, but slipped away as Tom's BMW, a perk from his years at the Croyden dealership, drew alongside with a gentle toot.

They bought Lucozade and Ribena at the chemist's, and located a box of Meltis New Berry Fruits, their mother's favourite candy, in case she could be tempted.

"Sunita's going to be a while with Mum." Gillian looked at her watch. "Let's just drop off the Lucozade for her, and then drive over and look at the ducks in Brynmill Park. Like when we were little."

The pond was still there, complete with panhandling ducks, beady eyes fixed sideways on them. Holding ice cream cones from the park kiosk, they sat on what could have been the same iron bench as that used by their mother or Olwen fifty years ago, while Gillian described to Tom how ill their mother seemed.

"She's probably dehydrated," he said, "It's surprising what that can do to you."

He took a bite of his ice cream. "Do you remember the rude monkey that used to be in the cage behind this bench?"

Gillian smiled. "We were never allowed to watch him, were we? There was a fox here too, in a pen behind the bushes on the other side of the pond. Remember? Sometimes you could smell it."

"What was the point of that? We couldn't look at the monkey, and no one could see the fox."

"Who knows?" Gillian licked her cone and looked at him sideways. "You threw my Koala bear, Ozzie, into this pond, Tom, and Mum wouldn't get him out because he'd be filthy. I was pretty upset."

"Sorry!" Tom sighed. "I seem to have spent my life saying 'sorry'."

He broke off a piece of cone and threw it to the ducks which squabbled as if it were their only source of nourishment for the day. "Do you remember Gill, when you didn't write for almost a year; that second year you were in Canada? What happened there? You've never told me."

She lowered her ice cream. "I've always felt bad about not writing, Tom, especially when you told me about Gladys and the baby. But Mum had already told me it was all over. No baby, and no more Gladys, and then I just shelved the whole thing, probably because I was so caught up with Doug."

"We're a right pair, aren't we?" He smiled at her over his cone. "But I never heard much about Doug; you sort of clammed up on that subject. Was it a rebound thing after Llewellyn? I've always felt you were more hurt by that jerk than you let on."

"I suppose I was on the rebound, really. But it seemed so wonderful at the start. I really thought I'd found true love at last, Tom. I forgot everybody and everything while I was living in that farmhouse with Doug. I'll tell you all about it later when we have more time. And about how Diana rescued me."

"Diana from school? I remember her. She came to see you at home one holiday. I thought she was smashing. What happened to her, do you know? Did you keep in touch?"

"Oh yes, we see each other from time to time, even though we live so far apart. She became an executive for a big travel agency and made enough money to retire early. Now she breeds Staffordshire bull terriers with her partner, Penny, on Vancouver Island."

"Oh I see." He smiled. "I can imagine." He crunched up the mini-cone at the bottom of his ice-cream and brushed his hands together. "I've got to go now. But when we've got time, I'd like to hear the story. I've often wondered."

As he gathered up the napkins and took them to the bin, Gillian looked across the grey pond to the bushes where the fox's cage had been, mentally reliving her disastrous attempt at giving her all.

SHE WAS FRYING BACON for Doug's breakfast when the phone rang, unusual at any time, let alone at eight in the morning. She picked up the phone, jerking the receiver away from her ear as a clear voice rang out, echoing around the bare kitchen the way it had years ago on the school hockey field. "That you, Gill?"

Afraid that The Voice of Authority, as Diana had been called at Deer Park, could be heard upstairs in the bedroom, Gillian almost whispered her reply, but her friend was too excited to take the hint. She was actually in Ottawa, she declared, and had managed to track Gillian down! She'd have to return to Vancouver in a few days, but she could come to see her that afternoon. Would that be possible? It'd be such fun to meet! They hadn't seen each other in such ages!

Gillian lowered the receiver, holding it in both hands, and looked out over the snow-covered fields. Doug was not keen on visitors, she knew, but surely he wouldn't want her to miss this chance of seeing her old friend again. Raising the phone, she gave Diana directions to the farmhouse and invited her to lunch. She squared her shoulders and went upstairs to the bedroom.

Doug was awake and awaiting her explanation for the call. "I'm not sure about that, honey." He sat up and settled himself against the pillows. "You'd better call her back and tell her not to come." He glanced out of the window. "The weather looks really bad. These early March storms can be the worst." He reached over and switched on the bedside radio.

"But, Doug, I don't know where she's staying." Gillian raised her voice over those of The Platters. "And anyway, she's probably left already."

With a sigh, he turned down the volume. "How come you didn't talk to me before inviting her here, Gill? You know I like it best when it's just the two of us." He held out his hand. "I thought you did too, my darling." His eyes were watchful. Choirboy eyes, Gillian called them, dark blue, heavily fringed with black lashes.

"I didn't want to disturb you," she said. "Besides, we're not really doing anything today." She sat down on the bed, still holding his hand. "Diana was my best friend at boarding school, Doug, and I haven't seen her since we left school six years ago. I really want her to come."

Turning his head, he raised the volume on the radio and closed his eyes.

The melancholy harmonizations accompanied her downstairs, followed by a severe-weather advisory.

"With any luck," Doug came into the kitchen five minutes later in his ratty dressing gown and broken-down carpet slippers, "she'll hear that storm warning on the car radio and turn back. I mean we wouldn't want her going into the ditch, would we?"

Gillian put his breakfast down smartly in front of him as the ancient percolator finished gargling. "Diana's very competent. She's been living out west for years. She'll cope with the snow."

He stabbed the two egg yolks so that they bled all over the plate and ate in silence, the ticking of the wooden wall clock the only other sound.

AN HOUR AND A HALF LATER, a car turned in through the gate Gillian had managed to pull open after clearing the driveway. "She's here!" she called out to Doug in the back room, and flung on her sheepskin coat and boots to skitter down the front steps.

Diana, in a bright red duffle coat, jumped out of the car, hugged her and held her at arm's length, looking her up and down. "Skinny as ever! Still that crazy hair! You haven't changed a bit, Gill."

"Neither have you." And indeed it was true in Diana's case. She had the same round face and rosy cheeks, her straight black hair still as short as at school, if rather more stylish. As they turned laughing towards the house, arms linked, Gillian saw Doug pull back from the window.

"What the hell's that?" Diana stopped to look at a metal structure beside the steps, consisting of four sleigh runners curving vertically away from an upright steel drum of the type used for storing toxic materials. Great lengths of rusty chains, their links at least three inches long, were welded to the tips of the runners, piling up on top of the drum before dropping down its sides into the snow.

"That's one of Doug's creations. He makes them out of metal things he finds around the property. Metal things sprout out of the ground here like the soldiers in that Greek myth."

"He's an *artist*?"

"Yes, he had an exhibition last year. Had a good review and sold three pieces. People in downtown Toronto put them in their gardens."

Gillian saw Diana look back askance as they went up the steps into the house.

Unshaven, his dark hair straggling over his collar, Doug was standing in the middle of the floor in corduroy pants, bald at the knees, and a grubby red and black plaid lumber jacket. He held a cigarette in one hand and a stubby bottle of Molson Export in the other. Gillian could not help wishing he had made more of an effort to brush up for her friend, as he had for his exhibition when, in black pants and turtleneck, he had attracted at least as much appreciative scrutiny as his creations.

"Doug, this is, Diana." She stood back for them to shake hands.

"Charmed I'm sure!" Ignoring Diana's outstretched hand he raised his beer bottle in salute and took a drag on his cigarette before ostentatiously blowing the smoke away from her. After a long swallow, he banged the bottle down on the counter and smiled his sudden dazzling smile. "Whatcha want to drink, Diane? How 'bout you, Gill? We must celebrate this great occasion!"

Maybe it was going to be all right after all. Gillian smiled back at him. "Let me get Diana comfortable first." She took her friend into the warmth of the back room to settle her in the capacious if threadbare armchair by the wood stove. "How was the drive?"

"It wasn't too bad, actually," Diana held out her hands to the warmth. "The car I rented is new and it's got good tires and a heater, but I borrowed chains and a snow shovel just in case. There is an awful lot of snow, though. Perhaps I should try to get back before it gets too late."

"I think you should." Doug came forward to chuck a massive log into the already pulsating stove. "There's a severe storm warning for later this afternoon, and the temperature's going down to minus thirty, not counting the wind factor. I don't want to sound inhospitable," he stood up, poker in hand, smiling at both of them, "but if I were you, I'd set off right away."

Diana laughed. "Well, maybe not right away, but well before dark."

Does she think he's joking? Gillian put her hand on the front of his jacket and lifted her face to look into his eyes. "Doug, please! Diana can't just turn around and go back. We want to talk and catch up."

He turned away without replying and stalked into the kitchen where she found him a few minutes later, standing at the front window, cigarette in hand, staring out at the snow through a cleared space in the frost feathers. Joining him, she could see the snow throwing its weight around. The driveway and road were already obliterated, and she could hear the wind keening through the gap over the front door. She jumped as he whizzed his bottle cap across the room into the open garbage bin.

At the same moment, Diana came in, holding out a bottle of wine. "I brought this for you and Gillian, Doug. I hope you like it."

He took the bottle of *Liebfraumilch*. "Oh, super." He put it on the counter behind the beer cartons. "Thanks a lot, Diane."

"It's Diana actually, Doug. I'm glad you like it. I know I do."

"I'm sure you do." Doug pointed to the road. "You know, *Diana,* I really think you should take my advice and go back right now."

She glanced at the window and did a double-take.

"It's not as bad as it looks." He opened the wine. "But it'll get worse. If you go right now, though, you should get back okay. Here, have one for the road." He filled a juice glass.

"Thank you. I'll save it to have with my lunch. Can I help you, Gill?"

He returned to the window with a fresh bottle of beer in his hand and lit another Marlborough. After a few puffs, he ground it out in the massive brown glass ashtray, already overflowing, which he had lifted the day before from the Wakefield Inn.

The women laid the battered pine table in front of the side window in the kitchen, exchanging news of old school friends: Anita had had another baby girl; Chris was performing in a jazz concert in Cardiff next month; the headmistress was retiring. As they seated themselves at the table, Gillian tried without success to catch Doug's eye. Attempting to draw him into conversation, she mentioned the family history surrounding the Clegg farmhouse, but he munched his way through the homemade tourtière, baked beans, and apple crumble without saying a word, sticking to his beer and refusing the wine.

After lunch they went into the back room to warm up, Diana again sitting, at Gillian's insistence, in the armchair, while Gillian and Doug took each end of the sagging, sawdust-leaking vinyl couch. Gillian slid sideways looks at the aquiline profile, willing Doug to say something.

"Darling," she turned to him eventually, touching his arm, "Don't you think Diana'd better stay? It's getting really dangerous out there."

"It's not that risky." He addressed an *objets trouvés* moosehead on the barnboard wall behind the woodstove. "She's got a good car, and the snow plow'll be along. There's still time to get back before the light fails."

Twisting her hair, she went to the back window. Snow tumbled over billowy fields, whitening the forest beyond. "But

Doug, look at it out there! She has to stay. I'd never forgive myself if she came to any harm!"

"Excuse me." Diana pointed to the woodstove. "I think the stove-pipe's turning red. Is that all right?

Seeing the familiar dull flush halfway up the black pipe, and hearing an ominous roaring, Gillian ran to close the damper. As the danger signs subsided, Doug closed his eyes. Shaking his head as if at the stupidity of others, he turned again to his beer.

"Do you not you have a dog?" Diana looked brightly from one to the other after a short silence. "I should have thought this was the perfect place for one."

Doug took another swig and studied the ceiling.

"We did have one, actually." Gillian cleared her throat and swallowed. "Nigel, a stray; a sort of black lab, with a sticking-up ear, but he disappeared. He went out one terribly cold night last winter, after a snow storm like this, and he never came back. I was working then, and had to stay in town because of the storm, but Doug stayed up all night, waiting and calling for him, didn't you, Doug? But he never came home." She took a deep breath and straightened her spine. She had looked for Nigel for months. Still did.

"That seems strange," Diana put her head on one side, her eyes on Doug, "to get lost so close to home. You'd think a dog would know his way."

"Who knows what happened." Doug looked away. "It was an idiot dog anyway. Tried to bite me once."

"He was only defending me." Gillian blinked hard and looked up at the ceiling. "He was still a puppy. He didn't know you were only joking."

"That's enough about the bloody dog!" He slammed down his bottle like a gavel on the wood floor. "If I could just have a bit of peace, I'd like to take a nap." He put his head back and closed his eyes. Diana made a moue at Gillian, and they removed themselves to the kitchen.

With their coats on, hands clasped around warming mugs of tea, they sat at the table as Diana caught up with Gillian's news. She had been very sorry to hear from Anita of Dr. Davies's sudden death from a heart attack. How was her mother managing on her own? Gillian explained that her mother had sold the house and gone to live with her own mother, since Gillian's grandfather had also died.

"I'm so sad about Daddy,' she said. "I loved him, but I didn't really know him, you know? We were evacuated and then away at school, and the times when we were at home he was always so busy, either working or playing tennis or badminton. Before I left, he and I were becoming closer, and I was glad of that, but I thought there was plenty of time, of course. And then he goes and drops dead on the tennis court." She blew her nose. "You know, I never thought they were very happy together, but Mummy was quite distraught when he died. At the funeral she kept saying, 'I'm sorry, Roy, I'm so sorry.' I've often wondered what she meant exactly." She topped up the teapot from the whistling kettle. "I found it easier to grieve for Grandpa actually. I was upset that Mummy didn't let me know in time to get home for that funeral. I'd have liked to have been there for Grandma's sake, and I know Tom would've been beside himself. He and Grandpa were very close."

"Ah, yes. Tom. Where's he stationed now?"

"Last I heard, he was in Germany. He might be a lieutenant by now."

"Married or anything?"

Gillian decided not to go into the business about Gladys. "Not that I know of. He's always had lots of girlfriends, but he's never stuck to any of them."

"Well, it's no shock that he's had lots of girlfriends. He's quite the dreamboat."

Gillian blinked. "I didn't know you were susceptible to masculine charms, Di."

"Well I'm not, but even I could see that. He's tall, dark, and handsome, and he has a sort of warmth about him. Do I gather you two don't communicate any more? You used to be pretty close. Being an only child myself, I always envied you that."

"We have kind of lost touch. I think my mother's given up on me too. I haven't written to either of them for months. Or to my Grandma."

After Diana turned her attention to Gillian's present life at the farmhouse, Gillian explained how she had met Doug at an exhibition in Ottawa, organized just over a year ago by the art teacher at the high school where she had been teaching English. He had been introduced to her as an artist, she said, and apparently had fallen in love with her at first sight, while she, for her part, had been immediately attracted by his melancholy intensity. He had persuaded her to visit the picturesque village of Wakefield near his home, and then to come and see where he lived.

"I was really struck by the lonely feel of the house," she said. "He told me his parents were both dead, his mother ten years before, of cancer, and his father soon after in a tractor accident. Some question of drunkenness, I gathered. His brother went out west around that time and never made contact again. Doug showed me a picture of the four of them." She rummaged in the shallow drawer under the table and produced a cracked and curling black and white photograph, taken when Doug was a skinny, worried-looking ten-year-old. His mother faced the camera, her hand on his shoulder, a resolute smile on her thin dark face. His father, rough-hewn and saturnine, glowered to the side as if sighting an invader, while his brother, a short, thickset teenager, leaned on a pitchfork, scowling at the photographer.

"If that didn't scare you off, nothing would," Diana said.

"I felt so sorry for him, Di. He was so alone and unhappy. He was still grieving for his mother—a native woman from the reservation near here—and hating his brute of a father. I felt I could make a difference. And I have. He says his life wasn't worth living until he met me." She described how a couple of months later Doug had persuaded her to stay over; then in quick succession, to move in and commute to work; and finally, to give up her job, and sell her car.

"I don't get it." Diana frowned, her clear, hazel eyes searching Gillian's. "You and he are so different. And you told me you loved teaching. So why on earth would you want to give up your job *and* your income, to come and live here? And why sell your car, for God's sake?" She broke off, her eyes resting thoughtfully on the small round bruises, one under each ear, which Gillian had tried unsuccessfully to conceal with makeup.

Gillian sank her chin down further into her polo-necked sweater and shrugged. "Oh I don't care about going anywhere, Di. Why waste money on the insurance? I'm happy enough simply to stay here with Doug; just the two of us, in this beautiful place. You should see it here in the summer, Di! Or in the fall! All the little sudden hills make me feel at home, and there are thousands of acres of wilderness out back, and rivers and lakes nearby. I love the winter here too. It's so sort of... *abundant*."

Diana put her mug down firmly. "Well, I know about that sort of thing myself," she said. "And that's all very well, but what I want to know is, does this life *suit* you, Gill?" She shot her a piercing look. "Are you really happy? You're even thinner than you were in school, and you seem awfully jumpy." Putting put her elbows on the table and counting on her fingers, she said in her carrying voice, "Let's see now: one, you've lost touch with your family; two, you've cut yourself off from your old friends, so that I had to come and find you; three, you gave up your teaching, that is to say, your independence; four, you never see your friends in Ottawa anymore, so you have no social life whatsoever; and five, you no longer even have a dog."

She sat back and looked around the shabby kitchen. Lowering her voice, she said, "Face it, Gill. You have no life at all. All you've got is Doug, who, even if he does weld stuff together, apparently has," she started on her fingers again, "no job, no steady income, no friends, and no family, not to mention no manners." She threw up her hands. "He's worse than Llewellyn if you ask me, and that's saying something, from what I hear."

"Steady on, Di." Gillian worked at enlarging the peephole in the fern-etched window. "You're not seeing him at his best today. Doug's different when it's just the two of us. He can be funny, and kind, and sensitive, and he sort of watches over me. I've never felt so interesting and important in all my life. And the main thing is, I know he'd never leave me or cheat on me like Llewellyn did. We're all in all to each other." She looked down into Diana's quizzical eyes. "He says we don't need anyone or anything else, not even money, now that we have the annuity Daddy left me. As he says," she paused, smiling at the memory, "We are 'a kingdom of two'."

Diana snorted into her mug. "'A kingdom of two'! Jesus Christ, Gill! What's happened to you? You used to have brains and some gumption, and now here you are, stuck in this freezing old farmhouse in the middle of nowhere. It's as if Elizabeth Bennett—or Jane Eyre, anyway—were throwing herself away on a *fake* Heathcliff! And you're so isolated here!" She slid a quick glance at the bruises. "I'm actually worried for you." She put her hand on Gillian's arm, lowering her voice. "Come away with me tomorrow morning, Gill, even if it's just for a day or so, to think things over; get a different perspective."

Before Gillian could say she had no intention of leaving, the kitchen door crashed back as Doug lurched into the room, his face crimson. He squinted down the outstretched arm and finger pointing unsteadily at Diana. "I heard that, you evil bitch! Get out of my house!" He jerked his arm at the door. "Now!"

Gillian could smell the beer on him from across the room. She saw Diana's colour flare up to match his as she jumped up, her chair clattering to the floor.

"Doug!" Gillian got up to face him, her heart pounding. "Stop it! You can't talk to Diana like that."

"Oh can't I?" He peered at her, his head wobbling. With surprising speed he grabbed the hair at the back of her head, pulling her face around so that it was just inches from his and blasted by his breath. "That woman has insulted me in my own home, and has tried to come between us." A savage jerk brought tears of pain to her eyes. "And if you're thinking of taking her side against me, you should know by now that with me it's all or nothing. Either you tell her to go, or," another jerk, "if you prefer to be with your butch friend," he released her so abruptly that she nearly fell, and pointed to the door, "you can go too."

Gillian turned her face to the hall where Diana, her face set, was pulling on her boots.

"I'm warning you, Gillian. If you step outside that door, you can never come back in."

She looked back at him in shock.

"You can freeze to death on the doorstep for all I care." He paused, refocusing his eyes on hers. "Like your fucking dog."

His gaze wavered and fell, and his arm dropped to his side as she stared at him, her mouth open and her eyes wide. In the hall behind her, Diana went still.

"I'm sorry, darling." His voice was high and thin. "I didn't mean it." His eyes filled with tears. "I can explain."

"How can you explain that? It was thirty-five below, and you shut Nigel out, and let him die! How could you, Doug? How *could* you? You knew I loved him."

"You loved him so much, I was jealous." He blinked his tear-drenched eyelashes. "You were always petting him and sweet-talking him."

"You killed him because you were *jealous*? I don't believe this!"

"As a matter of fact, I didn't actually *kill* him. I didn't know the stupid mutt would freeze to death, did I? Cross my heart! It was only because I love you so much that I just didn't bother to let him in. That, and a bit too much to drink, perhaps."

"There's no *perhaps* about it. You were drunk and heartless then, as you are now. And you let me go on looking for him for months, and all the time you *knew*!"

She turned to the door.

"Don't put a *dog* before me, Gill! Please don't go! Don't leave me! I can't live without you. You are my life." His voice broke. "Remember? We're 'a kingdom of two'!"

She turned back to look at him; at his pale face, outstretched hands, and pleading, tear-filled eyes. For a moment she hesitated, close to tears herself, but as the wind howled again in the door, she stiffened and turned away. In the hall, she flung on her coat and boots, and snatched her purse off the hook while Diana opened the door, grabbed the shovel, and ran down the snow-piled steps. Gillian looked around once and with shaking hands pulled the door shut behind her. Together, with surprising speed, they cleared the driveway down to the road and through the gate.

"Have you left anything important behind?" Diana peered through labouring wipers at what they trusted was the road.

"No." Gillian stared into the white dazzle ahead of them. "Nothing at all."

"Time to go." Tom looked up at the gathering clouds. "I'll drive you over to Saint Anne's, but I'm meeting Ian Martin this afternoon. I'll be there by four o'clock though." They hurried through the park to the car, the first, heavy drops of rain falling as they slammed the doors.

Dr. Gabriel was leaving her mother's room as Gillian arrived. He took her down the hall, away from the door, his face grave. "I'm glad to see you, Gillian. We need to talk." He led her to the recess by the bay window in the hall.

"Your mother's condition is worrying," he said. "Her lungs were much compromised to begin with, and we can't seem to shake that infection. Her heart's labouring too, due to pressure from fluid retention. Her kidney function's very weak, and the electrolytes are disturbingly low. She could be taken to the hospital to be stabilized and made *temporarily* more comfortable by the removal of the fluid. Or," he held his chin in one hand and looked into her eyes, "since she signed a form stating that she doesn't want extraordinary efforts made to keep her alive," he shifted his gaze to the window, "we could let nature take its course."

"No!" Gillian held onto the back of the chair. "Take her to the hospital! Give her some more time. She's not ready to die yet."

"I think her body is, Gillian, but I agree with you for now. I'll arrange for an ambulance to come sometime this afternoon, and she could be brought back tonight, if all goes well."

"What do you mean, 'if all goes well'?" Gillian clutched her elbows, staring at him.

He put a hand on her shoulder. "When someone's whole system is as weakened as your mother's is," he said, "you can never be sure. I think there's still some fight in her yet, but I can't offer you any promises. We just have to hope for the best."

Her mother was lying back on the pillows, her eyes shut, patches of rouge standing out sharply on her cheeks. Her eyes flew open at Gillian's approach, and she held out a shaking hand.

"Sunita tells me I've got to go to the hospital! What's wrong with me, Gillian? I shouldn't like to think I was *dying*! But I'm not, am I, Gillian? Dying?" She tightened her grip, a skunk-like odour rising from her as she strained upwards.

Gillian looked down into the red-rimmed eyes, and gently squeezed the frail hand. "You'll soon feel better, Mum. They'll fix you up at the hospital. That's why you're going."

Her mother relaxed into the pillows until her body was gripped and shaken by a fit of coughing.

The ambulance arrived at four o'clock. Leaving a message for Tom, Gillian went with her mother to the hospital, where the patient was immediately whisked off through a pair of swing doors.

"The procedure will be all over in about an hour, dear." A cherubic male nurse flitted through the doors about fifteen minutes later, dimpling as Tom lumbered up. "And then you can take your mum back to Saint Anne's. She's in very good hands there."

"How come they employ twelve-year-olds as nurses now?" Tom struggled with the plastic lid of a Styrofoam cup of machine-made tea as they settled on a bench for the wait. "I saw a lady doctor who didn't look much older either."

"*Woman* doctor, you mean." Gillian sipped the pale drink, grateful for the heat and for the unexpected sugar. "We're getting old, Tom!"

Forty-five minutes later, the cherub emerged pushing their mother on a gurney. "Here she is then." He patted the frail shoulder. "All set to go now, aren't you, sweetheart?"

Their mother was deathly pale, but her breathing was clearly easier. She smiled at the three of them. "I've turned the corner!"

AFTER THEY RETURNED TO LANGLAND and Gillian had assured Tom that, still suffering from jet lag, all she wanted was a bowl of cereal and an early night, he made a couple of calls on his cellphone. He came back into the kitchen, grinning and holding a blue and gold striped tie, his blazer over his arm. "I've got to rush into town, Gill. Vanna's actually at a loose end this evening, so I'm taking her to dinner at The Dragon."

Gillian fluttered her fingers in farewell. "Take it easy," she said through a mouthful of Weetabix.

Waiting for sleep to come, with Tweetie-Pie purring beside her, she turned her thoughts back to Doug. She had heard that he had sold the property after the farmhouse had gone up in flames, and had gone out west to look for his brother. She had heard no more of him after that until Diana's startling and recent report of a visit from him at her home near Comox, on Vancouver Island.

"Imagine my astonishment," Diana had written, "when I answered the door and found myself face-to-face with Doug Clegg! He was a bit grizzled and wrinkled, of course, but there was no mistaking that face. He didn't recognize me at first because I'm pretty grey now, alas, and getting a tad stout, but when he heard my voice, he went all quiet and thoughtful.

"'Are you who I think you are?' he says, 'Diana, the Abductor?'

"'That's me,' says I, 'And what can I do for Doug, the Dog-freezer?'

"Apparently he'd come to inquire about buying a couple of dogs to guard his place! Hah! As if! I learned later, that his and his brother's 'place' is a highly successful grow op in the forest behind Comox!

"My God, Gill! What a scene that was, all those years ago! And what a trip back to the city!"

BEFORE FINALLY DRIFTING OFF TO SLEEP, Gillian reflected on what a lucky escape she had been granted, and how fortunate she had been in the way things had worked out for her in Ottawa. To begin with, at any rate.

TWO DAYS AFTER DIANA'S Sunday-night departure from Ottawa, Gillian was hanging curtains and rearranging furniture in the apartment they had found. Small, but bright and high-ceilinged, with a bay window overlooking a narrow little valley of a park, it had immediately felt like home. She would have, for the first time in her life, a place of her own, and despite all that had happened she felt good. She placed a hooked rug, a Salvation Army find, in front of the fireplace, watered the white gardenia that had been Diana's house-warming gift, filled the shiny whistling kettle, and turned on the little Canadian Tire radio, Perry Como's "Catch a Falling Star" inspiring her to sing along and execute a sort of tap dance, such as she and Vanna used to practice years ago. Raucous barking rose up immediately from downstairs, quickly followed by a knock on her door.

Mrs. Armstrong, her landlady, who lived on the ground floor and was the owner of the old, brick three-storey house, stood smiling in the doorway, a plate of freshly made oatmeal cookies in her arthritic-looking hands. In a blue-grey cashmere twin set and coordinated tweed skirt, she looked exactly the sort of woman Gillian knew her mother would approve of.

"I want to apologize for Jack's barking," Mrs. Armstrong held out the plate, "and to give a proper welcome to my new neighbour." The chunky West Highland terrier at her feet twirled around, his claws clicking on the hardwood floor, his black nose pointing steadily up at the cookies.

Over Irish Breakfast tea in Gillian's new blue and white striped mugs, Mrs. Armstrong put her into the context of Rosedale Villa. The tall, bespectacled man in a sheepskin coat, whom Gillian had met the day before as he was leaving the house, was her son, Russ, who came to see her three times a week, "like clockwork." He was a scientist, she said, and worked at the National Research Council. The nervous-looking, middle-aged man who had doffed his beret at meeting Gillian on the stairs was Monsieur Laliberté, a flautist, who lived on the top floor, and played in the Ottawa Philharmonic Orchestra. When the weather got warmer, Mrs. Armstrong said, and the windows were open, they would have the pleasure of hearing him practice. Gillian sipped her tea and imagined sitting on the window-seat in the sunshine as haunting notes drifted down to the blossoming crab-apple trees below.

LUCK HAD ALSO BEEN WITH HER in the matter of finding work. A not-so-lucky, about-to-retire English teacher at one of the downtown high schools had slipped on the ice and broken her hip, and would not be finishing the school year. English teachers were hard to come by, according to Peter Fearnley, Gillian's previous principal, who said he could not offer her full-time teaching at his school but would be happy to recommend her for the position at Sir Charles Roberts High School.

She had found a comfortable place to live and a good job, both within a week.

That evening she put up her feet on an exotic little leather pouf she had found in a junk shop on Bank Street, and looked back over the past eight months. It could all have been a dream: the forgetting of all other ties; the living only in the present; the total absorption in each other, or rather in Doug, she now saw, since everything had always and only been about him.

Every time she thought of Doug, her heart jumped in panic. She knew Diana had been right when she said in the car that he was a dangerous man. She had gone further than that, using alarming psychological terminology, with which, looking back, it was hard to argue. Gillian tried to drown out that insistent voice in her head and be objective, but could not get past the image of Nigel freezing to death on the doorstep. Nor should she try to, she decided, blowing her nose. Diana was right. That was what Doug was.

She had not done well with men, she thought, settling herself deeper into the chair, or they by her. First there was Llewellyn, and, of course, James; and then Doug; jerks all three as it turned out. Perhaps, to be fair, they had thought they loved her. They had said they did, except for James, and even he had seemed to be holding out some sort of promise, but looking back, she was pretty sure there had been no real heart in any of it.

Gordon, on the other hand, had loved her, she felt certain, but the sad truth was that his devotion had irritated her; the way he hovered, ever alert, to be of service: to write her philosophy essay, carry her book-bag, pick up her dropped handkerchief; he was just asking for it. It had been the same with Eric, a colleague at her first Ottawa school, who was forever coincidentally bumping into her, asking if she needed help settling in, and finding excuses to talk, even going so far as to offer help with her marking. She had gone out with him a couple of times, but had retreated in fright at the prospect of being invited to dinner with his family, a flight that had resulted in a little poem, written in copper-plate on azure vellum:

You picked up my life like a paper bag;
looked into it,
found it empty,
crumpled it up,
and threw it away.

Appalled, she had crumpled it up and thrown it away, cutting off the poet completely.

It was true, though: like Groucho Marx scorning any club which would have him as a member, she trashed any true lovers, while the men she was attracted to just used her. She sank down further in her chair, brooding. Maybe she could write a poem too; one about the hopelessness of ever finding real love. She picked up a pad and the mottled-blue Waterman fountain pen her father had given her as a going-away-to-school gift, and stared for a long while at the blank piece of paper before beginning to scribble. Finally she wrote out the fair copy of her efforts:

Sleepless I lie within your arms.
You stir and sigh; the night grows cold.
The sphinx of thought stares down those charms
That sang of happiness, then told
That one is one; and love, the sense
Of loneliness grown more intense.

She threw down her pen, which rolled off the table. 'Arms' and 'charms'! 'Cold' and 'told' indeed! And so derivative! She was as hopeless at poetry as she was at love.

After a restorative cup of tea and one of Mrs. Armstrong's cookies, she returned to the subject of men. Wondering if a viable compromise might be possible perhaps at some time in the future, she retrieved her pen and printed two headings: *Users* and *Losers*. Llewellyn, James, and Doug, she put under the one; Gordon and Eric under the other. She had a feeling, looking at the *Users* list, that she had forgotten someone, but could not remember who it might be.

After mulling over the other men in her life, she added a third column for those who were neither users nor losers. She put her father in that column, and, of course, her grandfather, along with Mr. Fearnley and a few others. She would have included Tom, but remembered that unfortunately, as far as love was concerned at least, he belonged in the *Loser* column. In his letter at Christmas he had written about the awful business with Gladys. He would have to marry her, he wrote, because if the child was his, which it well might be, he wanted to look after it, and make sure it had a better childhood than his had been. No child of his was going to be neglected by anyone.

Despite the way things turned out, he must have been hurt and surprised to have had no reply. So must her grandmother; and Vanna, who had actually written, after more than a year of silence, exulting over her success in landing a place as an actress with the Swansea Repertory Company. Mrs. Farrell was another whom she had cut off in this way. She resolved to write to them all, apologizing for her neglect, and filling them in on what was happening in her life.

Only then did she remember that Tom's address in Germany, along with all the other letters, was still at the farmhouse. So were her photographs, her passport, her few good pieces of jewelry, her books, records, clothes, and a framed Picasso print she had always liked, called *Resting on Imperfection,* in which a woman sits with her hands around her knees, staring sphinx-like into the distance or the future.

SHE WAS TO START TEACHING the following Monday at Sir Charles Roberts School, a short bus ride away from the apartment. She would be teaching senior grades only: two grade thirteen classes, two grade twelves, and an enriched grade eleven; a heavy load entailing five large classes of over forty students and three different sets of lesson preparations. Her predecessor, Mrs. Kay Entwistle, apparently an indefatigable worker, had set written homework every week for each class besides assigning quizzes, exercises, and tests, and had sent Gillian the schedules and tests for all classes, along with sets of corrected essays. She would be a hard act to follow, Gillian knew, but she would take it one day at a time. She gathered her books together on the table and settled down to prepare for Monday.

AT THE START OF HER FIRST CLASS, Thirteen C, the students seemed so quiet and well-behaved that Gillian wondered why her predecessor had written, "Watch this lot!" above the class list. After introducing herself, she checked names and attendance, described what was ahead for the last weeks of the semester, and passed around mimeographed copies of Mrs. Entwistle's quiz on *Hamlet.*

"So far, so good," she thought, as she collected their answers before writing on the board the questions on Act Four, Scene Two. While they scribbled, heads bent, she looked over the quiz sheets.

The top paper, the last to have been handed in, offered in answer to the first question: *What is the gist of Laertes' advice to Ophelia?* the terse injunction, *Stay away from Macbeth!* The second question: *What is 'that undiscovered country from whose bourn no traveller returns*? had for answer, not *Death*, but *Poland*, heavily crossed out and replaced by *England*.

Keeping her head down and pressing her lips hard together, she glanced at the five rows of students, all seemingly bent over their work. She had better take a closer look at what they were doing.

In the first aisle she confiscated a knitting pattern for baby boots, a math textbook, and a *Mad* comic. She collected a Harlequin romance and Coles notes on *Hamlet* in the second aisle and nothing at all in the fully alerted third. Holding her scruffy spoils, she stood in front of the class.

"Why are you here?"

They glanced at her and at each other, muttering and sniggering.

"Write an honest, one-sentence answer to that query, with your name on it, please, and hand it in as you leave, together with your answers to Mrs. Entwistle's questions."

When the bell had rung, and they were jostling their way out, a thick-set youth, heavy black stubble on his chin, loomed over her desk. "I want my math book back," he said. "I've got an important test tomorrow." The other students nudged each other as they passed.

She looked at the name inside the cover. "I'm sorry Bruce White, but you must pay attention in my class."

"You'll be the sorry one if you don't give it me." He stared down at her and held out his hand for the book.

She gathered up the last of her papers. "You'll have it back next class, the same as everyone else."

"Is that so?" He raised his eyebrows and stared at her. "We'll see about that!" He lurched out of the room, his back-pack slamming against the door frame.

Marking the quizzes in the staff room at lunchtime and incidentally confirming her suspicion that Bruce White was the author of *Stay away from Macbeth!,* she became aware of an intensification of tobacco fumes as a pair of bony hands and wrists, protruding from threadbare tweed cuffs, appeared on the table in front of her.

A thin, grey-haired man leaned over the table, his prognathic face a few inches from hers.

"Be a good girl and give the lad his book back!" he said in one of those voices that can be heard clearly throughout any assembly hall. "He's going in for engineering. He doesn't need *Hamlet,* for Christ's sake, but he sure as hell needs all the math he can get!" He straightened up. "Besides, we've got a match against Ashburn tonight, and he, my dear, is our goalie. We don't want him off his form, do we?" He winked and held out his right hand, palm upwards, jiggling it at her. "Just give us the book, sweetheart, and I'll get it to him."

"As I understand it," Gillian rose to eye level with him, "he needs to pass Grade Thirteen English to go in for anything at all at the post-secondary level, and by the looks of it, if he doesn't give it his full attention and effort, he may very well *not* pass. Besides, he won't be studying anything much tonight if he has a match. He can have the book back tomorrow, as I told him."

"I see." He narrowed his eyes and gave her a penetrating look. "This does not end here." He turned on his heel and walked out of the room, the fingertips of his left hand clutching the cuff of his jacket. Interested eyes followed him and then swung back to her.

"Good for you!" Danielle, a French teacher, appeared beside her. "That's Phil Scott, the senior math master. He's probably off to tell on you to his pal, the principal. Come on, let's go to the cafeteria. It's lasagna day."

She was around Gillian's age, slim and dark, with a wide, humorous mouth and a husky voice. As they walked along the hallway between the battered lockers, Gillian told her about the quiz answers, eliciting a loud, throaty laugh.

At the end of the school day, Harold Brown, the principal, sent for her. A small, bald man with a hooked nose, he strutted around the large desk to his chair.

"You are young, Miss Davies," he said, thick glasses magnifying his round black eyes as he sat, tilting the chair back and balancing his hands on the rise of his pot-belly, "and have much to learn about how a school works. As this is your first day here, I will not make too much of this." He sat forward, raising his eyebrows at her. "But you must understand, my dear, that you need to understand the need for flexibility. All sides of the question need to be equally considered you know, not just your own side. Bruce White is a valued member of our school community and has made a valuable contribution to our athletic standing. So if you'd be so good, kindly hand over the book in question."

She felt in her bag and, without taking her eyes off him, silently handed over the dog-eared book. His glasses flashed as he looked away. "Thank you. Please close the door after you."

Weighed down by her heavy bag, she walked home through the slush rather than share the bus with students. She had no stomach for their lethal backpacks, their shrieks and shouts and foul language. She kicked a grey, disintegrating lump of ice out of her way. Why hadn't she said, "Would you like the Harlequin romance, the knitting pattern, the comic, and the Coles notes as well, so that all the other students involved can be equally considered?" Why was she challenged by students, called "sweetheart" by the likes of Phil Scott, and mutely, if mulishly, obedient to the orders of such a man as Harold Brown, the Human Budgie? Why, for that matter, she asked herself as she sloshed along, had she let herself be dismissed by Llewellyn without putting up any sort of a fight? And why had she been so blind about Doug? Why couldn't she be like Jane Austen's Emma, always confident of receiving the best treatment, because she 'would never put up with any other'? She was distracted from going further along that line of thought by a shower of slush thrown up on her by a car speeding around the corner at the crossroads.

That evening, after wearily finishing her preparation for the next day, she looked to see how the students in Thirteen C. accounted for their presence there. "Because i have no choice," she read; "There's nothing else to do"; "To hang out with my friends"; "So as I can get a really good job and make alot of money." Out of the few who claimed to enjoy learning for its own sake, one stood out: Joel Waterman had written, "I am here to read as much as I can before I have to go into my father's meat business. All I want to do is study literature; English is an *oasis* in my day!" Admiring the semicolon, along with the sentiment, she experienced a leap of the hope that springs eternal in the English teacher's breast.

Putting the papers away, she noticed the knitting pattern in her bag and took it out. As she smiled at the picture of the tiny booties, a worm of worry stirred in the back of her mind. So much had happened that last week that she had not thought about it until then, but wasn't she *late*? She looked in her diary. She was, in fact, five days late. Not that that was so very unusual; she was not always completely regular. When she had broken up with Llewellyn, the same thing had happened; she had been a week late then. These were similar circumstances. Probably the same cause: just stress. That made sense.

She turned her mind to the problem of getting her belongings back from the farmhouse, but at the thought of facing Doug her new-found sense of being somewhat in control of her life further evaporated. Doubts and worries sneaked, and circled, and sank their teeth into her. What if she could not get anything back, not even her passport? What if she lost her job, as perhaps she might after that cheeky stare in the principal's office? What if she could not get another? And then that most frightening of all possibilities reared up again. What if…? She ran her fingers through her hair and shook her head. It was too soon yet to worry about that. Probably was not going to happen anyway. She should forget it for now, and start writing those letters.

As she put pen to paper, the doorbell rang.

"I'm not going to stay. I'm just passing," Danielle brought a wave of cold fresh air in with her. "I missed you after school, and I want to know how things turned out. I remembered you said you lived here." She swept off her silver-fox hat and shook out her long, dark hair.

"I've only had my job for a day, and I think I could've lost it already." Gillian described her encounter with the principal.

"Don't worry about it. They need you. That was just a staff-room spat. We have them all the time at Sir Charles and they always blow over. You did fine, actually. The bully boys will leave you alone now, and you'll get some respect from the kids." After regaling Gillian with a snippet of gossip concerning Phil Scott and the female phys. ed. teacher, she put on her coat. "You okay for tomorrow? You look *un peu…*"

"I'm fine," Gillian said quickly as she saw her out. "Thanks for coming round." But she was exhausted. She had struggled all day to keep alert, and had slept for two hours as soon as she got home. Naturally she was worn out, though. A day like that would do anyone in.

The following day brought no reprieve from her fears, nor did the next, nor the day after. A week passed, and then another. By the end of the week after that, she had run out of hope. Brooding, she considered her options. Looking to Doug for help was out of the question. Imagining him with a child sent her, to her surprise, into mother-tiger mode. The same reaction arose to another equally improbable option; no one, especially not her, was going to harm her baby. She remembered what Tom had said, and now completely understood how he had felt about his putative child.

She began to worry about money. The baby would be born in October, so there could be no chance, obviously, of going back to work in September. On the positive side, thanks to her father's annuity plus some savings, she would probably be able to stay on in her apartment for a while anyway. Then what? Go home to Mother with a baby? *Absolutely not*! She would just have to wait and see.

SHE WAS PUTTING UP A CORK notice board in the kitchen the following Saturday when she heard a tap at the door. In a turtleneck sweater and cords, Russ Armstrong looked younger, and less of a stuffed shirt than she had thought.

"I heard you hammering, and wondered if perhaps you could do with a hand?"

There would be no harm in asking him in, she decided. Actually she could do with some help in putting up an awkwardly large mirror.

"I want to thank you for helping my mother bring in her shopping the other day, and for walking Jack the night of the freezing rain." He straightened the corkboard. "She gets very tired these days, and I worry about her." He stood back to check on his work. "I wish she'd come and live with me in Manor Park. There's plenty of room in my house, but I suppose she likes her independence."

Gillian put on the kettle. "Do you have a family?" She assumed that at his age, in his mid-thirties at least, and with a house of his own, that was likely.

"No, unfortunately, I don't." He took off his glasses and polished them with a spotlessly laundered handkerchief. "I've always been too busy studying, and then working, to have had any time for a personal life."

This was the first time she had met anyone like that, even at university. She asked what his work was, and learned that he worked in the field of helicopter icing.

"It's a serious problem," he said, "especially, of course, in northern countries. We've made great strides recently." He went on to describe in detail the huge rig they had constructed, with one hundred and sixty-one nozzles, to help provide icing protection. It seemed they were leading the field in that work. Over a mug of Maxwell House instant coffee, he told her more about the icing problem. She could not understand much of his explanations, but could see that his mother was right: he lived for his work.

After putting up the mirror, he looked around the apartment. "It's nice in here. You've made it very home-like. My place just looks like a hotel."

Having seen him to the door, she poured her coffee down the sink as usual those days. He just might be interesting, she thought as she washed and dried the mugs, as long as he stayed off the subject of ice-rigs. He was not bad-looking at all, and definitely not the demon-lover sort; neither user nor loser perhaps. If things were different, she might even encourage his possible overtures in the hope of finding that viable compromise she had been thinking about, although that was obviously out of the question now.

As it turned out, Russ would not have needed any encouraging. When his mother invited Gillian down for an afternoon cup of tea the next Saturday, it was he who opened the door, looking casually smart in a sports jacket and cavalry twill trousers such as her father liked to wear. A bit behind the times, but a tidy man, she thought; not like Doug.

They sat at the round, rosewood table, laid with gold-rimmed Royal Albert china of a dark blue, white, and orange pattern, dabbing their lips with hand-embroidered napkins, and passing around homemade scones and carrot cake.

When they returned to the fireside, Jack laid his red rubber ball at Gillian's feet, giving a bark of excitement when she rolled it over to Russ, who, after a moment's thought, bent down and rolled it back. Isobel, as she had asked to be called, watched the stout little dog scamper between them. "Poor Jack! He's not getting nearly enough exercise these days. My arthritis is really acting up."

"I could walk him." Gillian looked up. "I'd love to. I'm not getting enough exercise either."

Russ observed that there was a park nearby where dogs were safe to run free. It was a lovely day, he said. Perhaps the two of them could both take Jack there for half an hour or so before the sun went down? Isobel looked, smiling, from one to the other. Gillian thought of saying she had too much marking to do that day, but did not want to seem ungracious. Isobel had been very kind, it was indeed a lovely day, and a short walk would, in fact, do her good.

That was how it had started. Without any encouragement from her, one small thing had led to another on an almost daily basis until it became disconcertingly clear that, if not head over heels in love with her, Russ had intentions that she could not imagine were anything but honourable. She had tried to say that she was busy or had other engagements, but he was persistent, and in the circumstances it was difficult to snub or avoid him. She understood that short of moving across town, she could not run away from this. She had better tell him.

"YOU'RE LOOKING VERY LOVELY TONIGHT." Russ regarded her solemnly over the brilliant white tablecloth at the fashionable Italian restaurant he had chosen. He was not looking so bad himself, she thought, in his well-tailored grey suit, white shirt, and discreetly patterned, red silk tie. *Clean-cut* was the word that came to mind. Her mother would be impressed. If, on the other hand, he grew his hair, got rid of those round gold-rimmed glasses, and changed his suit for casual pants and shirt, she might even fancy him herself; if circumstances were different, of course.

She had been glad to find that she had no trouble fitting into her dress, retrieved from the farmhouse along with her other possessions the previous weekend when Danielle and her boyfriend, Pierre, had driven her out there. To her relief, Doug had not been around, having left everything on the steps, stuffed into two large garbage bags.

The dress, black georgette with a flared skirt and soft neckline, was one which her mother had taken upon herself to find for her, unasked, at Mrs. Rosenberg's little shop. "You should have at least one stylish thing to wear," she had said. "I don't suppose you'll find anything smart where you're going."

Gillian had never worn it, convinced it was strictly for funerals and would make her look at least forty; but when she tried it on that evening, adding the string of pearls her parents had given her for her twenty-first birthday, she was surprised to see that her mother had been right: the effect was far from frumpy, and the pearls were perfect. "Knowing that you're wearing good pearls always gives one confidence," her mother had said, an idea Gillian had scoffed at, but now found herself wishing could be true.

She began to worry that Russ would get the wrong impression: that he might think she had made a special effort to look good for him; that she fancied him even. He was looking rather nervous, tapping his fingers and loosening his tie. Was he planning to make some sort of move that evening? What would she say? Pulling herself together, she got down to the less daunting business of the menu, choosing a clear soup and a salad.

After he had finished off his veal marsala and spooned down his sabayon, Russ patted his mouth with the extra-large napkin and sat back, clearing his throat. "You know, I've never met anyone like you, Gillian. I mean before I met you." He looked at her over the little posy of red and white carnations as the candle flickered in its glass bowl. "You're the most, um, elegant girl I've ever met. And, and you're reserved. I really like that in a girl."

"Well, thank you." Gillian looked around for a washroom sign.

"You remind me of my mother." He smiled shyly, lifting his wineglass.

She checked the exit route. "That's nice."

"I'd be honoured … er, that is, I was wondering, Gillian, if you'd consider—what is it they call it?" he put his head on one side—"*going steady* with me? He placed his large, pale hands on the table, the nails irreproachable as always, unlike Doug's hands, with their scars from metalwork, and their hard-bitten, dirty nails, and Llewellyn's; light brown, slim, and nimble-fingered.

She sat up straight and clasped her hands on the table in front of her. "Russ," she said, "There's something I have to tell you."

AFTER SHE HAD SAID WHAT she had to say, he sat back, his face slack with astonishment. "I can't believe it! You seemed so refined."

"Well, even refined women get pregnant, you know." She put her napkin on the table. "I'm sure your mother, for example, has always been very refined."

"My mother …" he grimaced. "My mother's going to be so shocked!"

"Mine too. She's obviously not as refined as yours, since she's had *two* children, but she's not going to like this. But she's in another country. Maybe I won't tell her, and just present her one day with a *fait accompli.*"

"With a what?"

"A *fait accompli.* It's what comes after a fate worse than death."

"That isn't funny, Gillian."

People were always telling her that things were not funny.

"But what are you going to do?" He frowned. "How, er, pregnant are you actually?"

"Don't even think of it."

They sat in silence for a minute.

"So, there will be a baby." He looked into the distance. "If I may ask, does the father know about this?"

"No he doesn't, and he's not going to. Look, Russ, I think I'd better go home. I can get a taxi."

"Certainly not!" He beckoned to the waiter for the bill. "I'll drive you home, of course. It's the least I can do."

He was a nice man, she thought, sitting beside him in his Chevrolet. Maybe it really was a pity that she could not take this any further. To her surprise, as they said goodnight at the foot of the stairs, he put his arms around her and kissed her cheek, his lips soft, and his embrace, unlike those of Llewellyn or Doug, holding no hint of underlying danger. In his arms she felt safe. Suppressing a strong impulse to respond, she said goodnight, and went up to her apartment. Before she had closed her own, she heard him tap on his mother's door.

In bed, disarmed by that glimpse of security, she gave herself up, first to panic, and then to an overwhelming sense of loss. She grieved for Doug, alone again with his demons, and for poor faithful Nigel, waiting in vain on the doorstep for her to return. Sinking deeper than those heartaches, even deeper than the anguish of Llewellyn's desertion, she found herself sobbing like a little child for her mother: *"Don't go! Don't go! Don't leave me!"*

"I TOLD YOU I'D TURNED the corner! I'm a tough old bird!" Their mother was sitting up, smiling, as Gillian and Tom came to St. Anne's the next morning. She did indeed look better: her colour had improved, and her breathing was still easy. There was even a whiff of *Je Reviens* in the air as she beckoned them closer. "What have you two been up to?"

Gillian shot an amused look at Tom who had not come back to the bungalow until morning. "Oh, nothing, just an early night," she said. "By the way, Mum, did you know that Tweetie-Pie snores?"

"Actually, Mum, I went out to dinner last night. With Vanna!" Tom sat down, beaming at her. "We had a wonderful time!"

She stared at him, eyebrows raised. "Vanna? That Irish girl? Really, Tom!" She looked out of the window with a sniff. "Typical!"

"What the devil d'you mean by that?" Tom jumped to his feet, his face red. "Vanna is a brilliant and successful woman. She's made far more of her life than *you* ever did, with your—your coffee mornings and your cocktail parties and your fancy hats. Where would you have been if it hadn't been for Dad, eh? *Eh*?"

She glared furiously at him. "I would have been in Australia. Happy! Now please go away. And don't come back."

"Jesus Christ! No wonder Dad said you were a hell of a woman!" He slammed out of the room.

Telling herself it was not funny, Gillian caught up with him on the landing., "Don't listen to her, Tom! She's old, and sick, and not making any sense."

"She's never made any sense! I'm sick and tired of kowtowing to her. And I'm not having Vanna insulted like that." He was huffing and puffing, a thick vein standing out on his temple.

"Calm down. It's only Mum. Isn't it time we stopped stressing about her? She's probably not going to be with us much longer anyway."

"I know, but I'm not tiptoeing around her, walking on eggshells anymore."

"Well that's a good thing. Why should you, after all?"

He shrugged his shoulders, but he was less flushed. He grinned. "'I would have been in Australia' indeed! What the hell was that about?"

"Who knows?" She watched him go heavily down the stairs, his hand on the rail, something slipping again across the back of her mind.

Her mother was drying her eyes with a handkerchief. "That's right. Stick together. Never mind me. You were always thick as thieves, you two."

The memory slithered by once more, and this time Gillian caught it by the tail: her grandmother, looking sadly at a faded sepia photograph of two radiant young people who had also been thick as thieves. The laughing young man had gone to Australia, her grandmother had said, and had died there five years later.

Gillian sat down thoughtfully beside the bed. "Mum, you started telling me yesterday about the man who gave me the Koala bear. Who was he?"

Her mother looked down, carefully smoothing the satin ribbons of her bed jacket. "Oh, just an old friend. A distant relative, actually." She flicked a look at Gillian. "Why do you ask?"

"It seemed important to you, and I ..." Gillian broke off as the door opened wide.

"Your mum's really perked up after that procedure, hasn't she?" Sunita came in, her arms full. She put down her load, filled a stainless-steel bowl with hot water from the wash basin, and wrung out the face cloth. "You're looking rested too, Gillian. I won't be long here, but I'm going to freshen Iris up and change the sheets as well as see to her medications. Give us about half an hour."

Gillian walked to the Uplands shopping centre. After watching her mother and some of the other patients in the nursing home, she was appreciating the fact that she could walk, and briskly at that. Climbing the hill and enjoying the warmth of the sun on her face, she wondered about the man who had given her the bear. Could he be the young man in that photograph?

She was in the bookstore, searching unsuccessfully for any Canadian content, when a raised voice jolted her to attention. A middle-aged man was haranguing the young female cashier about an order that had not yet come in. She heard him say, "Do I make myself clear?" and saw a balding, grey-tonsured head thrust forward as the sallow-faced man turned and pushed past her, his pale eyes fixed on a distant goal.

It was the self-important swing of his shoulders as he left the shop that gave him away.

She had grieved all her life over *that?* She had wilted under the judgment of a future annoying old fart? She would have married him, and spent her whole life with him, would she? Hugging her elbows, she stood at the door and watched Llewellyn get into a Mercedes-Benz, the revelation further enhanced by the sight of a stout, equally angry-looking, black-haired woman in a red straw hat sitting at the wheel.

She bought up all the freesias in the grocer's shop for her mother and set off for St. Anne's, her arms full of the white yellow and purple blossoms. Despite their heady fragrance, her euphoria faded as she walked back in the noonday heat.

If only I had known! She thought of all the years she had spent held back by guilt, bruised by rejection, afraid to carve for herself, and unable to see her way; the waste of shame through which she had struggled all her life. To be fair, Llewellyn had not been the first cause of all that; he had been more of a symptom, she realized, as had Doug, and, after Doug, the dim purgatory of her marriage to Russ. She shook her head recalling the ten, trancelike years of their marriage, and the surreal awakening that had brought them to an end.

WATCHING *ZORBA THE GREEK* one summer night at Ottawa's Mayfair Cinema, Gillian saw that during those years of marriage to Russ, she had somehow mislaid her life. She was a ghost, drifting through the motions of domesticity while the living souls, clapping fervently, if stupidly, beside her in the cinema, for example, were surely caught up in the joys and pains of existence. They felt free to throw back their heads and belt out arias, or pop songs, or hymns. They jived to the pulse of disco lights and drums. Their teeth clenched on thorny roses, they swirled and swooped in sultry tangos. Cuddled on the sofa, they watched Wayne and Schuster, wiping tears of laughter from their eyes. They threw cast-iron pots at each other, and then, if they survived, made passionate love on the kitchen floor. They rejoiced and suffered with a blessed intensity, in heaven or in hell, while she, prim and pampered, languished in limbo in a genteel, white-frame house in Manor Park.

She walked to the car behind a middle-aged couple, at least ten years older than she was. The woman put her head on the man's shoulder as they walked in step, her arm tucked tightly under his. They were laughing in delight over the film, and Gillian knew that when they got home they would make love.

IN HER GLEAMING KITCHEN the next morning, she lifted the damp mass of hair off the back of her neck with a sigh and stirred lemon slices into a jug of iced tea. She drew out the long-handled spoon, pulling a face at her upside-down reflection in its back, and watched the drops of condensation trickle down the tall sides of the glass jug onto the shining, tomato-red countertop. An image of a stream tumbling down a cliff-face between wind-blown poppies was disrupted by the drone of the Hoover, as Mrs. Knight, her cleaning woman, apparently unfazed by the heat, began briskly vacuuming the upstairs hall.

Gillian blew down the front of her blouse. When she had immigrated she had thought the main problem with living in Ottawa would be the cold, but at that moment, even though it was still only June, she might as well be living in one of those hothouses, complete with banana trees, they used to have in the Educational Gardens in Swansea. Nine-year-old Bryn had found it hard to do his homework and to get to sleep the night before and had trailed off to school that morning, pale and bruise-eyed. She would ask Russ again about getting an air conditioner. He had given her the new Hoover as a present for her thirty-fifth birthday in April, so perhaps the air conditioner could be an advance Christmas gift. She would tell him that several other households in the neighbourhood had already acquired one.

With a pang she remembered the couple walking from the cinema the previous night. Ten years before, Russ had been so insistent that he loved her, and that he would think of her unborn child as his own that, believing she had found a man who was neither user nor loser, she had gladly agreed to marry him. To be fair, she reflected, he had been honest when he made those promises. He loved her as much as he could, she believed, and probably would have regarded a biological son just as numbly as he did Bryn.

She remembered an incident in Windsor Park when Bryn was about seven months old. Needing to tie her shoelace, she had handed the baby to Russ who, as usual, held out the wriggling bundle at some distance from his body as if afraid it might explode. At a warning shout, she looked up from her shoe to see a football, arcing end over end through the air, heading directly for Russ.

"Russ! Look out!" she yelled, and watched, appalled, as Russ, taking in the danger of being hit on the head by a large flying object, raised his arms and fended off the ball with the baby.

Still in shock, and giddy with relief since the ball had bounced off Bryn's well-diapered behind with no ill effect, apart from his ear-splitting objections, she had laughed off the incident, and for years, despite the recurring image of the flying ball and the baby in the air, had firmly told herself that she had been lucky to marry a decent, steady man who loved her.

He had certainly told her he loved her when he proposed marriage but apparently had felt no need to repeat himself, and lovemaking, if you could call it that, had long since become a thing of the past. He seemed satisfied with the routine of their life: a silent, hurried breakfast, packed lunches to take to the National Research Centre, and dinners of the sort that could be adjusted to his timetable. There was never a meal out, or a holiday trip. Restaurant meals were overpriced he said, and travel didn't appeal to him.

Isobel had come every Sunday until her final illness, four years before, to spend the day with them, bringing Jack with her, to Bryn's delight. Russ had agreed they would take over the care of Jack when Isobel became too ill to look after him, but when the old dog died, soon after Isobel, he said there would be no more dogs. Jack's barking had disturbed his rest, he said, and affected his ability to concentrate. Moreover, the animal was smelly, scruffy, and towards the end, incontinent. His mother's previous dog had died too, he remembered, after a similar deterioration. What was the point? He was, he said, allergic to cats.

He seemed to have no sense of family life; understandable perhaps, since before his marriage there had only been he and his mother, his father having died when he was a baby. When Tom had come to Ottawa that one time on BMW business, Gillian had hoped that the two practical-minded men might find something in common to talk about: engines, fuel consumption, metal fatigue... But for the whole three days that Tom had stayed with them, the conversation had been minimal and awkward and he had left looking sad and subdued.

Their social life was equally minimal. Danielle, still teaching at Sir Charles Roberts, but now married and living in nearby Lindenlea, came over occasionally for morning coffee, but Gillian's attempt at a dinner party for her and Pierre had been a failure.

Never one for small-talk, Russ had been polite but ill-at-ease, and conversation had been stilted over the shrimp cocktail, game-hens, and blueberry cheesecake Gillian had prepared in anticipation of a lively evening. While she served after-dinner coffee and liqueurs, Russ excused himself to check data, returning just as Pierre, who loved a joke, reached the punch line. Gillian saw Pierre's mouth snap shut and his vivid, mobile face freeze as Russ re-entered the room, and understood immediately that there would be no more such dinner parties. It was not just because Russ knew few French-Canadians; he was awkward and unresponsive with everyone he met. Socializing was not his sort of thing, he said. No more than it had been Doug's, she thought.

Work could have made her life less empty, but when, years before, she had suggested she could return to teaching once Bryn was at school full-time, Russ had dismissed the idea, arguing that unforeseen domestic concerns might interfere with his work. In any case, there was no need for it. He had looked complacently around at their well-appointed home. He could provide for all their wants.

Gillian had not argued. Perhaps Bryn needed her to be home, and she should be supportive of Russ, who was working harder than ever. She should appreciate what she had and not rock the boat.

THE SOUND OF THE VACUUM intensified and then stopped as Mrs. Knight arrived at the top of the stairs. There was another driven one, thought Gillian, wondering what motivated her cleaning woman to work with such fervour; a question which reminded her of a strange little discrepancy regarding Mrs. Knight. Her friend, or friendly acquaintance, Bernice, with whom she shared Mrs. Knight's services, and who lived in a shabby-genteel house in Ottawa's Sandy Hill, all hardwood floors, varnished panelling, and stained glass, had reported to her that Mrs. Knight had said her greatest pleasure lay in "helping to restore a beautiful old home to its former graciousness." Mrs. Knight had told Gillian, on the other hand, that she preferred houses like hers, where everything was fresh and new and came clean quickly. "Not like those big old houses where, however hard you work, it always looks shabby."

Turning her eyes from her reflected presence in the kitchen's shining surfaces, Gillian prepared lunch. She heard Mrs.

Knight bump the Hoover down the stairs, and saw her pause at the bottom beside the maidenhair fern, whisk a rag out of her apron pocket, and rub something, a finger-print maybe, off the oval hall mirror.

Knowing that Mrs. Knight would refuse anything more substantial, she laid out plates of lettuce and tomato and slices of the best, whole-grain bread, lightly buttered.

"I'll just have a little bit of lettuce, and a bit of bread and butter, and a nice cup of tea, if you have one," Mrs. Knight would say with a bright smile. "I'll have plenty to eat tonight when the family comes to supper."

Mrs. Knight was rightly proud of her family. Shirley, the eldest, was married to Nicholas, a very successful businessman, who had just bought a new Buick apparently, in which Mrs. Knight would be taken for a drive that evening. It seemed they had a lovely home on elegant Clemow Avenue, where they entertained important people like the mayor. Their six-year-old twins, Kimberly and Kendra, as bright as they were beautiful, were to start at a private girls' school, in the fall.

Doreen, her younger daughter, was articled with a highly respected law firm. She had been engaged to a brilliant young orthopedic surgeon, but had recently broken it off; Mrs. Knight was afraid that Doreen liked living at home too much for her own good.

The youngest, Norman, his mother's pride and joy, was doing his Master's degree in political science at Carleton University. According to Mrs. Knight, in looks and personality he took after his father, Victor, a gentle giant of a man with hair so blond it was almost white, and piercing blue eyes.

Victor had died, it seemed, when Shirley was ten and Norman barely two, and Mrs. Knight had raised the children single-handedly since then, struggling to keep to the ideals and hopes her husband had for them. Gillian and Bernice thought she was wonderful: a shining example of what was possible.

"You must be exhausted in this heat." Gillian pulled out a vinyl-topped stool for Mrs. Knight. "But we'll all be much more comfortable soon because my husband's buying us an air conditioner." This was not strictly true, but it felt good to say it. "Look, why don't you go home after lunch? With full pay, of course. It's much too hot for such heavy work, and you've already done much more than I expected."

"Oh, no, I'm not a bit tired. After all, I'm only fifty-five. I never run out of energy." Mrs. Knight looked mistily at the rounded, sky-blue refrigerator. "My husband used to call me 'the human dynamo'. He used to say it wore him out just looking at me dusting." She studied the hot-pink polish on her short, broken fingernails. "I told you he died of leukemia, didn't I?"

"No . . . No, I thought it was polio for some reason. You said he died when the children were very young. That must have been terribly hard for you."

Mrs. Knight stirred her tea thoughtfully. Gillian noticed, for the first time, brown blotches on the back of her hand, and heard a little clatter as she replaced the spoon. Her amber curls had lost their bounce, there was a film of sweat on her brow, and while her cheeks and lips were their usual geranium pink, her blue eyes had a confused look that Gillian had not seen before, the shadows under them too deep for makeup to hide.

"No, it was leukemia. It was my father that died of polio."

"Oh, I'm sorry. I must have got mixed up." Gillian poured Mrs. Knight another cup of tea.

The meal over, she collected the dishes. "I'll see to these. And please let me drive you home today for once. It's far too hot for you to have to stand at the bus stop."

"No. I like the bus, and I may want to drop in on a friend, but thanks just the same, Mrs. Armstrong. Now I'll be off upstairs to tackle that grouting. I'll have it spotless in no time."

"Please don't, Mrs. Knight. Not in this heat. Leave it until next week."

"Not to worry. I'd like to get it done."

TWO DAYS LATER, GILLIAN WAS cutting roses in the garden in her coolest sundress while waiting for Bryn to get home from school. She felt sweat break out between her shoulder blades as she walked over the yellowed lawn. Thunder rumbled continuously in the heavy air like distant bombing, while rain always seemed to be about to fall, but never did, and the poppies and peonies drooped and faded despite daily watering. She moved listlessly along the bed of roses, looking for the least wilted. As she leaned over to clip a sheltered crimson bloom, she heard the phone ring.

"I'm sorry, Gillian, but I've got some awful news." Bernice's usually crisp voice sounded fuzzy and hesitant. "It's Mrs. Knight. She's dead, Gillian! She dropped dead here, cleaning windows."

"Good God, Bernice! Cleaning windows? In this heat?"

"I know! I told her not to. Honestly, I did, Gillian; but she said she felt fine, and she wanted to do them because it's better when the sun isn't on them." Bernice took a shuddering breath. "You get a better shine she said."

Gillian sat down by the phone. "When did this happen?"

"About an hour ago. The ambulance has just gone."

"Oh, her poor family! And poor you! You must be feeling terrible." Gillian listened as Bernice unburdened herself tearfully at length. "We should send flowers," she said finally to Bernice. "And go to the funeral, of course." After Bernice rang off, Gillian shakily jammed the roses into a jug, crimson petals falling onto their own reflections in the gleaming, black and white tiled floor.

VISITATION TIME AT THE SMALL downtown funeral parlour coincided with both rush hour and the long-awaited downpour. Gillian was grateful that Russ, possibly feeling he should be sorry about Mrs. Knight, had uncharacteristically volunteered to be home when Bryn got back from school, and to stay until she returned. An accident on Bank Street necessitated a detour, and by the time she had found a parking place and hurried over swirling gutters and down streaming streets to the small funeral parlour, she was late for meeting Bernice. As she entered the dim front hall, breathless and flustered, a short, stout, middle-aged man stepped out from a doorway.

"You gotta be Mrs. Armstrong." He shook her hand. "I'm Norm Knight. Thanks for coming to pay your respects to my mother." He smoothed his thin, greying hair and tucked in his nylon shirt over a substantial belly.

This is Norman? Trying to hide her confusion, Gillian said, "I'm so sorry about your mother. She was a wonderful woman. I admired her so much."

"Yeah, that's what that other lady said. Would you like to see the remains?" He led her into a small, shadowy, visitation room where a dozen or so people, not including Bernice, turned sharply to stare at her.

The star of the occasion, clad in a silky white dress, lay in an open casket floating in a pool of illumination on a dais at the other end of the room. Accompanied by Norman, Gillian approached the casket to survey what seemed to be an artist's version of Mrs. Knight; the brassy curls subdued to auburn waves and the cheeks and faintly smiling lips beneath the patrician nose, tinted a pale, refined rose.

She peered at the name and dates on the placard in front of the coffin:

VICTORIA ELAINE KNIGHT 1905–1970.

She had talked to Mrs. Knight every week for years, and had thought she knew her, but had not even known her Christian name, or her true age.

Norman leaned forward. "She has a lovely face, eh?" He touched his mother's hand tenderly.

Dizzy from hurrying and from the heat, Gillian nodded and lowered her gaze to the oppressively sweet-smelling bouquet of lilies below the casket, and to the few, wilting wreaths. Sensing someone watching her, she looked up to see a dark-haired little woman in a beige crimplene suit standing nearby, next to a gaunt man in black pants and a white shirt, whom Gillian recognized as a waiter from La Roma. Behind them skulked a spotty teenaged boy in worn jeans. The woman stepped forward. Ice-blue eyes that, but for the expression, could have been Mrs. Knight's, bored into Gillian's with such hatred that she stepped quickly back, at which the woman turned and walked away, followed by the other two.

"That's my young sister, Doreen," Norman was back at her side, "and her husband and son. They're in a real state. Know what I mean? That's my father, Vince, over-there." He pointed to a swarthy little old man pouring himself a bumper glass of sherry from one of two bottles on a small table.

"Your father?"

"Yes. What's the matter? That other lady was the same. Looked real funny."

"I... I expect she was overcome, like me. We were both very fond of your mother."

"Yes, poor ladies." Norman was obviously trying to be fair. "My mother was ever so sorry for both of you." He left her side to guide his father away from the drinks table.

She was sorry for us? Gillian looked at the occupant of the casket, and then around the room, which seemed to have become peopled by trolls. There were those eyes again; this time on a stout, ginger-haired woman who glared across the casket at Gillian before contorting her face to mouth a single word:

"Murderer!

"Excuse me? What did you say?"

The woman rounded the casket at a trot to stand, breathing heavily, in front of Gillian. "I'm Shirley Knight," she said in a hoarse voice. "And I gotta tell ya, lady, my mom killed herself looking after you and your sort." She jabbed Gillian in the shoulder with a thick forefinger. "She'd drag herself home, half-dead from cleaning up after them parties you was always throwing in that friggin' mansion of yours. And you," another jab, "Madam," jab, "never lifted a finger, did you? Never gave her a break, not even in this friggin' heatwave. Never gave her a decent lunch, just that friggin' brown bread she hated, and a bit of lettuce. Never even offered to give her a drive home in that fancy new Buick you got. Not once!"

Gillian's knees shook as she backed away. "Did... did she say that?"

The woman narrowed her small, fierce eyes and rocked back on her white lace-ups. "Oh, she always had excuses for you. She was a saint! But I knew my mother. I knew you people was goin' to be the death of her." Her voice rose. "Usin' my poor, sick mother, a sixty-five-year-old woman, like a slave! Who the hell d' you think you are?" She thrust her jaw forward, her face inches from Gillian's. "You *killed* my mother!"

"Okay, Shirl. That's enough." Norman's voice came through the mist that filled Gillian's sight, and she felt the edge of a chair being pushed against the back of her buckling knees.

"You mustn't mind Shirley," Norman was saying as Gillian sat up after the room came back into focus. "She's real upset, being the youngest and all. We all are. You gotta understand."

Gillian sat for a while, trying to recover her composure while at the same time struggling to make sense of Mrs. Knight's upside-down, back-to-front, inside-out world in which the only recognizable element was Norman's decency. She rose from the chair, clinging to its back.

"Thank you, Norman." She looked into his dark eyes. "I'm sorry if I've caused your family any distress by coming here today." Deciding that the actual ceremony was a conclusion best foregone, she made her way shakily down the room through a gamut of outraged glares. Leaning against the door frame, she looked back at Mrs. Knight's family, and over and beyond them to Mrs. Knight herself, serene in her shining little craft, floating above the swirl of muddy waters below.

DRIVING HOME, SHE BROODED on the dénouement to the story of Victoria Elaine Knight, heroic widowed mother of brilliantly successful offspring, saintly victim of slave-drivers. What must her life have been to drive her to weave that gleaming web from the meagre rags of truth? Why, moreover, had she herself not picked up on the improbabilities and contradictions in Mrs. Knight's narratives that seemed so obvious now? Clearly she had chosen to just enjoy the story rather than bother to read between the lines.

You are so cool-hearted. She shook her head and drove faster, despite the continuing downpour. Forgetting that the car radio had been turned up to full volume the day before for Bryn's benefit, she switched it on. Vibrations shook the car, bass notes thumping her in the solar plexus.

The words, the melody, and the deep, trembling voice of the famous singer, young and beautiful then, with everything before him, swept her back to her arrival in Ottawa, twenty-two years old, homesick and lonely, but full of hope. She dashed the tears from her eyes with the backs of her hands as the wipers flailed ineffectively against sheets of rain. Where was her hope now? Who loved her tender? What dreams had been fulfilled? She slowed down. Her life was a shadowy sham, and she was sick of it. She stopped the car in her driveway, dried her eyes, and sat up straight.

Bryn was sitting on his school bag at the back door, dark hair plastered to his head, eyelashes starry-wet, white shirt clinging transparently to his chest. He beamed and waved as she got out and, with a leap of love, she wondered, as often before, how she and Doug between them had managed to produce such a sweetheart.

"Hi, Mom! How was the funeral?" His smile disappeared as he saw traces of tears. "Did it make you very sad?"

For once, she controlled her everything's-just-fine reflex. "Yes," she said, "It was very sad. I'll tell you about it one day." She bent to stroke the dripping hair off his wide, white forehead with its scattering of pin-point freckles. "I'm so sorry, darling, that you had to wait in the rain like this. Dad must have forgotten."

"Big surprise, eh?" He grinned. "But I didn't mind. I never got this wet before with my clothes on! And it's not cold. Anyway, I knew you'd be home soon."

She looked at her son, soaked and smiling on the doorstep, trying to keep his homework dry by sitting on it, and swept him up into a big hug. "Come on, Sunshine. We can do better than this! Let's get you dry, and then we'll go to McDonald's for supper. Just the two of us."

Gillian placed the freesias beside her on the bench in the front garden of Saint Anne's, and gave in to the temptation to rest a while before going in to see her mother. Reluctant to move, her bones aching a little, she sat in the shade, remembering the long, lonely years after she had left Russ, and the way Simon had come into her life.

On her way home from the school where she had taught for the last twenty years, Gillian picked her way along an Ottawa side street, still slushy and salt-strewn in March. Stopping in front of a shop window crowded with old volumes, she studied a display of thirty or so travel books: *Exploring Quebec City; Old Edinburgh; Istanbul;* Jan Morris's *Oxford.* About to move on, she spotted a little book at the back of the display, its title half-obscured by a pile of Fodors, possibly an early edition of George Borrow's 1872 travelogue, *Wild Wales.*

It was one of those dim, musty, tunnel-like shops, going way back. Bookshelves, crammed floor-to-ceiling, lined each side of two narrow aisles and most of the back wall. Strips of threadbare carpet of indistinguishable pattern and colour covered the uneven floor between the aisles. Bare bulbs provided just enough light for her to browse the shelves and see that she was alone with the books in peace and silence.

Remember me! She nearly dropped the book she was holding. From somewhere at the back of the shop, the rich soprano voice rose up in the aria of the abandoned queen in Purcell's *Dido and Aeneas*. *Remember me!* the diva sang again, *But, ah! forget my fate!* With a click, the music was turned off.

Replacing the book, Gillian drifted distractedly along the aisles before stopping at the novels. Still unsettled, she pulled a pristine edition of *Dance of the Happy Shades* off the shelf in the Canadian section and tucked it under her arm before checking for the presence of other favourites. Among the American authors, she leafed through an Edith Wharton novel before moving on to the British section, where complete sets of classics weighed down the shelves. Feeling something brush against her leg, she looked down into the golden eyes of a long-haired, grey tabby, the size of a schnauzer, with lynx-like tufts on its ears.

"That is my cat, Jeffrey." A stocky man, of about her height, curly black hairs mixed with gray sprouting over the top of his white T-shirt, came down the passageway from the back. "I didn't realize there was anyone here. I trust you're not allergic?"

She shook her head and bent to stroke the cat, which rose on its hind legs to receive the caress. Looking up, she asked if that was indeed a copy of *Wild Wales* that she had seen in the window.

His eyes were very dark, the whites clear under short spiked eyelashes. He smiled, showing equally white teeth. "I thought twice about putting that in the window, but it rounded out the display and I didn't think anyone would notice. It's pretty special."

"I know." Now she had to have it.

"You from Wales?" He glanced at her as she nodded. "I thought I could hear something in your voice. Hang on while I get it."

While he was gone, she moved on to the religion section, less dusty and better organized than the rest, and surprisingly extensive, she thought, even by second-hand bookstore standards. Christianity, Judaism, Islam, and Buddhism were all richly represented, together with an especially large collection of books on Hinduism.

After taking the little green and gold book from his hand and scrutinizing the first page, she looked up. "Is religion a special interest of yours?"

"It is. All religions." He ran his hand over some thin, yellow paperbacks, hesitated, and then turned to look at her. "But I'm most interested in the school of Indian thought called Advaita Vedanta."

"Oh? What attracts you so much to that?"

A blaring of horns from outside was followed by a bang.

"Oh, you know… 'That thou art'."

Angry shouts rose up in the street.

"I'm sorry? What does that mean?"

After a pause he said, against the wail of an approaching siren, "It means that what you seek is what you are. You don't need to go searching, because what you're looking for is already inside you. In your soul, if you want to put it that way."

What you seek is what you are. "What's the best book to read about that?"

He took down one of the paperbacks. "This'll expand on the idea, but in the end it all comes down to those three words." His eyes held hers for a moment. "That thou art."

At the counter he gave her change out of an ornate antique till and placed the three books in a brown paper bag. "I hope you enjoy them." He handed her the bag with another quick glance. "And I hope you'll come back."

"I will." She hugged the books to her breast as she left the shop.

THAT FIRST EXCHANGE HAD BEEN followed by a further visit a week later and by others after that, until she developed the habit of dropping in at the bookstore for a browse and a bookish chat on her way home from school.

She was trolling through the Enid Blyton titles in the children's literature section one afternoon in early April when Simon approached her down an aisle. He had recently had his hair cut very short, and instead of his usual T-shirt, was wearing a white shirt, brand new, judging by its brilliance and evenly spaced creases. He looked younger, she thought, and vulnerable.

He cleared his throat. "Um, I thought I'd make some coffee, and I, er, I wondered if you'd like a cup?"

She took a seat on one of the two battered chairs in a little room at the back of the shop while he attended to plugging in the kettle and checking the insides of two thick mugs. He opened a jar of Nescafé and sniffed the milk carton he took from the otherwise empty mini-refrigerator. "Would you rather have tea? I've got Red Rose tea bags."

"No. Coffee'd be lovely." She looked around the room. Besides the chairs, a small, rickety table, and Jeffrey, there was an electric fire, one bar turned on, and a battered filing cabinet. On top of the cabinet, next to a little radio, stood a framed black and white photograph of a couple, arm-in-arm.

"That's my wife, Rachel, with me," Simon said.

She got up to see it better and to hide her sudden, shocked dismay. She saw a younger, slimmer Simon smiling down at a small dark fine-featured woman who, although she was facing the photographer, somehow gave the impression of having no eyes. They were there physically, of course, and could have been beautiful, had they not been somehow blank, like the eyes of a Greek statue.

"That photo was taken a few years ago," Simon said, "as you can probably see; before Rachel became too ill to stay here. She's now in a nursing home for Alzheimer's patients." He handed her a mug. "Sugar?"

She shook her head, still looking at the photograph.

He took it from her and replaced it on the cabinet before sitting down. "We lived here, above the shop, for years—I still do—and I looked after her as long as I could, but I had to give up." He stirred his black coffee vigorously before taking a gulp. "She'd wander about down here in the night, looking for a particular book, crying and pulling shelves apart, desperate to find it, but she could never remember what it was. She said she'd know it when she saw it." Coffee splashed as he put down his mug. "She started saying I'd hidden it, screaming at me to tell her where I'd put it." He stopped with a grimace. "But I'm sorry. I shouldn't be telling you all this."

"Please go on. I want to hear."

His eyes on the photograph, he described how he had come down in the early hours of one morning to find her rummaging around in the filing cabinet, her nightgown and shawl trailing and the fire turned on full. That, he said, was the moment he knew they could not go on like that. "But really, I don't know why I'm unburdening myself to you like this, Gillian. I never talk about it to anyone. It was just that... well, the way you looked at the photograph caught me off guard."

She lowered her eyes. "So what did you decide to do?"

He meshed his fingers, pulling them against each other. "I would have sold up and looked after her twenty-four-seven, but she ... she turned against me. It got so that just the sight of me upset her to the point where she'd physically attack me."

He stood up, collected the mugs, and restarted the kettle. Over his shoulder he said, "I visit her every day after I've closed the store, but most of the time now, she hasn't a clue who I am. Only," he paused, a mug in one hand, the milk carton in the other, "once in a while she asks me where have I been all these years. 'Where did you go Simon? Why did you leave me?' That sort of thing." He turned around. "I loved her, you know, and still do. But sometimes I wonder now what it is that I love. Is it just memories?" He shook his head. "I don't know any more."

He put the refilled mugs on the table and sat down.

"Do you have children, Simon?"

"Rachel has a daughter from a previous marriage, but Sarah's stopped visiting her mother, and I can't say I blame her."

"I'm sorry. It must be hard for you to bear."

He shrugged. "I read, I meditate, and I look after my shop. I try to live in the moment, although after the way I've been talking, you'll probably find that hard to believe." He lowered his head and spread his hands on the table. "For the most part, I accept the way things are, and I'm not unhappy."

His hands were broad and strong, with fine black hairs across the back. His wedding ring gleamed dully. Holding her breath, Gillian reached out to put her hand on his, touching him for the first time, feeling the spring of hairs and the warmth of his skin. "You know what Edith Wharton says? 'If you make up your mind not to be happy ...' "

He looked up with a quick grin and they finished the quotation together: "'there is no reason why you should not have a fairly good time'." Laughing, they finished their coffee.

Taking the mugs to the sink, Gillian noticed a sheet of notepaper under the photograph, a few lines centred on it. She picked it up and read aloud,

Eyes stretched wide, straining
to catch a memory's tail;
another one
gone.

"Simon …"

He stood up and held out his arms. His sleeves were rolled up and his collar open. A coffee stain on his shirt, shocking against its whiteness, made her want to weep.

While the little refrigerator hummed and Jeffrey rubbed against their legs, Simon took her hands and pressed them against his heart to feel how it beat. They stood, foreheads touching, eyes closed, barely breathing until Gillian said, "Take off that shirt, Simon, so that I can wash away the stain before it sets."

"Gillian?"

She opened her eyes with a start to see a little woman of about her own age, built like a hen, standing before her in the front garden of Saint Anne's. The artificial poppies nodding in a straw hat perched on the dry black curls matched those on her dress, their scarlet shade picked up by fingernails and by the toenails peeking out of patent-leather high-heeled sandals.

"It *is* Gillian, isn't it? Gillian Davies? Remember me?"

Jolted back from her other world, Gillian looked into the bright, black eyes in front of her, and blinked.

"Gladys? Is that *you*?"

Placing the freesias on the grass, Gladys sat next to her. "My Robbie said he saw you sitting here, and I thought I'd have a look-see. How are you then, Gillian? And how's you mam? I been thinking about her. And about you too."

She shifted her stout little body around to face Gillian and pursed her lips. "Now that I'm getting on a bit, see, Gillian, and looking back, like, there's things I want to say." She smoothed the dress on her short broad lap. "We 'ad somethin' in common, you know, Gillian. More'n people would think. Know what I mean?" She flashed Gillian a look. "Din't do us no good, neither of us, all that with Angus, did it?"

All that with Angus?

"What did you say?" Prickling with shock, Gillian stared at her. "You mean …? Oh my God, Gladys! It was you too? Both of us? Oh, I'm so sorry!"

Sparrows chirped and flitted about in the tree above them as they looked at each other. Gillian took Gladys's small, work-worn hand in hers. "We were handed to him on a plate, weren't we?"

Together they slowly shook their heads. "But how did you know about me, Gladys? What did he tell you?"

"He took me to the barn, and I seen you doll there. He told me you really liked all that, and that I would too."

Gillian shuddered. "Gladys," she said after a pause, "Can I ask you this? Don't answer if you don't want to, but did he … did he go further than just … molesting you?"

Gladys straightened her hat. "'e got around to it in the end. Yes. How 'bout you?"

"Jesus, Gladys! He actually *raped* you? Dear God! I don't know what to say!" Gillian turned her head away, closing her eyes and swallowing hard, an icy tingle running down her back. "But as for me …" She shook her head and turned back to Gladys. "No, he didn't rape me, just everything but. I knew he fully intended to. I was very, very lucky to be able to leave when I did." She looked into the round, dark eyes. "I am so terribly sorry, Gladys!"

"Well likewise, indeed, Gillian." Gladys gave her shoulders a shake and grinned suddenly, an aging imp. "Hey! Mebbe we could bring a court case? Sock it to him! Rub his nose in it! Wouldn't I just like that!" She wrinkled her nose. "Bit late now, though, I suppose, innit?" She stood up, straightening her dress. "Anyhow, I just wanted to tell you that I never told nobody about all that. And I'm very happy to have had this little chat with you finally."

"Me too, Gladys! Thank you for coming to find me." Gillian hugged her. "I'm glad everything worked out so well for you in the end."

"And for you, too, by the looks of you. We survived anyhow!" Gladys grinned. "Tell you mam I was asking after her. God bless!"

Gillian watched her bustle away on little pointed feet. Many things about her old *bête noir* made sense now. Seeing her in this new light as a small, defenseless child, and remembering Gladys's reckless teenaged self, Gillian was seized by a murderous rage.

TURNING BACK TO THE NURSING home, she pulled herself together in preparation for what she might find inside. Pressing a Kleenex over her hot face, she scraped her hair back, tying it firmly before picking up the wilting flowers.

She could hear the cry as she approached the stairs: her mother's voice, shouting one word, or perhaps uttering a cry of pain, over and over: "*Yey*-ya! *Yey*-ya!" Reaching the landing at a run, she met Sunita, who put a steadying hand on her arm.

"I'm afraid your mum's not doing well at all." Her eyes were wary and sympathetic. "Dr. Gabriel says it's pneumonia. I've given her the sedative he said she should have, so she'll probably sleep soon. I'll just be in the hall office if you need me." She took the freesias. "Let me put those in water for you."

Her mother, flushed and dishevelled, was calling out the same word repeatedly in a hoarse and shockingly loud voice. She seemed to see someone in front of her, and to be struggling to reach him. "*Yey*-ya!" She held out her arms. "*Yey*-ya! Don't go! Wait for me! Don't leave me!"

Don't leave me?

"I'm here, Mum. I won't leave you." Gillian put her arms around her mother's shoulders and managed to get her lying back and covered with the sheet. She wiped the burning forehead with a cool, damp cloth and moistened the dry lips with slivers of ice, until her mother, struggling feebly to sit up, cried out again. "*Yey*-ya!"

Gillian repeated the syllables aloud to herself, "*Yey*-ya."

She jumped up, clasping her hands over her mouth.

Ieuan! The laughing young man with his arm around her mother in her grandmother's album.

Ieuan, who had come back when she was four, and who had died so young in Australia.

She turned to her mother, desperate to ask about him, but her mother was in a different place and time, and could not hear or answer. "I'm sorry. I'm sorry," she kept saying, her head turning from side to side on the pillow as she plucked incessantly at the sheet. "I'm so sorry, Ieuan." As Gillian leaned over to smooth the hair off her mother's forehead, the dazed eyes focused on Gillian's face. They stilled and opened wide in amazement. A shaking hand reached up to cradle Gillian's cheek. "Oh Ieuan, *cariad!*" her mother whispered. "So old!"

Gillian fell back, holding her burning cheek.

SO THAT WAS IT! THAT WAS THE MYSTERY behind the coldness and unhappiness, the tension and resentment; the discomfort about her appearance, and now about Alice's. Here, at her mother's deathbed, well into middle age herself, Gillian looked back over their largely separate lives as mother and daughter and saw how they had circled and avoided each other, hugging their own poisonous secrets. Looking down at her mother, quiet now, her ravaged face relaxing into a suggestion of its former beauty, she grieved for the waste of life, and of love; for her mother and father, for Ieuan, for Tom, and herself; their lives all damaged by that choice the young Iris had made.

Her mother had fallen into a restless, drugged slumber, the fever clearly worse and her breathing rougher as pneumonia tightened its grip. As the hours went by, Sunita, who had extended her shift, came in several times during the evening and night to check on her and help Gillian make her more comfortable. Not sure what difference it made, Gillian continued wiping her mother's face, and moistening her lips, until at last the old woman fell into what seemed a deeper sleep. Finally, after releasing her hair and loosening her waistband, Gillian managed to sleep also, in the armchair she had pulled up to the bedside.

In the morning, she saw a further change. The fever seemed to have subsided, but her mother's cheeks and mouth were even more fallen-in, her breathing a soft rattle, her restless fingers still. As Gillian stirred, her mother's eyes opened and dwelt on her.

"Gillian," she said, her blue lips barely moving. "Gillian …"

There was a soft tap at the door. Tom came quietly into the room and Gillian embraced him. As they stood at each side of their mother's bed, looking down at her, Gillian took her hand, surprised and moved to feel an answering pressure.

"Mum," Tom took her other hand. "It's Tom."

Her lips opened, but not her eyes. "No time now."

Gillian and Tom looked at each other.

"I'm sorry," he said awkwardly. "I don't want to be a nuisance."

Faint but unmistakable, the words were heard, "Always a nuisance."

Turning a grimace into a crooked smile, Tom retreated to the window to stand with his back to the room. Drawing her hand out of her mother's, Gillian went to his side and put her arm around him.

When she returned to the bedside, the coldness of her mother's hand chilled her. The closed eyes had sunk further back in their sockets, the nails were blue. The bedclothes barely moved over a form that seemed to have shrunk to little more than that of a child under the sheets.

"Tom," Gillian said. "Come here with me." They stood together, hand in hand, Tom weeping, Gillian dry-eyed, watching the marble features lose their strain as the rattling breaths grew ever shallower and further apart, until, after one last sigh, they stopped.

AS THEY PREPARED TO LEAVE THE ROOM after fetching a tearful Sunita, Tom picked a silver-framed photograph off the chest of drawers, a black and white portrait of their mother in film-star pose, beautiful as they first remembered her.

"Could I have this?"

"Of course you can, Tom. Take anything you want."

They stood heads together, in front of the dressing-table mirror, regarding the photograph.

"She certainly knew she was beautiful," Tom said.

Looking up, they caught each other's eyes in the mirror and smiled ruefully. There was none of the youthful radiance of that old photograph in their reflected images, Gillian saw, but their mother's winged eyebrows and high cheekbones were still to be seen in Tom's countenance, as were Ieuan's curly hair, thin features, and wide eyes in her own. As she looked, she saw those green eyes fill with tears.

"WELL, GILL, WE NEITHER OF US GOT what we wanted." After the funeral, Tom sat beside Vanna on the sofa in her living room. "But, you know, I find I don't really care all that much anymore." He took Vanna's hand and raised it to his lips.

Gillian looked from one to the other in disbelief. Not since childhood had she seen Vanna smile so happily and openly, without a trace of irony or mockery. "Is this for real?"

"As real as it gets." Vanna held Tom's hand in both of hers. "This is it now. No more running, no more searching. What I wanted was right in front of me, and I couldn't see it until now."

It was not quite, 'That thou art', Gillian thought, but close enough. "Well that's wonderful! I'm thrilled for you both! Promise me you'll come and visit me in Ottawa as soon as you can."

"We're planning on it." Tom topped up her wine glass as Vanna went to check on the sausage rolls, their choice of comfort food. "How about you, Gill?" He was serious again. "Are you all right?"

"I am. I never did have that talk with Mum, but that can't be helped now, and like you, I don't seem to mind so much." She turned to face him. "I've learned something else, though, Tom, which you should know."

After she told him about Ieuan, he came over to sit on the wide arm of her chair, his hand around her shoulders. "Good Lord, Gill! I don't know what to say." He looked into her eyes. "But how do you feel about it?"

"It was so long ago, and we're getting so much older, that, to tell you the truth, Tom, all I feel, now that I'm over the shock, is a sense of waste, and pity. Pity for everyone involved, including and especially poor Dad."

"Right. Poor Dad." Tom blew his nose. "I remember now you telling me about that photograph, after we visited Grandma that day. Did Grandma know d'you think?" He wiped his eyes. "Did Dad?"

They heard a clunk from the oven door, and a savoury smell wafted in from the kitchen as they looked at each other.

"So that was the mystery man she'd have been so happy with in Australia." He got up, smiling sadly. "Poor Mum! Perhaps she would." He set off for the kitchen but stopped and turned back. "So you think that this Ieuan came back to see her when you were four, and tried to persuade her to leave Dad, and take us back to Australia with him, but she refused?" His eyes widened. "Because of me, do you think? I must have complicated the issue, mustn't I, *nuisance* that I was."

"I think she was too scared, Tom. Imagine leaving your home and everyone you know, to set off across the world into the Great Unknown with two small children. And then she might've had to live in relative poverty with Ieuan. After all, remember, she left him in the first place to marry Dad, who must've already been pretty well off by then."

"I say!" Tom grinned. "Do you wish she'd gone with him, Gill? Think about it! We could've been little Australian children, larking about in the sunshine with our pet kangaroo! No evacuation, no boarding school…."

"…and a happy mother." Gillian twisted her hair. "But then, a different father, Tom. And no Bryn and Carol, or Alice. Or Simon."

"Or Vanna!" A smile spread over Tom's face as he shrugged his broad shoulders. "Well, it's all water under the bridge now, isn't it? Let's drink to that, eh? Where are you, Vanna? Come and join us!" He opened another bottle of wine and filled their glasses rather too generously, necessitating some hasty mopping-up. They clinked glasses.

"To water under the bridge."

AFTER HER RETURN TO OTTAWA, Gillian to her surprise brooded constantly, going back over her life and picking retroactive fights. She turned on herself for being a self-centred loser, while her anger against her mother grew rather than abated. Curdled with unrequited love and under-acknowledged grief, it seethed in a tightly lidded cauldron, the toxic mixture thickened with fury against Angus for what he did to Gladys. At times the focus of this rage shifted completely onto him and onto his mother. Had that woman really not seen what went on? Forgotten details came back to Gillian: how his mother would let him come into the bathroom while she sponged down the children; how she had tucked the Shirley Temple doll into his bed, giggling in a way that had struck Gillian even then as inappropriate. But it was Angus's crime against Gladys that burned Gillian the most as she pictured Gladys suffering in ways far worse than she herself had known.

She was at odds in her relationship with Simon, too. Although he had still kept the apartment over the bookstore, he had spent more and more time at her house during the last months, and she had been happy with that until she went back to Wales. After her return, however, she told him she was upset over her mother's death and needed more space.

"You must suit yourself, of course," he replied stiffly, and returned to his apartment over the shop, leaving her more or less alone after that. She understood and felt the magnitude of her loss, but could not summon up the will to turn things around. "So what?" she argued with herself. He was a lovely man: kind and sensitive and cultured, and she had thought she loved him, but she was no good at relationships; they always failed in the end, so what was the point of hanging on where there was no longer any joy or peace?

She became increasingly aggravated also by Carol's determined cheerfulness and by Bryn's anxious solicitude. She was all right, she told them irritably; she just wanted to be left alone. In the end they stopped inviting her to join them in the evenings and at weekends. Worse still, the company of Alice, once her delight, now made her uneasy to the point where she avoided the child, in whose eyes she now fancied she saw a cold, strange look. She saw, too, how cherished the little girl was, and how protected; how she was the focus of her parents' concerns, her welfare always their first priority. Everything in that house revolved about Alice. If they were not careful, she thought, they would find she ruled the roost. Without a doubt, the child would become horribly spoiled and self-important.

Christmas was the worst time. She managed to bah-humbug her way through the season until the unavoidable mid-day Christmas dinner at Bryn and Carol's home when the foolish hilarity, the grossly extravagant feast, and the threat of Christmas crackers and games drove her to leave early.

She walked Dora by the river in Windsor Park. Under a darkening sky, the ice-bound willows creaking in the north wind, and the hard snow groaning under her boots, she strode on until the dog stopped, holding up an ice-packed paw, mutely imploring that they return home.

Her work was in trouble too: her colleagues boring and her students insufferable. That last semester, arguing with a student about the meaning of a word, she had come close to a serious misdemeanour. The girl had objected loudly in class to Gillian's correction of the word *emphasize* in the sentence, "*I can emphasize with my friends' problems.*" Gillian had explained her reason, writing all the forms of the words *empathy* and *emphasis,* in columns on the board, and doing a sort of riff to demonstrate their distinct uses, only to hear the girl say, "Whatever. That's still what it means to me." Others in the class declared that that was what it meant to them too, so what was the big deal? When Gillian suggested, tight-lipped, that they look it up in the dictionary, the girl said, against a background of nodding heads, that she didn't care what it said in the dictionary, that it was what *emphasize* meant to her, so that was what it meant. Period.

That was when Gillian said, "Do you want a smack?"

There was a communal intake of breath, all eyes fixed on her. Switching quickly into damage-control mode, she added "... is what I'd have been able to get away with saying at one time, but now I think I have to say, 'You have a right to your opinion'."

"You still saying I'm wrong, or what?" The girl was a scrapper.

"What I'm saying," Gillian stated, "is that I'm emphasizing with your point of view."

She got away with it, but only just, and the incident showed her she was in danger of losing her balance, at the very least. For the rest of the winter she would focus on her work and on avoiding aggravation.

APRIL ARRIVED WITH ITS THREATS and promises, bringing with it Alice's sixth birthday. Gillian tried to take an interest in the party preparations, but as at Christmas, the whole thing seemed absurdly overblown. Once more, the expenditure of time and effort offended her: the extravagant gifts, so carefully chosen, wrapped in irrationally expensive paper, the loot bags, the junk food, the balloons and paper-chains, and the inane tape of Alice's favourite songs playing non-stop.

Seeing her irritation at the music, Bryn changed the tape to one of a Mozart symphony that sounded to her like a bluebottle trapped on a windowpane.

"It's only once a year," Carol said, seeing Gillian's expression as she surveyed the fairy cakes, the Rice Krispie squares, and the bowls of varicoloured Jell-O and of Smarties spread on the table. "Do you want to come and see the cake I made for her?"

"No," Gillian said. "I'll wait for the grand entrance."

Carol pressed her lips tight together and tucked a stray wisp of ultra-blonde hair into her chignon. She kept her eyes down and went back into the kitchen. Gillian knew her daughter-in-law felt rebuffed, but it was not right, all this fuss and celebration over a six-year-old. Where was the child anyway? Instead of running to greet her as she used to, she had disappeared upstairs when Gillian arrived. Getting all primped up, Gillian supposed. Twenty little guests would be arriving in half an hour or so, all of them no doubt similarly over-privileged.

INCOMPREHENSIBLY CLOSE TO TEARS, Gillian watched from the shadows, as her granddaughter came down the stairs to greet the first arrivals. A little slip of a thing in an opalescent dress and silver ballet shoes, her exuberant ash-blonde hair held back by a glittering tiara, Alice received her guests like the princess she no doubt felt herself to be. The hallway was quickly filling up with other princesses, all set to party.

Later, unavoidably in the thick of it, Gillian endured the non-stop screaming and kaleidoscopic activity as best she could until, after the games, the absurd meal, the blowing out of candles on the Disneyland cake and the screeching of "Happy Birthday to you!", the time came for the opening of the gifts.

Against a background of comments from visiting mothers on how much the child took after her, Gillian watched her granddaughter opening presents. Alice seemed delighted with them all, and thanked each giver graciously, as she had been taught, until she opened the last of her gifts, a handsome, lavishly-illustrated storybook from her best friend, Tiffany; the same book, Gillian saw with concern, as the one Alice had already received that morning from her Aunt Kelly, Carol's sister. Gillian saw her granddaughter look up from the opened package, her eyes clouding over with uncertainty and her smile of anticipatory delight wavering into a grimace of distress at not knowing what to say.

The awkward moment was soon over, and Alice was her laughing, chattering self again, but Gillian had left the party. She stood rigid, staring blankly at the dark panelling in the hallway of Bryn's house. Through the window of those distressed green eyes she had seen another six-year-old. In a stained, draggle-hemmed kilt and grubby yellow jersey, her hair cropped short for fear of nits from school, that child was crouched behind bales of straw in the dirt of an old barn, praying in vain to be made invisible.

Standing in the hallway, Gillian began to tremble, her heart pounding. She had never seen her childhood self that way before, always having unconsciously judged herself as an unwilling, but nonetheless responsible and guilty partner in the shameful goings-on. But she had been Alice's age, for Christ's sake! Just a little child! The long-simmering anger, now directed exclusively at Angus and on her own behalf, rather than on Gladys's, boiled up and overflowed. Leaning her head against the banisters, she hung onto them until the shaking stopped.

Pleading a headache, she left the festivities. Bryn followed her to the door, offering to take her home.

"Don't you worry about me," she said. "You just enjoy the party." She heard, appalled, her mother's voice.

She went straight home to phone the travel agent, talk to Simon, and prepare for a second return journey to Wales.

Bryn drove her to the airport, leaning forward from time to time to peer sideways into her face, unable to understand why she was going back so soon. "What happened at Alice's party, Mom?" he said as they drew up, as she had requested, at Departures. "You haven't been the same since you came back from Wales last summer, but I'm sure something at the party upset you even more. Was it something we did?"

"Of course not, darling. You never upset me. It was all about me and my unresolved problems." She turned to face him. “I’m truly sorry about the way I’ve been acting this winter, Bryn. Tell Alice I love her to bits, would you? And please explain to Carol that I was very upset at the party by a memory of something that happened to me at Alice’s age. We’ll talk more about it when I come back. Now, just let me off here would you, love? I’ll be back soon.”

He handed over her carry-on bag, a frown of concern still on his handsome face. “What about Dora? Shall we take her? And shall we meet you off the plane?”

“Simon’s going to move back in. He’ll meet me when I get back.” She saw his face light up at that news, and kissing him goodbye, thought how like Tom he was becoming. “Don’t worry, Bryn,” she said, “It’s just that there’s something I have to do in Wales. There’s a place I need to see.”

“’Ere we are then.” The bus driver turned around in his seat with a grin as Gillian made her way up the empty bus to the exit. “Croesffordd! The great metrolops! Knows somebody ’ere, does you, luv?”

“No, I don’t think so. Not now.” Gillian looked back from the pavement at his round, smiling face, fighting an urge to get back on the bus.

Don’t go! Don’t leave me!

“Oh. Well that explains it then, dunnit?” He waved a freckled hand. “I’ll be back at four o’clock sharp. Orrite? Cheers!” The bus rumbled away from the crossroads, past the row of stone cottages, on the final leg of its journey from Swansea to Brecon.

Shivering in the sharp breeze, she buttoned up her Aquascutum raincoat against the threat of an April shower and clutched her handbag. Standing on the corner where the bus had left her, she looked around at the tiny village she had first seen fifty years before. Down the road facing her was the little stone school where everything had been taught in Welsh. On the opposite corner, the chapel, Ebenezer, looked just as grey and grim as the first time she saw it. She turned to check if, by any chance, the square jars of sweets with their amber barley-sugar twists, brown and white striped humbugs and multicoloured 'boilings' still stood in the shop window behind her, but saw only a pale ghostly shape glooming back at her from the papered glass.

Thumbs tightly clenched, chin tucked in, she set off up the steep, narrow road between high, rough hedges, until she came to the turnoff for Maenordy. A cuckoo started up in the distance as she set foot after foot on the winding drive. She pressed on over stunted dandelions pushing through the gravel and past straggling rhododendrons until she rounded a bend and the house appeared.

She stood still, unsure. That was not how she remembered it. This was a dingy, off-white building, the slates on its roof uneven and broken, an attic window cracked. Brambles arched among the roses, the lawn around the bed high with the skeletons of last summer's weeds. On the other side of the house, however, the barn was strangely untouched by time, the monkey puzzle tree still standing beside it. Hand over mouth, she backed away, but stopped. She had not come this far, just to slink back home. Angus would surely not be here now, and this was where her search must begin.

She forced her heavy feet to approach and climb the stone steps up to the oak door, and her cold, stiff fingers to lift the brass fox-head knocker which fell with a heavy clunk, triggering loud barks. When the door opened, it seemed for a moment that Dinah, the beloved Springer spaniel of her memory, rushed out, waggling her whole body in ecstasy at her return.

"Daisy, behave!" A fresh-faced, dark-haired young woman in jeans and red sweatshirt smiled at Gillian. "Can I help you?"

Gillian cleared her dry throat. Her voice came out high and tight. "If it's not inconvenient, I wondered if it would be possible for me to look around the house and grounds, and maybe ask a few questions." She tried to smile. "I was, um, evacuated here with my brother when I was six years old, during the war, when Dr. and Mrs. Macpherson lived here."

"Oh they still do," the young woman said breezily. "Come in, and I'll tell them you're here. What name will I give?"

"Tell them I'm Gillian Davies." Twiddling and tugging the hair behind her ear, she watched the young woman cross the gloomy hall to the inner rooms. *They still do?* Even allowing for a child's perspective, they had been middle-aged fifty years ago. They must be around a hundred years old by now. She had not reckoned on meeting them again. She had not reckoned on meeting anyone from that time right away; just on seeing the place, being there again, and beginning her hunt for Angus. Trembling, she bent to stroke the silky brown and white head, so familiar and comforting, of Dinah's descendent.

The young woman was back. "Dr. Macpherson says please to come in." She led Gillian through the mouldy-smelling stone passage, to the back of the house, and into the kitchen.

Smiling at her, seated at the same scrubbed, battered white-pine table, set on the same slate flagstones she remembered, were two people: a faded, elderly woman, draped in a beige, hand-knitted cardigan, her wispy, grey-blonde hair piled on top of her head; and a tall, rusty-haired man who could indeed have been the Dr. Macpherson she remembered, except that he looked to be in his late sixties, if that. He stood up to greet her, reaching out large, long-fingered hands.

"Gillian!" He clasped her cold hand in both of his. "What an incredible surprise! How lovely to see you again! Come and sit down. Have a cup of tea." He pulled out a chair and patted a quilted cushion of blue and yellow squares onto which she sank.

"I'd know you anywhere," she heard Angus say, as if from far away. "Same hair. Same eyes. Still the same old Gillian, eh? Let me introduce my wife, Janet, and," he indicated the young woman, "my daughter-in-law, Rhiannon."

They were all still smiling away as Gillian felt herself fading. Part of her seemed to have floated up to the far corner of the ceiling, watching and listening, while the rest of her sat at the table with those people. Angus was asking where she lived now, if she were married and had any children, and if she worked. The part of her on the ceiling observed that she seemed to be answering sensibly enough, saying that she lived in Ottawa, had one son, taught high school English, and so on. She heard Angus explain that that he had succeeded his father as the only doctor in the district, and that his son, Ian, a solicitor, was living with them at Maenordy with Rhiannon and their little daughter.

With their little daughter? Here, in this house? Gillian pulled herself together. "Did you say your granddaughter lives here with you?"

"Yes, Sally. She's asleep just now. She's almost three years old. A real little beauty, just like her mother," he said, with a twinkle at Rhiannon, who rolled her eyes. "How about you? Any grandchildren?"

Gillian looked away, her stomach contracting. "Just the one. A girl. Six years old." She was damned if she'd tell him any more about Alice.

"Six years old, eh?" Angus's small brown eyes brightened. "I hope she takes after you. What's her name?"

"No. She does not take after me. Not in any way. She's plump, and dark, and her name," she looked straight at him, "is Gladys."

"Gladys, eh?" He chuckled. "There used to be a Gladys here in the village in your time. D'you remember? Lovely little girl!" He pushed his mug over to Rhiannon for a refill.

Gillian put her hand down on the dog's shoulder, the weight of its warm body against her leg grounding her. "I remember Gladys," she said.

Flapping and cawing, a flock of rooks, caught up in some corvidian drama, descended onto a dead tree near the window. Rhiannon hurried over to shut out the din.

"So you were here for a year, Gillian?" Janet said timidly into the silence that followed. "Was it very hard for you to be away from home for so long?" Her face was kind and full of soft little wrinkles.

"Of course it wasn't," Angus snapped. "She had the time of her life."

Janet subsided, biting her lip, but Rhiannon, topping up the Brown Betty teapot from the kettle on the red Aga range, asked over her shoulder, "And how did you find Mrs. Macpherson senior?" She raised an eyebrow. "Was she ever so strict with you?"

"Oh, Mother had her old-school ways, but she had a heart of gold," Angus said. "She looked after them wonderfully."

Heart of gold! Gillian sat up straight, feeling her cheeks burn with anger. "She was more than strict," she heard herself say. "She neglected us, and she beat us."

Rhiannon gave a startled snort, and Janet shot a frightened glance at Angus.

Exhilarated by this access of courage, Gillian took the offensive further. "And that's not all," she said, staring straight at Angus, a pulse thumping in her throat.

Narrowing his eyes, he looked hard at her for a moment from under his beetling eyebrows before producing the crooked smile she remembered so well. "I tell you what." He shot out his arm and looked at his watch. "It's not even noon, and I'm not due at the surgery until one-thirty. Why don't you and I pop over to the Hare and Hounds in Brecon, Gillian, and have a spot of lunch? We can have a good chat about old times, eh?" He took hold of her elbow and steered her out of the kitchen in seconds as Janet and Rhiannon sat open-mouthed over their unfinished cups of tea.

Gillian studied the cracks and stains on the wall of the house until, with a throaty purr, a forest-green vintage sports car crunched out of the darkness of the barn onto the gravel, dazzling in a sudden gleam of sunshine.

"How d'you like her?" Angus put down the hood and jauntily opened the passenger door, slinging her handbag into the minimal back seat. "It's a Jaguar E-Type. You won't see too many of these around I can tell you. Cost me a fortune!" As they roared off, Gillian turned in her soft leather seat to look back at the dilapidated house. The seven-mile drive to Brecon on a narrow, winding, hilly road took five terrifying minutes.

JUDGING BY THE CLATTER of crockery and the sound of conversation and laughter, the Hare and Hounds was already almost full. Angus must be gambling, rightly perhaps, that she was too well brought-up to make a scene in public, the presence of so many strangers sure to inhibit her from even raising the subject, let alone forcing a confrontation.

He spoke to the landlord who grinned, looked Gillian up and down, and slapped Angus on the back before leading them through a barrage of waves, greetings, and handshakes for the doctor, to a table for two in a far corner of the low-ceilinged, dark-timbered dining room.

A beaming teenaged waiter, an immaculate napkin over his arm, appeared as soon as they sat down. Angus ordered a whisky on the rocks and a lamb curry for himself, insisting on a schooner of sherry for Gillian whose churning stomach wanted nothing to eat or drink. In the silence that followed, he smiled complacently across the table at her until, as she reached shakily for her water glass, he placed his huge hand firmly over hers, red hairs still thick across his wrist. Her mind lurched away, again attempting flight, but she held steady this time, concentrating on the weave of the linen tablecloth.

"Let me say again, Gillian, how delighted I am to see you." He raised his glass. "I've often wondered how you and your brother were doing. You were such lovely children!"

A hairbrush thwacks Tommy's bare bottom; a hand around her ankle drags her back.

She wrenched her hand free. "And I've often wondered, Angus, how, between you and your mother, Tommy and I survived that year."

"You can leave my mother out of this!" He glared at her. "It was very good of her to take you in." He looked away, his face softening, the boy in him suddenly visible. "I cared for her at home until she died, you know. Ten years ago that was. She lived to be ninety-four, Gillian; marvellous to the end. "He blew his nose. "She was a wonderful woman!"

If you say so. Gillian rubbed her hand, momentarily disconcerted by this alternate view of Mrs. Macpherson. Could she, just a child after all, have somehow got the whole thing wrong?

"Thank you, Gareth," Angus gave a nod as the waiter put down their drinks. "How's that young sister of yours?" He smacked his lips after taking a gulp.

The waiter's round, spotty face lit up. "Megan's fine, thank you, sir. She's been a bit off form lately, but she seems okay again now. Thank you very much." He retreated to take a stand nearby.

"Nice boy," Angus patted his lips with the large white napkin. "Oldest of six. Know the family." He put his head on one side with a smile, and reality returned to Gillian in a rush.

"We had a lot of fun together, didn't we, Gillian?" he said, "D'you remember? Exploring the woods and fields, riding the bike, and so forth."

And so forth?

Thought he could brazen it out, did he?

Railroad her into treating this as a pleasant social occasion?

That she had learned nothing in fifty years?

Folding her arms, she stared at him for a good five seconds while he kept up his smiling front. "Angus," she said in a loud, clear voice, "I was six years old. How dare you talk to me about fun! Shall I remind you what your idea of fun consisted of?"

He jerked back, frowning and shaking his head almost imperceptibly while making little shushing movements with his hands. Beads of sweat broke out on his forehead as his eyes darted about the room, and she realized that there and then, in that tavern, surrounded by his friends and acquaintances, she could finish him. A couple of middle-aged women immediately in her line of vision were already staring with open curiosity, while at least two more tables were easily within earshot. The waiter remained at his post behind Angus.

Angus rallied, took another swallow, and wiped his face with the napkin. "Oh, come on now, Gillian." He bared his teeth in a conspiratorial smile, keeping his voice low. "There's no need to carry on as if I ruined your life. Actually, you seem to have done rather well for yourself. I mean, look at you." He held out a hand. "Elegant, healthy, obviously well off; married, I gather, and with a family and a profession to boot. What more could you ask, eh?" He sat back, still smiling.

What more could I ask?

The back of her neck prickled and her face burned.

Is he insane?

Clutching her napkin, she leaned forward, her eyes fixed on his. "I'll tell you what more I could ask, Angus." Despite the nearness of the waiter, and the distinct drop in the volume of noise around them, she raised her voice. "I could ask to have been left alone to grow up unashamed and unafraid; sure of myself, and," twisting the napkin, "... *proud* of myself."

As Angus glanced to either side, loosening his tie, she pressed on. "I could ask to be not just someone who can get by and keep up appearances, but someone who can live her life freely, and," she swallowed, "and *joyfully*. And most of all, Angus," she stared into his furious, frightened eyes, "I could ask to be someone who'd be able not just to fight, but to *win*." She threw down the napkin, pushed her untouched sherry away, and planted her hands on the table, ready to rise.

She had never seen a man sweat like that. Large whitish drops sprang out on his forehead and ran together to slide down his face. "Gillian," he whispered, "Don't go! Listen to me." He wiped his brow, managing a nod at two women at the nearest table who promptly lowered their eyes. No doubt he would tell them later that she had turned out to have been a madwoman. He turned his eyes back to her. "There's something I must say to you."

"What?" She sat back, seeing his age catch up with him in front of her.

Waving away the waiter's attempt to top up Gillian's glass, he glanced around and leaned forward.

"You have never been far from my thoughts."

What was that? She had never been far from his thoughts? She blinked and looked away to where, beyond the latticed window, the sun shone on trees and traffic and shop fronts, and on people going about their normal daily business. She blinked again and looked back at the lined, blotched face.

Was this some sort of acknowledgement?

An apology, even?

He shovelled in a forkful of curry, and took another gulp of whisky as she slaked her mouth with water, watching him.

"The truth is Gillian," he swallowed the last of his mouthful and wiped his lips, "all my life you have haunted me, whether I'm awake or asleep. In a way, you know, it's you who have ruined *my* life, and not the other way round."

She stared at him in disbelief.

"And as for the shame," he cocked his head, "consider this, if you will. It was not *I*, you know, who made you … uncomfortable, but society in general, and your shaming mother in particular." He raised his eyebrows, nodding agreement with his own argument. "Anyway," he went on, "what we did was just natural, eh? After all, I was only eighteen." He sat back with a smirk and saluted someone across the room.

She straightened her back, narrowing her eyes. The man had no idea whatsoever of what he had done to her, or worse still to Gladys; their feelings unimaginable to him and of no interest. "I see," she said, "So you're not at fault, is that it? In fact you're the victim. You were just innocently doing what was natural." She gripped the arms of her chair and leaned forward. "Natural, Angus? *All that?* It may have been natural for you, maybe; but for a six-year-old? Forget the fucking sophistry! You knew it was wrong."

A woman with a long pheasant feather in her mannish hat got up from across the room to sit at the table behind Angus, the other two making room for her without a word.

Angus drained his cut-glass tumbler and held it up, eyeing Gillian with a small, twisted smile as the white-faced waiter came forward and slipped away with the glass. "If you think that was so very bad," he said quietly, "you should count yourself lucky." He leaned closer. "Did you ever consider, Gillian, how amazingly well I controlled myself with you, so little, and fragile, and … *accessible* as you were?" He raised his eyebrows. "There certainly could've been *more* cause for so-called complaint in your case, couldn't there?" He sat back.

More cause for complaint?

In your case?

Those words, and the easy way he said them, along with the smile, revealed suddenly to Gillian that what had happened to her, and to Gladys, all that time ago had not been, as she had assumed, a matter of raging adolescent hormones, but the start of something much darker. Registering what he meant by "*more* cause for complaint," she realized that there must have been other, perhaps many other, little girls since that time, who had suffered not only her lot, but Gladys's; and that there could be more to come. Remembering Sally, the 'real little beauty', she jumped up and stood over Angus, staring down at him.

The buzz of conversation died, and the clatter of knives and forks around them ceased. As faces, near and far, lifted and turned towards them, she said loudly and distinctly, her voice shaking, but growing louder with every question, "With how many other little girls did you so considerately restrain yourself, Angus?"

A high laugh and the clink of glasses came from the bar at the far end of the dining room. A child wailed out in the street.

"In how many cases could it have been *much worse*?"

The pheasant feather shot up, quivering.

Seeing again the audacious little seven-year-old Gladys, she pressed on, her voice rising to a shout at the last word.

"How many little girls have you actually *raped?"*

She turned and walked out through the hushed room, her cheeks flaming but her head high.

A few minutes later, watching from the hotel entrance, she saw him lean heavily on the door of his absurd car, head bowed, before stiffly lowering himself in. Her eyes followed his slow retreat down the hill to the hospital.

Re-entering the bar, she called a taxi to take her back to Maenordy.

From under the monkey puzzle tree, she watched the taxi rattle away. Her stomach clenching and her palms wet, she turned to face the house. She knew what she had to say to Janet and Rhiannon now that she had grasped the full truth about Angus, but could not imagine how to say it. How could she explain to Janet that her husband of forty-odd years preyed on little girls? How tell Rhiannon that she was placing her daughter in horrible danger? Would they believe her? What if they did not? Would she be coldly, or furiously, driven away? Or, if they did accept what she said, could they handle it? Rhiannon seemed resilient enough, but Janet had struck Gillian as fragile and exhausted. Whatever the case, there was no turning back now.

Tucking in her chin and drawing a deep breath, she climbed the steps to lift again the fox-head knocker. Rhiannon opened the door, a solemn, red-cheeked child astride her hip, the wriggling dog at her feet. "Back so soon?" Eyebrows raised, she smiled at Gillian and looked beyond her for Angus.

"Angus has gone to the hospital," Gillian said. "But I've come back because I need to talk to you and Janet alone."

Rhiannon's smile faded. She stood aside to let Gillian into the hallway as Janet, her hair trailing from its bun and dark smudges on her apron, emerged from the door to the back of the house.

"Gillian wants to talk to us," Rhiannon said.

Janet stood still, her hand on the doorknob.

"Is there somewhere we could sit down?" Gillian looked around the austere entrance hall with its grandfather clock, narrow table, and single, upright chair.

Janet hesitated, her hand at her throat. She looked for a moment at the closed door to the reception room, furnished, as Gillian remembered, with black leather armchairs, cold and hard as boulders, but led them instead down the passage to the kitchen. They sat again at the table, Rhiannon pushing aside the heap of half-polished silverware. Sally scuttled under the table to play with her toy monkey on the small threadbare rug, while the dog took up its former place, leaning against Gillian's leg.

Taking off her apron, and tucking her hair back from her face, Janet sat down at the head of the table. She pursed her mouth and straightened her faded, Liberty-print blouse before clasping her hands in front of her on the table. "What's all this about, Gillian?" She put her head on one side, and raised her eyebrows as if addressing a wayward element of the local Women's Institute.

Gillian saw fully, with dismay, what she was about to do to this nice woman, her social life and local standing obliterated with one stroke, her careful shoring-up all swept away. People would turn away from her in the street. Shopkeepers would pretend not to see her. It would be a brave friend who would stand by her now in this small, tight community. Closing her eyes for a moment, Gillian put her hand on the dog's head, feeling, beneath the warmth and softness, the hardness of its skull.

"When I was evacuated here," she looked from one puzzled face to the other, "I had some very . . . damaging experiences."

Janet stiffened, her eyes fixed on the Aga, while Rhiannon stared at Gillian in astonishment. "What was it that happened to you here, then, Gillian?" she said. "And, if I might ask, what business is it of ours?"

Janet's chair screeched on the slates as she stood up. "Would anyone like a cup of tea?" she asked with a nervous, social smile.

"No, thank you." Gillian and Rhiannon spoke as one, and Janet sat down again, picking up a dessert spoon and turning it over.

There was a stir under the table. Sally was popping her monkey into the dog's face. "Hello!" she piped, "My name's George. D'you wanna play wi'me, Daisy?"

The dog turned its head up and away as if embarrassed.

"I'll give you a present!"

Daisy buried her muzzle under Gillian's elbow as the little girl returned, pouting, to sit at her mother's feet.

"Janet," Gillian said, "Rhiannon. I have to tell both of you about what happened to me here all that time ago because I'm afraid it is very much your business. Because of Sally."

Rhiannon froze, her hand on Sally's head, then looked up sharply. Janet scrutinized the back of the spoon handle as if doubting its provenance.

"Please believe me," Gillian went on resolutely, "I had no intention of upsetting you when I arrived this morning. I just wanted to find Angus and settle an old score. But after listening to the way he talked at the Hare and Hounds, I knew I'd no choice but to come here and tell you what…" she dropped her eyes to the scrubbed, battered tabletop, then looked straight at Janet, "what he did to me when I was six and seven years old."

The spoon dropped with a clatter as Janet stared at Gillian. She had turned so white that Rhiannon ran to fetch a glass of water which Janet took with a trembling hand, spilling some on her blouse as she raised it to her lips, the glass rattling against her teeth.

"I'm so sorry, Janet," Gillian said, "but for Sally's sake, you must listen to me."

"Jack and Jill went up the hill…" a little voice rose up from under the table.

The slates at Gillian's feet shimmered in dark iridescence. She blinked, and raised her head.

"You should both know, "she said, looking from Janet to Rhiannon, "that whenever Angus was home from boarding school that year, he molested me."

"Jesus wept!" Rhiannon clapped her hand over her mouth, staring at Gillian. Janet bent to pick up the spoon.

"I don't mean just one little fumble, either," Gillian went on doggedly, "but systematically, and repeatedly, whenever he could get me alone, which was often. And after I left," she said, trying to control the tremor in her voice, "he did the same thing to another little evacuee in the village, except," she kept her eyes on Janet, "that he actually *raped* her."

A bare branch rapped on the window pane as dead leaves whirled by on the wind.

"He never!" Rhiannon stepped back, her fingers across her mouth, staring at Gillian. She sat down hard on her chair.

Janet got to her feet. Pulling open the neck of her blouse, she hurried, slipshod, to the window to stand with her back to them, hunched over, clasping her elbows, the drooping hem of her skirt visibly trembling. "That's impossible!" She spun around. Her colour rose as she faced Gillian, head high. "Who do you think you are, you ... you *mischief-maker!* Coming here out of the blue like this, and saying these terrible things about my husband without a shred of evidence! You must be mad! Or maybe you think you can blackmail an innocent man? Yes! That's more like it! I'm going to call the police right now!" She set off towards the passage.

"Janet," Gillian moved in front of her. "That woman told me herself about the rape some months ago in Swansea, and will confirm what I've just said. Her name then was Gladys Jones."

A magpie landed with a flutter on the branch outside the casement, bending the twigs and seeming to peer into the room. *"One for sorrow ... "* the old rhyme came into Gillian's head as she saw Janet turn back to grip the windowsill, her knuckles white.

"Ah! I see it all now!" Janet said over her shoulder, "I *did* meet a very common young girl called Gladys Jones the first time I came here, before we got married. I didn't like her one bit. I thought then that she was very shifty-looking. I'm not surprised that *she's* involved in this." She faced Gillian again, a tall, gaunt figure, backed up against the sill, her face whiter than ever, but her head still high. "I think that you've been plotting with this Gladys Jones, and that you've made up this whole horrible thing between you."

Gillian shook her head. "Tell me, Janet," she said steadily, "Was there never any problem at all concerning Angus's treatment of little girls? Were there no complaints of that sort in all the years you've lived here? No strange, angry phone calls? No mothers coming to the door?"

Janet bridled and opened her mouth, but closed it, her eyes wide and her fingers pressing against her lips.

"What?" Rhiannon said. "*What,* Janet?"

"Nothing." Janet turned her back on them, her shoulders hunched and her head low.

"It's terrible, what you're telling us, Gillian," Rhiannon said after a pause, running the tip of a knife into the soft white wood on the tabletop. "But if it did happen, that was half a century ago, when he was still in his teens." She looked up. "There'd be no danger now, of course, of anything like that happening again."

A soft clunk came from the Aga as the anthracite shifted and collapsed on itself.

Janet turned, nodding vehemently. "That's right, Rhiannon! He was just a boy! A young lad! That's all water under the bridge now." She arched her neck, her face red and her hair trailing loose. "Why are you trying to wreck our lives like this?" she hissed. "*Why*?"

Gillian put her finger on the maze-like marks Rhiannon had made on the tabletop. "I'm sorry, Janet, I know this is a terrible thing for you to hear, but there's more. There's something worse that I must tell you…"

Rhiannon fixed horrified eyes on Gillian, as Janet, her colour still high, twisted away to stare out at the garden.

"From the way Angus spoke to me at the pub," Gillian said to Janet's back, then to Rhiannon's white face, "I realized that that sort of behaviour is not over. Not at all! I'm afraid it's… well, it's…" she squared her shoulders. "I think it is, and always has been a…" she directed her words to Janet's rigid form, "… a way of life for him."

"What?" Rhiannon leapt up. "Bloody hell! *A way of life,* you say? You mean you think he's *still doing that*? Oh my God!" She snatched up Sally and backed away, her face flooded with colour and her eyes blazing. "That fucking bastard! Jesus! I could kill him!"

Sally began to whimper.

"Rhiannon!" Janet cried. "For shame! You don't mean to say you believe any of this… this *preposterous* story? This is your *father-in-law* we're talking about here, Rhiannon! Sally's grandpa! You live in his house! How can you even *think* such things?"

Rhiannon looked away for a moment, her lips trembling, "I don't know," she said. "I'm not sure, but…" With Sally's head buried in her neck, she turned to face Janet. Shaking her head slowly, she said over the child's sobs, "I'm sorry, Janet, but something here rings true to me. A lot of things are beginning to make sense and sort of fit together." She sat down. "Now that I think of it, without knowing why—just a feeling I had—I never liked to leave Sally alone with Angus. To tell you the truth," she stroked the little girl's back to calm her. "I can't stand seeing those big old hands on her—or the way he looks at her, now she's stopped being a baby. And he's always bringing her presents and treats…" She closed her eyes. "And the other day," she looked at Gillian, "while I was soaping Sally in the bath, he came in and asked if he could help! Of course I said no." She shuddered, putting her head against Sally's. "Oh, dear God!"

Gillian shivered too at the image conjured up. She had come none too soon.

Janet tearfully reached out a supplicating hand. "Rhiannon! Please! Don't do this!"

Rhiannon kissed the child's cheek before settling her down on her lap. She turned to face her mother-in-law. "No, I'm sorry, Janet, but terrible as it is, what she's saying, I have to believe Gillian."

The telephone shrilled in the entrance hall. Gillian and Rhiannon exchanged a quick, almost shame-faced glance as Janet stumbled off down the passage. That would be Angus, probably, Gillian thought, sounding the waters at home.

Janet returned, her face as white as the handkerchief she was twisting in her hands. "That was some man wanting to get hold of Angus." She collapsed onto a chair. "He sounded very angry." She put her head in her hands. "I can't bear this! It's a nightmare!" She turned on Gillian. "This is all *your* doing! You've already spread rumours about him in the village, haven't you? Telling these obscene lies to everyone you met down there!"

Gillian kept silent.

Janet raised desperate, reddened eyes. "It must be you. Who else would say such things?"

Quite a lot of people actually now that the matter's been opened up. Gillian saw again the appalled faces in the Hare and Hounds, and the waiter, standing behind Angus, wringing his napkin like the neck of a chicken. But all that was out of her hands now. Apart from making a statement to the police, which she could do in Swansea, she had done what she had to do. Suddenly aware of the time, she looked at her watch. If she were to catch the return bus, she should leave soon.

WITH SALLY AND THE DOG RUNNING about in the strong fresh wind, Gillian and Rhiannon walked in front of the house. Wiping her eyes, Rhiannon tucked away Gillian's home address and phone number and hugged her so hard that Gillian felt a rib bend before they kissed each other goodbye.

As Gillian reached the first turn in the drive, Sally cried out that the monkey wanted to give her a goodbye kiss too and ran holding out her toy, a wide, confident smile on her face, clearly not a child to whom anything untoward had yet happened. Gillian kissed the monkey, and Sally too, who scrambled back to wave with her mother from underneath the monkey puzzle tree.

That tree was not what it had been, Gillian saw as she waved back. Lower limbs had been lopped off, the remaining branches had lost their manic thrust, and the sparse, browning needles were entirely missing from the top. This wind could blow it down.

Despite the shock and grief behind her, she looked up at the blue sky with an open face as she turned out of the driveway and onto the road. It was over. She had felled the giant. Her raincoat billowing behind her, she walked away from Maenordy and down to the crossroads to begin her journey home.

Acknowledgements

My heartfelt thanks go to my husband, Alistair, and my sons, Edward and David, as well as to my friends for their help and support throughout this whole process. I am grateful also to Ivan E. Coyote, whose upbeat writing course got me started; to the remarkable Mary Borsky and the members of her workshop, whose generous encouragement and feedback kept me going; and above all, to John Metcalf, my editor, who pushed me further than I knew I could go. Thanks also to all at Biblioasis, especially Tara Murpy, for their work in bringing the book to fruition.

SILVIA ZANON

Sonia Tilson was born in Swansea, South Wales, and educated at Monmouth School for Girls and the University of Wales at Swansea. In 1964 she came to Canada where she has taught English at various levels, mostly in Ottawa. *The Monkey Puzzle Tree* is her first book.